A GRAVE ROAST

ORCHARD HOLLOW  1

A.N. SAGE

**CAULDRON
PRESS**

A Grave Roast

Orchard Hollow, book 1

ISBN 978-1-989868-29-4 (Paperback Edition)

ISBN 978-1-989868-28-7 (Electronic Edition)

Cover and interior art by Cauldron Press

www.cauldronpress.ca

Editing by Inessa Sage

www.inessasage.com

© A.N. Sage and ansage.ca

CONTENTS

CHAPTER 1

Orchard Hollow was like any other small town except for one thing: we had magic. Set between rolling hills and the clashing waves of an angry sea, it was easy to miss it on a map. So easy that those who found it made it a point to come back year after year, their egos pampered believing they were privy to a secret no one else knew. The joke was that most who set foot in Orchard Hollow, even its own human residents, were clueless to the world hiding in the shadows.

That's right, kids! Despite what your parents wanted you to believe, the things that go bump in the night were not fairy tales. At least they weren't in my hometown.

Much like my mother and her mother before her, I came from a long line of witches. Powerful, do-not-mess-with-me witches that wielded magic like no one's business. Unfortunately, I didn't inherit the badassery gene. Something that was more than proven today, or, as I liked to call it, the worst day of my life.

Sweat beaded off my forehead, and I wiped it with the sleeve of my torn blouse as I watched the angry mob that stared me down. Okay, maybe that was a slight exaggeration. It was more of a lineup of early birds waiting for their morning lattes while I desperately tried to fix an espresso machine that refused to cooperate. It had only been three days since I opened the tiny cafe on Cliff Row and I was already drowning. I looked down at my soaked jeans, then back to the leaking machine. Literally drowning.

"How much longer is this going to take, Piper? I can't be late to open the salon!" a shrill voice carried over the crowd.

I looked up, my teeth grinding hard at the sight of Nancy Steeles—hair salon owner and town executive chief of gossip. Great. With her at the helm, news of my incompetence would be all over the town by lunch. I rolled up my sleeves and tried to power the machine on again, with no luck. "Doing my best here, Nance!" I announced, coating the bitterness in my voice with powdered sugar. "How about a scone on the house while you wait?"

Nancy's nostrils flared, but she reached her grabby little hands for the scone display on the front counter. Not that it surprised me; Nancy wanted her hands on everything that was mine. Ever since the day she started dating Bobby Kale in high school, when she knew I had a crush on him. That was pretty much the end of our friendship, and I thanked her for it ever since. It didn't take long for Bobby to dump her entitled butt for the next best thing, so her selfishness spared me the heartache. Nancy, however, didn't see it that way and made it her mission to make me her public enemy for the rest of our high school days. Even years later, I was sure she only came to the cafe to watch me fail. Not like that was hard to do most of the time. I was pushing forty with my birthday looming on the horizon, was more single than a Kraft cheese slice, and had my mother's sordid life tainting my every move. After all, not many witches could say their so-called role model dumped them for a questionable coven to practice black magic.

My gaze caught the words Bean Me Up etched on the large glass window, and I smiled. This place was my only true accomplishment. Unlike the small farmhouse I inherited from my grandmother, I got the cafe on my own. Well, with the help of a hefty loan from the bank, but still. It wasn't big, and it wasn't anything like the hipster places they had in King City, but it was all mine. Three, currently occupied, barstools shaped like spaceship command chairs lined the front window beneath a stainless steel bar. Behind them, the exposed brick wall held shelves that I curated with some of my favorite astrology posters and alien figurines. At the center of the cafe sat two bistro tables, each with a bouquet of fresh flowers tucked into moon shaped vases.

I twisted the rag I was holding to cover the leaking steamer handle and tied it in a knot. "Sorry, folks! I'm going to try something in the back real quick!" I hollered. Then, pointing to the tray of scones Nancy eyed greedily, added, "Help yourself to some scones."

Hurrying into the back room, I closed the door behind me and ducked into the office. My shoulders slumped, and I felt anxiety eat away at me as my gaze landed on the wooden cupboard next to my desk. I slid around it, white knuckling the brass handles of the wide doors. Sucking in a breath, I opened the cupboard, pulling out an iron pot and a small wooden box containing a mix of herbs. My brain hurt trying to remember the spell my grandmother cast to fix broken things. *Think, Piper. Think.* I poured half a cup of moon water into the pot and added a dash of cinnamon, four cloves of garlic, a sprig of rosemary, and a pinch of salt. My fingers grazed the brooch on my sweater—a gift from gran—and I felt the magic of the Addison family course through me. Carefully, I placed my finger in the pot and stirred, willing the magic to spread from my body and into the potion.

My hand shook and a zap of electricity burst from my finger and into the pot. The iron creaked; and the pot vibrated violently, the liquid inside sloshing from side to side.

"Crap!" I yelped, yanking my hand out.

As per usual, I was a moment too late.

No sooner had I pulled my clumsy arm out than the pot turned over, the liquid I brewed pouring over the side. Stream shot out of the pot like a burst dam. I thought back to the ingredients. *Was it one cup of moon water or one teaspoon?*

A moment later, I got my answer.

Water burst from my makeshift cauldron, hitting every available wall. From its force, the door to the office burst open, and a gust of wind blasted the broken espresso machine. I tried to keep my frantic thoughts contained and get control of the magic, but it was no use. I knew how this would play out too well from years of being a magical disappointment. The wind surrounded the espresso machine, and I saw confused looks on the faces of several patrons as they checked to see if a fan turned on above them. Then it all went to hell in a handbasket.

The espresso machine hissed and moaned; the small towel I had wrapped over the steamer coming loose. Frigid water flew in all directions, soaking my sparkly new counters and hitting Nancy right in the mouth.

If I wasn't so mortified, I might have laughed.

"What in the actual hell, Piper?" she snapped.

I ran from the room, shutting the door tightly behind me. As I handed her a stack of napkins, I blushed. "I'm so sorry! Here, let me clean that up."

"Don't touch me!" Nancy shooed me away. "This is the worst service I've ever had. Wait until the girls hear about this."

By *girls*, she meant her coven. In case I forgot to mention, Nancy was a witch, and not the kind that started with a capital B. The thing about Orchard Hollow was that you never knew who had magic and who didn't. The town drew in the paranormal because of the immense energy stored in the web of ley lines running under it; but just because you had magic in your family didn't mean that you were lucky enough to wield it. Or in my case, that you were any good at it. When I was little, I asked gran to explain it and the way she put it was that every paranormal family had an extra magic gene hidden away in their cells. Being close to a powerful energy source like the ley lines unlocked it for some people, but not for others. A magical Russian roulette of sorts.

It was pretty much impossible to tell who had powers and who didn't unless they made it clear. Nancy Steeles made it as clear as she could whenever she had a chance to. No shock there. In fact, it would surprise me there was a paranormal left in town who wasn't aware of her magic.

Most humans assumed her an eccentric and brushed it off, but I knew different. She once told me her coven would never accept me and that I'd end up a lonely old witch like the other women in my family.

I never even asked to join them. Weirdo. Unlike my sad excuse for a mom, a coven was not on my goals list.

"Don't worry about her. She'll get over it," a gruff voice said behind me.

I spun around to see Daniel wiping the wet counter as best he could with a soggy napkin. His platinum hair was slicked back, and he wore his usual black turtleneck and leather trench coat, even though it wasn't all that cool outside. When he reached for another napkin, I grabbed it from his hands. "You don't have to help. I got it, really." I wiped the counter in a pathetic attempt to clear the water, proving quickly that I, in fact, did not have it. "Heading to work?"

Daniel looked over his shoulder at the Rose Hollow Hotel across the street. "Uh-huh. Bright and early, as usual." He winked. "Ghosts never sleep."

I stifled a laugh. Daniel was a tour guide at Orchard Hollow's very own haunted hotel. There was certainly not one ghost on the premise, but it brought in tourists by the herd and made for good business. I didn't remember the hotel having the same reputation when I was young and my mind raced, trying to recall when the rumors started. One thing I knew, without a doubt, haunted was a stretch. Dusty and old, but not haunted. And I would know since I had the unfortunate predilection to see ghosts despite my best efforts not to. A parting gift from one of the Addison ancestors—a witch that could walk the veil between life and death.

"Piper?"

My cheeks burned as I shook myself back to attention. "Sorry. And sorry about today. I don't know what happened to the machine."

"Want me to check it out after work?" Daniel asked. "Try something... uncommon?"

His eyes narrowed to a pin, and I knew what he meant instantly. Daniel was a warlock and, while witches and warlocks did not get along, Daniel wasn't all that bad. Unlike most other warlocks, he never made me feel as though he hated my guts because my magic pulled from the earth while his depended entirely on the ley lines. Warlocks were an egotistical kind and looked their noses down on anyone who did not have to sacrifice their own energy to work spells.

I thought they were jealous of witches because when we cast we didn't have to haul butt to a ley line to replenish our energy. We didn't have plug-and-play magic.

"Hello?"

"I did it again, huh?" I asked sheepishly. "Anyway, no worries. I'll get someone from the company on the phone today, see if they can send a technician in to take a look. Thank you, though!"

"Any time." Daniel's lips curled up. "Mind if I hit you up for a bottle of water?"

I wiped my wet palms on my jeans and grabbed a bottle of cold water from the fridge. Placing it on the counter, I slid it over to Daniel. He reached for his wallet, but I waved him off. "On me. To make up for this hot mess."

As Daniel walked away with the bottle in hand, he looked back at me over his shoulder. His eyes darkened, and I sensed there was more he wanted to say but held back. Maybe it was the crowd or maybe he didn't want to be any later for work, yet something was there. Then again, who knew with warlocks? They were a broody bunch.

More so than vampires and even werewolves, which was hard to imagine.

I tossed a damp towel over my shoulder and walked to the center of the cafe. "Sorry, folks. Looks like I have to close up for the day until I can get this machine fixed. I promise I'll do my best to get it up and running by tomorrow, so stop by then!"

Ushering people out the door, I flipped the open sign over and turned the lock. Exhausted, I slid a chair out and perched at the bar, looking out the window down Cliff Row. Small, quaint shops lined the street; some already open for business. With fall looming on the horizon, Orchard Hollow was still very much in tourist mode, so the people living here had to be on their best behavior. Shops opened earlier and stayed open later. Everyone had a smile on. Even the beach was cleaner than in the off season. Past the street, you could hear the clapping of waves against the rocky cliffs that held our little slice of heaven in place and beyond them... Well, who knew? I haven't left Orchard Hollow since the day I was born in it.

"One day," I whispered into the quiet cafe.

"One day, what?"

I gasped, clutching a hand to my chest as I twisted on the barstool to face the counter. There, clear as day, stood Stella Rutherford. Her pearl necklace shined in the gleam of the overhead pendant lights and her tennis skirt swayed behind her as she sauntered over to the espresso machine. I had never seen Stella wear anything else. Then again, I didn't think ghosts could change outfits.

Squinting, I tried to see through her and couldn't. She must have been having a good day because when Stella was weak, or off, or however ghosts worked, she was almost transparent. Today, though, she was as solid as the craptastic espresso machine she now leaned against. Days like these were rare, and I told myself to enjoy it while I could. When Stella was solid, she wasn't as annoying. And trust me, nothing was more annoying than a ghost no one else but you could see; especially when that ghost had an attitude. To make matters worse, Stella wasn't any ghost—she was my familiar.

Because I couldn't get a cat or an owl like other witches.

Garbage powers and a ghost familiar. That sounded about right.

I couldn't remember the exact day Stella Rutherford entered my life, though I'm certain it was a gloomy one. There were no signs of her arriving, she simply appeared one day and never left. It took us a while to figure out the reason she was the only ghost I could see; we were linked. Gran was already gone by then and since I didn't exactly have paranormal friends, there was no one I could ask. Stella and I spent some time trying to make her crossover and when we couldn't, we accepted our fate.

I was still getting used to her random appearances.

Stella knocked on the metal backing of the espresso machine. "I told you to shell out for the better model."

"First, don't sneak up on me, you creep. You're going to give me a heart attack. Second, and I know this one is hard for you to understand, but some of us don't have unlimited bank accounts to do with as we please. Some of us didn't marry rich."

Stella scoffed. She actually freaking scoffed at me. "Please, don't bore me with your sad poor girl stories. I don't think I can handle it today."

I deadpanned. "Why? What happened?"

"It's back."

Draping my head in my hands, I rubbed my eyes and dragged my lids down. "Ugh, again?"

"That's what I said."

"Where is he?"

Stella pointed to the office, and I cringed. As if on cue, a loud bang sounded from inside, followed by the sound of an object rolling across the floor. I jumped from the barstool and bolted for the back door. As I swung it open, my chest tightened, and my eyes bulged from their sockets. The wooden cupboard that held all my magical supplies lay turned over on the ground. Herbs and candles and crystals covered the office floor and a sticky substance, likely honey, oozed from the cupboard and onto the brand-new carpet I rolled out only that morning.

My gaze knifed to the furry creature sitting atop the cupboard, and I saw red. Ignoring me, the chubby raccoon reached across to pull a dried berry off a sprig he found on the ground, cramming it in his already full mouth.

I groaned and leaned against the doorframe, sliding down to the floor. "Harry Houdini, I'm going to kill you."

CHAPTER 2

My knees hit the ground, and I ducked out of the way just in time for a chunk of amethyst to come flying overhead. It nicked my cheek, and I hissed, shielding my head as the crystal bounced off the wall behind me and tumbled to the floor. "Stop that right now, you beast!"

The raccoon tilted his head, and I swore I saw the slightest of smiles under his whiskers. He picked up another crystal, this one larger and with more sharp ends, and tossed it my way. I rolled on the ground, avoiding another attack from the trash panda. His grabby fingers reached into the open side of the cupboard to pull out a ball of red yarn. Bringing it up to his wet nose, he sniffed it a few times, then licked it for good measure. Gross.

"Get the jars," Stella instructed from the doorway, pointing to a collection of glass jars the rascal hadn't touched yet. "They make for better weapons."

I glared at her. "Whose side are you on?"

"The winning side, darling. Obviously."

Luckily, ghosts didn't speak raccoon, and Harry Houdini chucked the ball at my face instead. As it flew, it came apart and red yarn stretched from me to Harry. His black eyes shone, and he lunged for the string, rolling around in it like a clumsy piglet. The distraction gave me a moment to collect myself, and I hopped to my feet, grabbing the first thing I could think of. With a broom in my hand, I pointed it at the raccoon and said, "Last chance or I yeet your furry butt out of here."

That got his attention.

Harry's lips parted, and he chittered sounds I didn't understand but was certain was the raccoon equivalent of "This isn't over, you witch." He climbed out from under the yarn and backed away from me, his chubby body knocking things over as he waddled. When Harry reached the door leading to the alley, he gave me one last narrowed eyed glare and slid through the thin crack, disappearing from view. I ran after him to look outside. The alley was empty. I waited to see if he would emerge from one of the garbage bins to take his revenge, but Harry left the same way he came, like a freaking ninja.

"Is it gone?" Stella asked when I came back inside the office.

"Pulled a Houdini again," I replied. "He'll be back at sundown, I'm sure."

She blew on her nails and gave them a once over, satisfied with what she saw. "I don't know why you don't magic that thing gone."

"Because I don't want to kill an innocent animal. And because I don't do black magic. Oh, and because I don't remember asking your opinion."

Stella rolled her eyes, then shrugged. "You're not like her, Piper."

My stomach rolled at her words. My very frustrating and very judgmental ghost familiar knew me better than anyone. Probably because she watched me when I didn't know she was there, but I tried not to think about that part. What I thought of was that while she was right and I was nothing like my wayward mother, it didn't stop me from thinking a part of her must be in me. We were the same blood, after all. Same magical gene; same family. Then again, grandma was an Addison too and she cut ties with mom long before I did when we found out what she was up to in King City.

Still, what was that saying? Apple, tree and whatever.

"Wait," I said, "did you just pay me a compliment?"

"Lord, no. When?"

"When you said I'm not like mom."

Stella blinked her doe eyes and pushed away from the doorway. As she walked, her skirt bounced to reveal her long, slender legs. For a woman in her late fifties, she sure aged well. Especially considering her deadly situation. Slowly, Stella leaned in until she was inches from my face. "I meant because you're not all that great at the witching thing."

She waved her arm over me as though she was presenting a sidekick in a magic show, and it made me want to broom her butt out of the cafe faster than I did Harry's. Instead, I slapped her hand away and grinned when Stella's face soured as my fingers sliced through her corporeal body. There was still so much I didn't understand about the realm of the dead, but from what Stella told me, touching anything that had a heartbeat hurt like hell.

"Watch it," she sniped.

"You too," I bit back. "Where were you this morning, anyway?"

Stella's face darkened, and she pointed her sharp nose at the ceiling. "Oh, you know, here and there."

"Back in the woods again?"

The woods at the end of Orchard Row were deep and spooky, and even on a sunny day, people avoided them like the plague. Except for a few runners—or nut jobs if you asked me—they remained abandoned and wild. Stella, when she was alive, was one of those runners. Until she wasn't. She never talked about the day she died, though it wasn't for my lack of inquisition. All she knew was she was out for a morning jog before hitting the tennis courts and the next thing she recalled was waking up in the woods, looking down at her own body. Dead as nails.

When she nodded without meeting my eyes, I asked, "Any luck remembering?"

"Oh, please," Stella said. "Why bother? No one wants to think about death, darling. It's almost as tragic as wearing last season's shoes to this season's runway."

I had no idea what any of that meant, but I assumed the conversation was over. This was how it always went with Stella when I asked her about that dark day. I prodded. She gave me stuffy answers, then we went our separate ways. I wasn't sure why I thought today would go differently. Instead of spending the next hour annoyed with her, I brushed off the back of my jeans and headed out of the office and into the cafe. "I'll be back later to clean all this up.

Going to stop by the hardware store to see if Sasha can give us a hand with the machine."

"Give *you* a hand," Stella corrected. "I claim no ownership of that rusty old thing."

The walk down Cliff Row at this hour of the morning was a breath of fresh air. While some places were open, most were still locked up or setting up for the day. As I passed the only souvenir shop on the strip, I shot a small head nod to Sunny, who was already out and about fixing the postcard display for what I assumed was the millionth time. Sunny, an older woman with an even older cat who enjoyed lounging in the shop's window, was usually fixing something. She was a self-declared perfectionist, and I was pretty certain this was the reason her business continued to thrive even in the off season. Somehow, Sunny knew what to put on display to attract tourists and locals alike. When it wasn't colorful postcards, it was plush bears for Valentine's Day or pumpkin carving kits for Halloween. Sunny's displays changed with the seasons and were some-what of a staple in Orchard Hollow since I was a kid. You never knew what you'd find in the Shop of Curiosities and Gifts.

Sunny gave me a quick wave and turned back to her task, allowing me to move along with no small talk. That was another thing I liked about the woman, she was all business and no nonsense.

Laughter sounded across the street, and I turned to watch a man and a woman buckle a toddler into a stroller. The dad made faces, making the little boy break out in hysterics while the mom tried to maneuver straps over his wriggling arms. After a few attempts, she gave up and joined in on their games. The family wasn't one I knew from town and when I saw them roll the stroller into the Rose Hollow Hotel; I realized they were only visiting for the season. Gran said that Orchard Hollow was the place to be until it wasn't; nothing could be closer to the truth. During high season, the place boomed with cheerful laughs and hundreds of families, much like the one I watched. But when the cold weather picked up, we were a ghost town.

As I walked, Ray's smoothie shop door swung open and almost hit me straight in the jaw. I jumped to the opposite end of the sidewalk and watched as the burly man carried out a massive chalk board with today's specials, plunking it down on the cement with a thud.

"Ready for business?" I asked.

Ray wiped his brow and turned to face me; his red nose even redder in the light of the rising sun. "As ready as ever, Miss Addison," he said. "How goes it in the cafe?"

"Already hit a snatch," I admitted. "The espresso machine broke down this morning."

"Ah, yes. I heard about that."

How in the name of all that is good did he hear about my failure? I shook my head. "Nancy?"

Ray nodded. "Who else?"

We shared a laugh, and I continued moving along, giving Ray the opportunity to finish setting everything up before he got hit with a wave of people in desperate need of greens in a cup. While I wasn't sure, the brute way in which Ray operated made me wonder if he might have been a werewolf, or at least bore the gene in his lineage. Mostly, werewolves kept to themselves and didn't mingle with others. Especially not vampires. Those two had a thing out for one another for as long as time existed.

The things fairy tales got wrong were their depiction of werewolves. The paranormals were painted as wild creatures having no control over their hunger for flesh when they couldn't be further from it. Aside from the full moon, werewolves were more in control of their magic than all of us. And they were fully vegetarian, which was why they didn't mesh well with vampires who often regarded humans as a blood buffet given the chance.

But they were also moody as hell, so you know...

I hurried past Nancy's salon before she could spot me and rushed across the street. As I walked by the wide glass doors of Orchard Hollow's bank, my heart sank to my feet. The loan I had to take out to set up the cafe was likely nothing major for some people, but for me, it meant putting everything on the line. Before this, I worked a few dead-end jobs that led nowhere and if it wasn't for grandma leaving me her farmhouse when she passed, I would have ended up on the streets. When the loan got approved, I knew what I was taking on, but I also assumed that opening a cafe on a street where there wasn't one would be a solid business plan.

So far, I was way off the mark.

Light voices carried toward me, and I noticed Daniel walking down the street with Isabella Beaumont at his side. It was such a rare sight to see the owner of the Rose Hollow Hotel out and about; I couldn't help but stare. The woman was absolutely gorgeous. Her long, black hair barely moved as she swayed her hips from side to side, emphasizing the perfect fit of her pencil skirt. Only Isabella could make walking in four-inch heels a piece of cake and I had to pick my jaw off the floor when she hopped over a puddle in the atrocious things to avoid getting them wet. I'd have been face first on the ground by now, and that's without the jumping.

"Oh, hey, Piper," Daniel said as they passed me.

"Hi, you two. No tours this morning?"

Daniel and Isabella exchanged glances, then looked in opposite directions. "We have some lined up for the afternoon, big bachelorette party," Daniel said. "I needed to get a new chew toy for Margaret the Third, and Isabella joined me for the walk." He pointed to a bright pink bag with the local pet shop's logo on it. The paw stamped in gold foil reflected the light and the abundance of tissue paper sticking out the top made Daniel sound like a one-man band when he moved.

I didn't bother asking what toy he purchased because, knowing Daniel and his obsession with the yuppy Chihuahua, it cost more than my entire wardrobe. Aside from her obnoxious name, the dog was sure living the life. I looked to Isabella. "Good to see you again," I said.

I meant it. Isabella was almost never in town and operated the hotel out of the city. As far as I knew, Daniel became her right-hand man when he joined the hotel team and handled all the daily affairs. Seeing her was rarer than spotting a unicorn.

Those weren't real, by the way.

The hotel owner made no eye contact with me. "You as well..."

"Piper," I said. "I met you a couple of weeks ago down at the diner."

"Ah, yes," Isabella said, though I doubted she remembered. The way she acted made me wonder if she and Stella had been friends when Stella was still alive. It made sense for the two aristocrats to flock to one another. I made a note to ask my familiar about it later. "We should get going, Daniel. I need a word with the staff about the Facebook post."

I arched an eyebrow at Daniel, hoping he'd fill me in, but all he said was, "Another ghost sighting gone wrong."

When the two bid me goodbye and walked away, I took out my phone and pulled up the Rose Hollow Hotel's Facebook page. It was easy enough to find the post Isabella mentioned since it had almost a million likes and thousands of shares. Some woman wrote about a ghostly encounter at the hotel where she claimed two shadowy figures came to her room at night. This wasn't anything new and quite similar to other stories told by guests. Shadowy figures, screaming down the halls, the sound of blood dripping. All were tales emphasized by the eccentricity of online ghost chasing communities. Though I was sure this article struck a chord with Isabella since it seemed to have gone viral overnight.

"You know what they say," Stella said, appearing out of thin air beside me, "any press is good press."

I swung my head and talked out of the side of my mouth. "I thought we discussed you doing this in public. People are going to lock me up if they see me talking to myself. Remember what happened to my great-great-aunt?"

"You discussed, and I listened."

"And what happened to the listening part?"

Stella looked down the street. "I didn't like what I heard. Besides, your stuffy aunt was likely nuts, and that's why they locked her up. Not because she said she could talk to the dead."

"Either way, it's not a good look. Why are you even here? I told you I'll be back after the hardware store?"

"I got bored. That cafe of yours is nothing to look at and you chased today's entertainment away with a broom, remember?" Stella's face appeared more gaunt than usual, and her lips drooped a little as she looked off into the distance. "Why don't you call the company you bought the machine from and have them fix it?"

"Because they will probably ask me to pay for the service and I can't afford any added expenses right now."

Stella pointed to gran's brooch, a hefty-sized rose made entirely of rubies. "You'd have a lot more to work with if you took my advice and sold that gaudy thing."

I covered the brooch with my hand and sighed. "I'm not sure if you're playing dense or if dying made you slower. My family's brooch is not for sale. It literally holds our magic and without it, I will have almost no power at all. And before you suggest it, as I mentioned many times before, every family with the paranormal gene gets only one talisman to hold their power. It passes to the first-born child and moves down the generations. It's an honor to carry one and I can't transfer it to a less expensive item to fit your fancy. Ley lines or not, we have our limits. I know you were human when you died, but I'd think being a ghost would make you want to learn more about how all this stuff works."

"Not really." Stella shrugged. "And trust me, even with the brooch, you're not the best witch out there."

If she wasn't a ghost, I'd have elbowed Stella right in her perfect nose. "Why don't you go haunt the hotel and give it some credibility for a change? I don't need a chaperone."

Stella crossed her arms and pouted the lips; two puffy pillows I was sure cost a fortune. "No, thank you. That place gives me the creeps. See you at home."

With that, she vanished, leaving me alone to enjoy

the rest of the morning. Without Stella's commentary and the street as quiet as it could be, I walked the rest of the way to the hardware store with a skip in my step. I may have been bad at witching and had little in the bank, but there was one thing I got from mom that I didn't completely hate. I bounced back on my feet no matter what life threw at me.

If the espresso machine thought it could mess up my plans to succeed in this hole of a town, it had another think coming. I was an Addison, and an Addison never gave up. With that thought in my head, I sped until I was almost jogging. *New plan, Piper. Fix the machine, reopen the shop, and make the best lattes this town has ever had. Then go home and practice your magic.*

There was no way I was going to let Stella be right. Not if it was the last thing I did.

CHAPTER 3

"Your pump is shot. And there is something wrong with the water tank filtration, but I can't tell without taking the whole thing apart," Sasha said, his thick Eastern European accent emphasizing each vowel.

Sasha wiped his hands on his faded jeans and tossed the screwdriver he held on to the counter. I winced as it hit the marble with a ding and rested my head in my hands, leaning further on one of the bistro tables. "In other words?"

"No coffee."

"Great," I mumbled. "Any chance you can fix it?"

He shook his head and tucked his thick glasses into the front pocket of his plaid shirt. "I don't think so.

Sorry, Piper. If it was the pump alone, I might have been able to patch it up, but this is way out of my comfort zone."

My shoulders drooped, and I let out a long sigh, my chin flattening out on the table. I was relieved Stella didn't stick around to rub it in and make sure I knew she was right. Somehow, I had to come up with enough money to fix the machine if I had any hope of opening the cafe again. This day could not get any worse.

"Thanks anyway," I told Sasha. "I'd offer you a drink for your troubles, but you know."

"Don't sweat it, kid," he said. "Really wish I could help. Come by for dinner sometime, no? Anya would love to see you again. Last time we saw each other was..."

He trailed off, rubbing the rear of his neck. Goose-bumps covered my arms, and I rolled the sleeves of my sweater down. The last time I saw Sasha and Anya, his wife, was at gran's funeral. The day was a fog, but I remembered Anya offering to come by with a few dinners, allowing me to adjust to life without gran. She was well-loved in the town, especially in the para-normal community and though Sasha and Anya were as human as they came, they still gravitated towards her. Gran had a way about her that was hard to resist, and the shadow she cast when she died covered me whole.

I watched Sasha leave, waving goodbye from the doorway before turning back to the cafe. I tidied up most of the office while waiting for him to drop in and it was already so late the sun was a red spot on the horizon. Placing a few muffins into a to-go box—no point wasting them—I walked out, locking the front the door behind me. The cool air of the evening slammed into me, and I sucked in a deep breath, smiling as the sea salt hit the back of my throat. Since it took Sasha some time to tinker with the machine, Cliff Row was completely abandoned by the time I walked the few blocks down to where I parked my beaten-up old beetle. The thing barely drove, but it got me from the farmhouse to the cafe, and that was all that mattered.

Thoughts of failure clouded my mind as I walked, and I tried not to dwell on the fact that I might need to drop every penny I had left in savings to get the cafe opened again. I was so wrapped up in self-pity, I didn't notice the person walking toward me until it was too late.

My head hit a hard object and the muffin box flew out of my hands. It fell on the ground, muffins exploding everywhere. I rubbed my forehead. "Shoot! I'm so sor—"

I froze.

It seemed my clumsy butt had delivered me into a fresh new hell because I ran over a complete stranger. Not any stranger, too. A very attractive one at that. Wonderful. I didn't recognize his face and briefly wondered if he was visiting town. He didn't dress like someone from these parts; his hair was closely trimmed and under his tweed coat, the smallest hint of a suit peeked out. No one wore a suit in Orchard Hollow unless an occasion called for it.

The baffled man smiled and bent over to pick up what was left of the muffins. I ducked down quickly, hoping to grab it first, so he didn't go to any trouble to help when I was the one that bulldozer'd over him. As I did, our heads clunked together and the man let out a low yelp, the red mark on his forehead matching my own.

I clasped my mouth with my palm. "I'm so sorry!" I reached for the box at the same time as he did, and we bumped heads again.

Are you freaking kidding me right now?!?

The man leaned away from me and gestured to the box; I gathered the muffin corpses and shut the lid. We stood up carefully, keeping our heads far away from each before one of us got a concussion.

"You alright?" the man asked.

I nodded. "Yep. Mortified, but good. Is your head okay?"

"I'll live."

He extended a hand, and I took it slowly. As I did, I realized I was touching something soft and wet and looked down to see a squished muffin between our palms. *Oh, sweet mother of...* What was actually wrong with me? I grabbed the muffin he handed over and shoved it into the box with the rest. Cheeks burning, I said, "Thanks. Sorry I tried to kill you."

The man laughed and rubbed his hands together, pieces of muffin falling to the ground. "I'm Joe, by the way."

"Piper," I said. This time, I kept my dumb hands to myself and only stared at him like an idiot. Joe had a rugged handsomeness about him that was rare in these parts. A town full of paranormals drew in a crowd that was over the top, but Joe didn't seem to have that going for him. He also seemed very, well, human. I looked at the box in my hands and said, "I own Bean Me Up, the cafe right over there. Come by for coffee sometime, on the house to make up for this."

For someone who didn't have a functioning espresso machine, I was sure handing out coffees freely.

"I might take you up on that," Joe said. "I moved here about a week ago and haven't got out much."

"Oh? Where did you move from?"

Stop snooping, it's uncouth. I could all but hear Stella's voice in my ears, even though she was nowhere nearby. Still, it was rare for people to move here unless they had paranormal genes and were drawn to the power of the ley lines. In fact, other than the Signet sisters, he was the first to move to Orchard Hollow in over a decade.

Joe eyed me and creased his brow. I assumed it was because I drifted off into thought again. I tried to recover by smiling, with way too many teeth showing. Yikes. Finally, his lips curled at the edges, and he said, "King City."

"Ooooh! Big city boy, huh?"

Please stop talking now.

Joe chuckled. "Not anymore, I guess. I even bought a bookstore to prove it."

My eyes rounded, and I looked down the street at the small bookshop sign jutting out into the street. It couldn't be. "Brooks books?" I asked.

"That's the one!" Joe said enthusiastically.

This was quite the development. Liam Brooks operated Brooks Books for as long as I could remember. It was a lovely store with plenty of fun reads, but that wasn't what made it so special. Paranormals often frequented the bookstore, and it was a gathering for those who wished to meet other magical people in town. Liam himself was human, but from what I recalled, he had a few vampires in the family. His magic gene never kicked in, though that didn't stop him from stocking the bookstore with plenty of tomes on the paranormal. If you had a question about magic, Liam was your guy and Brooks Books was the spot to find it. When Liam passed away of old age last year, the store remained closed, and we all assumed it would stay that way.

But now, random cute-man Joe was taking over? It seemed off.

"Congrats," I said. "It's a great store. Very popular in these parts."

"So I hear. My uncle owned it, and it seemed a waste to see it stay closed. It took me a while to get the guts to move, but here I am." Joe gestured to the street. "Ready to take on Orchard Hollow one book at a time."

"Did you run a bookstore back in the city?"

"Not even close," Joe admitted. "I was a criminal defense lawyer. This is a much-needed change." He looked at his watch, then back to me. "I should get going, though. Nice to meet you, Piper. I'll stop by the cafe!"

I almost told him not to since Bean Me Up was closed until I could get my pathetic life together, but kept my mouth shut. As I walked to my car, I thought about Joe and his sudden arrival in Orchard Hollow. Fresh blood in this place was quite rare, and I felt sorry for Joe since he was about to become the town's gossip. I cringed, thinking about Nancy Steeles. Cute guy, no wedding ring? She was going to be all over Joe like butter on toast.

For the rest of the way home, I tried hard not to think about why I noticed the empty ring finger on the new bookshop owner.

The farmhouse was dark and quiet when I finally made it home; I trudged up the creaky porch steps, glancing at the empty field beyond it. Gran never did much farming on the lush land she owned, but she managed to keep a stocked greenhouse not too far from the main house. After she passed, I decided to maintain it as best I could and, for a few rose bushes that refused to cooperate, didn't do a bad job. Gran always said a witch without a greenhouse was a witch without a plan, and it stuck.

Granted, she actually knew how to use plants in her magic and all I could manage was a nice smelling pot of boiling flower water.

It wasn't for a lack of trying. If I did one thing as a witch, it was to keep attempting to get a hold of my magic. Mom, with all her shortcomings, was very much like gran—powerful without even lifting a finger. Until the day mom left Orchard Hollow and joined up with the coven that shall not be spoken of, people in town considered her and gran to be the strongest witches in the town. Possibly even the country. Especially gran. As far as the stories went, she once killed an ancient vampire by binding his magic to an old vase and smashing it to bits. Killing a vampire was hard enough; killing an old one was almost unheard of. It got gran a bit of a reputation around these parts, and I was confident it was why no vampire ever messed with the Addison women.

As far as the vampire community went, we were off limits.

Not that Orchard Hollow wasn't peaceful. For a town full of paranormals, it was very docile. Aside from the few silly feuds between some members, paranormals kept to themselves. Staying under the radar served everyone's best interests, so it made sense we didn't have as many issues as the big cities had. No one ever read stories of unexplained human deaths in Orchard Hollow because no one dared disturb the tranquility of this place.

We were the Switzerland of the paranormal world.

I checked the mailbox on my way in and found it empty, as usual. There was an ache in my chest as I let the metal top slam shut, disappointment spreading through my body. Mom hadn't written in six months. For a while after she left, she kept up with postcards and letters, refusing to email because technology was not her friend. Every one of her notes came with requests, usually for money, sometimes for spell ingredients which gran refused to provide. Then the mail stopped.

It should have relieved me to be free of the burden that was Sylvie Addison, but I kind of missed hearing from her. As selfish as those postcards had been, at least she was thinking of me.

I left my boots in the doorway and stepped indoors, inhaling the smell of old wood that wafted from inside the house. The farmhouse smelled like a cabin, all cozy and warm and full of secrets. There was a wraparound porch that offered the best views of the fields surrounding the home, and I often sat on the small bench on it, curled up with a book and a cup of coffee. Past the fields, trees surrounded the land; deep inside, the ley lines spread under Orchard Hollow. Gran said our farmhouse was special because of how close it was to the ley lines, and it was why our magic was so strong. I was certain she didn't mean me when she said it.

There were three bedrooms in the farmhouse. Two upstairs that gran and I occupied when she was alive. Now the second bedroom sat empty, and I could not for the life of me find a use for it. The bedroom downstairs was mom's though gran remodeled it into a spell room days after she left. Dwelling on the past was not gran's thing, so where once was a bed now stood a table with a giant cauldron on top. The bookcases no longer held books but rows upon rows of potions, and the table mom used as a makeup stand was draped in black velvet and held a crystal glass and decks of tarot cards.

Everything had a new life.

The living room and kitchen were a large open space, so when I cooked meals in the evenings, the entire downstairs smelled of whatever concoction I came up with. Unfortunately, the same could be said for the potions I struggled to brew that often filled the house with vile smells and made me gag for days after.

Tonight, the house only lightly reeked of burnt dandelion; an enormous relief to my senses.

No sooner had I put my purse down than a loud, annoyed sigh sounded from the kitchen. I rolled my eyes and turned around. "Hello, Stella."

"Finally," the ghost said. "I'd been waiting for hours."

"What? No happy hour with the other ghosts tonight?" I teased.

Stella's chin tensed. "I don't have friends because I'm dead," she said. "What's your excuse?"

I waved her off and walked to the fridge, pulling out a Tupperware of leftovers from the night before. Before sitting down to eat, I put an espresso maker on the stove and loaded it up with beans I ground that morning. When the pot boiled, I inhaled the deep smell, poured out an abysmal amount into an even larger mug, and sat down at the kitchen table. As I dug into the cold noodles, I avoided Stella's disapproving glares. It was hard enough to eat the tasteless food without her side eye. Shoving another forkful in my mouth, I chewed it quickly and tossed the empty box into the sink to wash later.

"I take it by your less than cheerful demeanor you had no luck getting the machine fixed?" Stella asked.

"Nope," I answered. Then, before she could start in on me, added, "I'll figure it out tomorrow."

Stella's gaze fell to the brooch on my sweater, but she kept her opinions to herself. Shocking. Not giving her a chance to reconsider, I grabbed a flashlight off the kitchen counter and walked to the back porch entrance. "Be right back," I told Stella. "Going to get some ingredients for a spell."

At my back, I heard her mumble, but her words didn't reach me, which was a good thing since I doubted it was anything nice. I turned the flashlight on, pointed it toward the greenhouse and walked down the grass-lined path until I reached it. Opening the door let out the fresh smell of flowers and herbs and for a second, I thought I smelled poppy seeds in the air.

Panic set in and I scanned the greenhouse, back relaxing when I realized it was only the walnuts I had crushed here yesterday. The last thing I needed was an allergic reaction and considering how intolerable poppies were to witches, and that I was here all alone, if any got in somehow, I'd be in trouble.

I walked over to where the crushed walnuts lay and dusted them off the makeshift wood counter that ran along the center of the greenhouse. On either side of the crammed space, plants sprouted from mismatched pots. Some trailed to the ceiling, while others fell to the ground in green tendrils. Toward the rear of the greenhouse, petals of red and orange and yellow filled the windowsill as autumn flowers took their moment to shine. I breathed in the greenhouse like it was a lifeline. Memories of being here with gran hit me hard, and I opened my eyes wide, recounting the herbs I needed for the spell. It was a simple enough mending spell I was hoping to try on the stupid espresso machine in the morning.

I picked out a sprig of lavender and a clump of goldenrod and was about to search for the next two ingredients when my phone rang in my pocket. Holding the flashlight in my teeth, I picked it up and looked at the screen, a number I didn't recognize flashing across. I was about to let it go to voicemail, but something told me to answer.

"Hello?" I asked as I pressed the phone to my ear.

For a moment, the other end was silent, and I thought the person hung up on me. When they spoke, I almost didn't recognize the voice. "Piper, I need your help. It's important."

CHAPTER 4

"**A**re you there?" Daniel asked on the other end of the phone.

I shook my head and picked my jaw off the floor, surprised to hear from him. Eyes wide, I put the flashlight on the small wooden bench and sat down. "I'm here. You caught me off guard." When Daniel said nothing, I asked, "How did you get this number?"

Daniel was a fine person to chat with about remedial things, but he and I were not friends by any stretch of the word. In fact, in most circles, people would assume we hated each other on account of me being a witch and him being a warlock. No matter how nice Daniel was, deep down, I kind of assumed he was only nice to me because of gran's stellar reputation.

"Olivia gave it to me a while back, in case I needed to reach you."

Thanks for the heads up, gran. I rolled my eyes. "Okay, sure. What's going on? You said you needed my help?"

Daniel fell silent again, and I cleared my throat to urge him to continue. Not that I didn't have time to speak; I was getting eager to hear why he called me. It was so out of the blue I half expected him to say it was a misdial or a crank call. Instead, he sighed deeply, thinking longer before speaking.

"Not on the phone," he said.

Strange. Why call at all if he couldn't talk unless it was in person? The entire incident felt fishy, and I didn't like where it was headed. Warlocks were an odd bunch, and most witches did not trust them. Though I didn't exactly roll with other witches on account of my poor ability to witch, there was something to be said about their collective opinion. Still, gran gave Daniel my number so she must have thought he was a decent guy.

Unless she felt obligated to.

Sometimes I wished I could see ghosts other than Stella so I could ask gran some questions. Like, what was the secret ingredient in her blueberry pies? Did she really cast a spell on the Orchard Hollow mayor when he wanted to cancel the Christmas parade that one year? And most importantly, why in the name of everything magic did she go around handing my number out to warlocks?

I banished the wayward thoughts and turned my attention back to the phone. "Why did you call if you can't talk about it? You're killing me here, Daniel."

"Trust me, it's better to talk in person. There's a lot to explain. It's important, more important than even I realized."

Cryptic much? I sighed. "Okay, so what do you propose? Pistols at dawn? Come alone?"

Daniel muttered a stretch of curses under his breath.

"Sorry," I said. "I just find this entire thing bizarre. You call me out of the blue when I didn't even know you had my number, tell me you have something very important to tell me, but can't actually say it? It sounds like a big hoax. Why me?"

"I'll explain everything tomorrow," Daniel said. "Can we meet in the cafe when you open?"

I laughed before I could stop myself. "You'll have to be more specific. The cafe won't be opening for some time."

"Right, the machine. How about six tomorrow?"

"In the morning?"

"Of course. When else?"

The call went from hoax to annoyance in under sixty seconds. I wasn't a morning person and the idea of getting up early when I didn't have to made me break out in hives. It was hard enough to wrap my head around being up that early to open the cafe every day, but to do so on a forced day off was blasphemy. I twirled the flashlight on the bench and the light bounced around the greenhouse, making it seem like I was putting out an S.O.S. I slammed my hand over it, realizing too late that Stella might have seen it. Sure enough, my annoying familiar appeared in front of me with her arms crossed in seconds.

She pointed to the phone and mouthed, "Who is it?"

I waved her off, and she stormed away; though I noticed she didn't leave and lingered near the greenhouse door, eavesdropping.

Paying her no mind, I pressed the phone closer to my ear and said as quietly as I could, "Tomorrow at six is fine. I'll see you there. And no more games, please."

"I promise, I will tell you everything tomorrow," Daniel said. "Oh, and Piper?"

"Yeah?"

"Keep this in the family."

Then the line went dead, leaving me wondering what I just took part in.

"Who was it?" Stella asked, reappearing in front of me as soon as Daniel hung up. "Someone cute?"

"It was Daniel, calm down."

She patted her mouth in a fake yawn. "The warlock? How boring. Please don't tell me you're dating the man who believes a leather trench coat is an acceptable fashion statement? I know you're about to hit the dreaded four-oh, but I don't think you should stoop that low."

I squeezed my lips into a tight line and stared her down. "I'm not seeing anyone. Besides, Daniel is not into women, and he definitely is not into witches. Trust me."

"Then why call you?"

"I honestly have no idea," I admitted. "He said he has important information, but he can't tell me in person. He wants to meet tomorrow at the cafe to explain."

Stella cocked her hip to the side. "Cryptic."

"That's what I said! It's weird, right?"

The more I thought about it, the more it bothered me. Things didn't sit right, and Daniel's voice was not the same voice I was used to hearing every day. He sounded panicked and if I didn't know any better, I'd say a little afraid. But why? What could a warlock with as much experience with magic as Daniel be afraid of?

Each second passing made me wish I didn't let him hang up so quickly; I should have dug a little further, pressed him for more information. What if Daniel was in trouble and I did nothing to help? I was sure there wasn't much he needed from me, but I could have at least lent an ear. I could have been more like gran and put myself on the line to help a fellow neighbor and instead I made dumb little jokes and got off the phone with him as soon as possible.

For once, I was relieved not to have seen gran's ghost since she passed. She'd be so ashamed of me right now.

Fingers trembling, I called the last number in my phone history and listened for the dial tone. It rang five times, then went to voicemail, Daniel's cheerful voice on the other end. I hung up and tried again, getting the same response.

He probably didn't want to waste any more time talking to me. Daniel sounded adamant about needing to speak in person and here I was, tripping over myself to get a hold of him. Perhaps the best thing I could do to help was practice a bit of patience. With much regret, I forced myself to stand up and gathered the rest of the ingredients I came for while Stella scowled from the doorway. What I needed tonight was a distraction and what better one than possibly setting the house on fire while trying another spell?

CHAPTER 5

My eyes were half shut when I unlocked the cafe doors and turned on the overhead lights. The brightness overpowered my senses, and I hissed like a wild animal ready to attack. I rubbed my pounding head and walked over to the counter, casting a glance at the espresso machine.

"Delightful time to pick not to work," I mumbled and plugged an electric kettle in.

When in doubt, instant caffeinate.

Pouring a steaming mug of instant coffee, I topped it off with a dollop of cream and took a big gulp. The roof of my mouth burned, but it was so worth it. Sweet, sweet coffee for the win. I could already feel the tension at my temples lighten and my mood improve. Even the perils of Bean Me Up didn't seem as dire as they did when I first walked in and I glanced at the coffee-cup-shaped clock hanging over the door with a tiny bean on each arm, scowling.

It was six fifteen. Daniel was late.

Instead of wasting time waiting on the warlock, I pulled out my laptop from under the counter and searched for the maker of the espresso machine online. It took ten minutes to track down a customer service number and then another fifteen on hold. By the time I got done jumping through hoops to explain my problem to a much too cheerful automated voice, my coffee cup was almost empty.

"Diamond Coffee, how can I help you today?" a woman's soft voice sounded on the line.

Throat tight and full, I tried to regain some level of enthusiasm, even though it was still early, and I very much wanted to crawl back into bed. I would have rather been talking to Stella than having this conversation, but big girl problems required big girl solutions, so I straightened my back and did what mom taught me—fake it, fake it, fake it.

"Hi there," I said sweetly. "I purchased one of your machines from a reseller a few weeks ago, and it seems to have died on me."

"Hmm," the woman said. That should have been

my first red flag. "What's the make, model and serial number, please?"

I walked over to the machine and read out the numbers etched on the back.

"Hmm-hmm." Another red flag. The woman typed on her computer and was silent for what felt like forever. Finally, she said, "I see here this model is discontinued."

"Okay. Do you have someone that can come out to fix it or somewhere I can drop it off to be looked at?"

There was more typing and more silence. I grit my teeth, white knuckling the phone in anticipation. "I'm afraid because you didn't purchase the machine directly from us there's not much we can do," the woman declared.

My jaw snapped. "What do you mean? The store I bought it from said if I have any problems, to reach out to you."

"Where did you say you got it from?"

"A reseller in King City. Let me find the name of the store." Walking briskly to the back office, I rummaged through the desk until I found the receipt for the machine and read out the name and address to the representative.

This was when the red flag of all red flags dropped in my lap. The woman sighed. Full on sighed, and this time, there was no typing on the other end of the phone. "Oh, dear," she said. "I don't know how to tell you this, but I'm afraid you may have been duped. We don't provide machines to any business by that name. I'm also sorry to be the one to break it, but our company does not stock discontinued items; if you purchased one, it didn't come from us. We have had instances where people," she paused, "where some people acquired our machines in less than legal ways and have attempted to sell them to the public. In most cases, when someone lets us know about this, we can report it, but unfortunately a few had been known to sneak through the cracks."

"I'm sorry, what?" My stomach turned and my heart raced in my rib cage. "Are you telling I was sold a stolen machine? How is that even possible? This place had a website and everything!"

"I'm afraid I don't know," the woman said. "Have you tried contacting them?"

"Not yet," I admitted. "I will do so today. Are you sure there isn't someone on your end I can have look at it? I'm in a bit of a time crunch."

"I would love to have better news for you, but since the machine is discontinued and has been for quite some time, we would not have the parts to fix anything that might be wrong with it. And due to how it was purchased, I'm afraid our warranty would not apply."

The headache that was almost gone was back in full swing and I held onto the desk for support. My vision blurred at the edges, and I wanted to scream into a void for ten minutes straight. I also wanted to put a hex on the guy who sold me the stupid machine, but of course that was not in my witch arsenal. My mind was still racing when a scurry of small feet sounded near the back exit. I turned my head, eyes flashing to Harry Houdini's chubby body skittering across the office toward the stash of cookies I hid in the bookcase. He expertly positioned his back feet on the bottom shelf and stretched his arms high in the air, his skinny fingers clawing at the bag.

"I'm sorry, can I call you back?" I asked the representative.

"Of course. Thank you for calling Diamond Coffee. I hope you have a—"

I hung up and yipped toward Harry, grabbing the broom on my way. He saw me coming and jumped away from the cookies, tiny feet running away to hide behind a large box of paper coffee cups lining the office wall. I heard him clamber around and the box shook as he squeezed his robust behind into the tiny crevice.

"You're going to get yourself stuck in there!" I warned him.

If he understood me, he didn't care because Harry

continued to press himself further and further behind the box and make chittering noises as he did so. If someone were to walk in right now, they'd think I was trying to hurt the sneaky monster. Little did they know, Harry was a guest you had to set rules with. If you let him think he had the upper hand, he'd expect the red carpet rolled out for every uninvited visit.

I couldn't remember when Harry became a regular at Bean Me Up. Sometime during the renovation process, when I worked late nights to get the cafe ready for opening. I vaguely recalled half a pizza being stolen one night and then finding Harry lounging in the back office covered in crumbs the next morning. The only good part about my dinner going to waste was Stella discovering the petty thief and screaming bloody murder until I got him out of the cafe.

It was great.

Broom in hand, I reached for the box to move it out of the way, then noticed strange marks on the tile floor. The beast had dragged dirt all over the office when he came in. His paw prints stretched from the box where he hid all the way to the exit I was certain I locked the night before.

"Now you can pick locks?" I asked.

It was then I realized what struck me as odd about his footprints. It wasn't mud that outlined the tiny shapes of Harry's feet, but something else, something red and sticky looking. I bent down and reached my finger in one print, then thought better of it. The last thing I needed was to get sick off whatever the trash panda found in the garbage out back. Standing, I shook a fist at Harry, who remained out of sight and walked to the back door. The plan was to leave it wide open and hope he decided to leave on his own accord. Or if all things lined up, to get Stella in here and scare her senseless.

That plan went out the window hella fast.

As I neared the door, I noticed one of the garbage cans turned over on the ground. Burnt coffee beans covered the alley, and Harry Houdini's prints ran all the way from the door to what looked to be a dress shoe abandoned on the ground. My eyes traveled over the alley. The dumpster was slightly shifted from its spot, the edge of it sticking out further into the alley, and a dark stain on its edge drew my attention. It dripped down to the ground like soot. Near to it, several bags of torn garbage lined a trail from the dumpster to the shoe.

I glanced back at Harry's hiding spot. "What did you get into this morning?"

Slowly, I walked into the alley and approached the mess Harry left behind. My pulse skyrocketed and my heart beat so hard, I thought it was going to tear through my ribcage. Behind the turned over garbage can lay the shoe I saw from the doorway, but that wasn't the end of it.

Attached to the shoe were long, black pants and an entire human body.

Daniel's.

And from the looks of it, he wasn't breathing and hadn't been in quite some time.

Bright lights danced across the brick wall of Bean Me Up and I watched, horrified, as Sheriff Romero taped off the back alley. Or as it was now referred to, the crime scene. I wasn't sure if the Orchard Hollow police force was understaffed or if the sheriff put in a personal appearance due to the nature of what I discovered, but whatever it was, he was taking his sweet time out there. I stayed in the doorway, half in, half out of the cafe and stared, refusing to leave.

Not because I wanted to see the sheriff inspect Daniel's body to confirm what I already knew was true —he was very much not alive. I stuck around because my feet would not work. My entire body stayed glued to one spot since I made the call to the police. Every once in a while, I looked behind me into the office, checking for Harry. The raccoon either sneaked by without me or Sheriff Romero noticing, or he was still hiding, safe from the world and the crap shoot that was the alley. My gaze found his paw prints and my stomach rolled.

Blood. That was what Harry dragged throughout my office.

I touched nothing after I called the cops. Since my nights often involved binge watching crime documentaries, there was no way I was going to implicate myself in whatever was going on here. Though judging by Harry's bloody prints on the tile and the way the sheriff kept glancing in my direction, things were not looking so hot for team Piper. Behind me, the cafe felt exceptionally quiet, and I wondered why Stella chose this moment to stay away. I was going out of my mind, anxiety drowning out every thought with its loud shouts. At this point, arguing with Stella would have been a welcome reprise from the crazy cycle of my worried thoughts.

Which said a lot about how poorly I was doing.

The sheriff did another walk around the alley, then turned on his heels and moseyed in my direction. His thick-rimmed glasses hung so low on his nose I thought they were going to drop as he walked. As he neared me, Romero tipped his head and rolled forward on the balls of his feet. "Tell me again what happened."

I sucked a breath into my paper-thin lungs.

"Last night Daniel called me and said he wanted to talk and to meet him here," I explained.

"And he didn't say why he couldn't tell you over the phone?"

I shook my head from side to side. "No. He said he wanted to do it in person. I tried to call him back after he hung up, but it went to voicemail, so I figured I'd see him in the morning and find out what the urgency was."

Romero jotted notes in the small notepad in his hands and then flicked his stony gaze to mine. "And prior to this, you have never spoken to Mr. Tse on the phone?"

"Not at all. I didn't even know he had my number."

"Which he got from," the sheriff looked back through his notes, "your late grandmother, correct?"

"Yes," I said. "But I had no idea she gave it to him or why. Anyway, when I came in, Daniel was nowhere to be found, so I went about my business. I was on the phone with the coffee company about my machine when I noticed Harry Houdini come inside—"

The sheriff held a hand up to stop me. "Is that the raccoon?"

"Yes, sorry. It's a long story."

"Is this a pet?"

My eyes widened in shock, and I tried not to laugh in his face. "Oh, definitely not! He's a nuisance, at most. Came with the place and refused to leave. No matter what I do to keep him out, he always finds his way in. So now we're stuck together, I suppose."

"Alright. You spotted the raccoon, and then what happened?"

"I chased the little guy into that corner." I pointed to the box. "Then I noticed the prints and went to check out what he dragged in."

"And that's when you found Mr. Tse."

I nodded.

"You didn't touch anything?"

"Absolutely not," I said. "I know how this works."

The look Romero gave me told me he believed I did not know how anything worked, let alone a police investigation where a dead body was involved. He checked his phone and said, "Give me one moment. Don't go anywhere."

I froze in my spot and watched the sheriff walk down the alley to greet a man in a dark navy shirt and pants. The two exchanged words, all while staring me down, then walked toward Daniel's body. While Romero stood off to the side, the other man bent over the body and surveyed it. With the sheriff in my direct sightline, it was hard to tell what the man was doing or read his expression, but occasionally, he would whisper to Romero and the sheriff would scribble in his pad again. After an eternity of standing ramrod straight, Sheriff Romero came to see me once more. "Miss Addison, I'm going to have to be frank here," he said. "I have many questions and very few answers."

"But I told you everything I know," I said. "What happened to Daniel? Was it an accident? How long was he out here for?"

My head spun and my eyes watered. I held to the doorway for support and tried not to act like a lunatic because I was pretty sure I knew how bad this looked for me. A small town like Orchard Hollow didn't have dead bodies showing up in alleyways. It wasn't our way. *Why did I tell him about Harry? I made myself look absolutely insane!*

"I'm afraid I don't yet have those answers, and even if I did, I would not be privy to share them with you. I do, however, have some questions, ones that the coroner is not yet able to answer but will after a full examination."

A chill racked my body.

"I'll be frank," the sheriff said blandly. "I know all about the darker side of Orchard Hollow, as well as your family's part in it."

"I'm sorry, sheriff, what darker side are you referring to?"

Romero's stern look grounded me in my place. "I think we both know what I mean," he said. "There are few humans who have been entrusted with the knowledge of your kind, and my position means that I am to be one of them. It is important to the town that I have all the information I need to do my job."

"Okay," I said shakily.

"That said, there are things about Mr. Tse's condition that strike me as suspicious. Your discovery of his body being one of them."

My stance widened, and the fear I felt before was replaced with absolute shock. Did this man think I had something to do with Daniel's death? The thought was so incredulous it was ridiculous, but Sheriff Romero's burning eyes made me quickly realize he had other ideas. "All I did was agree to meet him today," I said.

"Perhaps. Yet you two were not friends, according to you, and combine that with the witch and warlock situation... You must admit it looks awfully strange that he would be found dead in the back alley of your business."

I had no words. For the first time in my life, I was speechless.

"Miss Addison, I'm need you to do me a favor."

"Of course," I said. "Anything."

The sheriff pocketed his notebook and tapped a finger on the tip of the gold star pinned to his uniform. His dark eyes narrowed with a singular purpose. He looked at me again, and I wished he didn't. Cold air gripped my bones and my legs buckled under the weight of my heavy heart. At my back, the scurry of tiny feet running away echoed in my ears. *Ladies and gentlemen, Houdini has left the building.*

I struggled to smile but my lips refused to cooperate and when the sheriff spoke again, there was no chance I would ever smile again. "I'm going to ask you to close the cafe until further notice," he said. "And I need you to follow me to the station. We need to have a proper chat about what happened here this morning."

CHAPTER 6

Harry Houdini

On most days, you wouldn't catch me dead out and about at this early hour. Today, however, the sun was still hiding, and clouds shielded the town in a murky shade of gray. They looked like marshmallows, and my stomach growled. I looked up, sniffing the air. Winter was on its way.

My thick fur did a decent job protecting me from the cold and as I ninja'd my way from one dark spot to the next, my mouth salivated. So close. A few more blocks and I'd be at the alley behind the cafe, rummaging through a few days' worth of delicious goodness.

Never for the life of me could I get over the things humans threw out. Who would dispose of perfectly good food was beyond me. The witch had a particular knack for delivering the best tasting meals on the strip, which was why I frequented her alley most often.

That and she kept a bag of cookies in her office that was ridiculously easy to snatch.

If not for the transparent woman she spent time with, I'd have moved into the cafe a long time ago. I never understood why the witch enjoyed the obnoxious female so much or why she kept her around. She didn't seem to have any real talent, and she reeked of decay, a scent even *I* could not get used to.

Hind leg walkers. Go figure.

I scooted around a turned over garbage can and stuck a paw out, feeling inside. Empty. My nose wrinkled, and I turned on my heels, speeding up as I neared the alley. Above me, the sun showed its ugly face, and my vision flickered, though my will stayed strong. Nothing was impeding a sweet, sweet meal, and I knew the witch was bound to have an excellent selection ready for the taking. Yesterday there wasn't much going on in the cafe and for a second, I worried I might need to find another take out place to dine in. It wasn't the worst idea, considering it would free me of the incessant see-through woman that seemed determined to ruin my day every chance she got. If it was only the witch and I, I'd like it better.

Turning the corner, I nudged the side of the building with my side and crept into the alley. Here, the sun hid behind the rooftop, and I found it easier to navigate. I'd have to return at night when my senses were sharper to make sure I got all I could out of the situation, but for now, a snack would do.

I tip toed to the closest dumpster and clawed at the sides. My fingers stretched upward, but I still couldn't quite get a grasp to pull myself up. Looking around, I spotted a garbage can on its side and my teeth chattered with excitement.

Success will be mine!

Hurrying to get my paws on whatever awaited me, I pushed around the can and stopped. The smell that hit my nostrils made me wish I didn't eat the last bite of watermelon behind the fruit stand because it was all coming back up now. Gross.

What is that vile scent? Sniffing the air, I tried to find the yummy trail of treats I usually smelled here, but my nose was filled with a nasty combination of lemons and musk—two things I wouldn't be caught dead eating.

I snapped my jaw shut and stepped around the can. What I found was not even remotely close to what I expected. Instead of the usual discarded scones and croissants lay what looked like a human. As I inched closer, I confirmed that this, in fact, was not a croissant but a man leisurely lying behind the garbage can. I wondered if perhaps he also arrived for food and my legs tensed, worrying my meal had been eaten by the stranger.

When I noticed a few stray scones lying on the ground beside him, I relaxed. I leapt at the pastries and shoved one in my mouth, chewing it fast before I was found out. *Finder keepers, loser!* Glancing at the man, I realized he wasn't waking and moved in closer. My nose swiveled to the sky, wondering if the upcoming daylight knocked him out into a deep slumber.

In truth, I was getting awfully tired myself.

As I tried to sniff out the man, I caught the scent of something dreadful and my face scrunched. My blurry eyes traveled over the man's body, and I nearly dropped the scone in my paw when I saw the oozing red liquid around him. Careful not to lose a decent meal, I shoved the second scone in my mouth and clenched my teeth.

This was not good.

The man still wasn't moving, and I was pretty sure he never would again. I'd seen my fair share of roadkill; this guy was no different from a squirrel who met the unlucky end of a truck tire. I glanced at the cafe back door. *The witch would want to know about this.*

Scone still tucked inside my cheek, I pressed my feet into the red liquid and proceeded toward the door, looking behind me to make sure the trail was easy to spot. If she couldn't figure out this out, it was on her. I climbed up the protruding bricks on the side of the building and gripped the door handle, twisting it as I'd done many times before. The door opened, and I dropped to the ground, squeezing through the opening to get inside. Somewhere in the cafe, there was a rattle, and I made my way to the front, ready to warn the witch of the stranger in the alley. I was halfway there when my nose sniffed out a familiar scent. I stopped in my tracks. My head twisted to the shelves lining one wall.

Hmm, cookies... What was I doing again?

It didn't matter anymore and couldn't have been that important because all I could think of now was getting my paws on that yummy chocolate chip and spicy cinnamon. My legs stretched and stretched, and my fingers reached for the bag, scratching at the paper to get it closer to me. Suddenly, the fur on my back stood on end.

I wasn't alone.

Eyes traveling to the office door, I jumped back from the shelf at the same time as the witch sped up toward me. She may have had longer legs, but there was no way she'd be able to get me from behind the boxes she kept stacked here. I skidded around one box and slid into the space between it and the wall.

"You're going to get yourself stuck in there!" I heard her yell.

Pushing further, I snaked my body far enough away where she couldn't reach me, even with the apparatus she referred to as *the broom*. While the witch continued to shout, I twisted around and made myself comfortable. My eyes sparkled in the darkness, and I fished my paw from under me, bringing the prize I scored in front of my face. As luck would have it, I sneaked away not one, but two cookies before the witch came in.

Everything was coming up Harry.

CHAPTER
7

The police station was only a short walk from Bean Me Up, but since the sheriff drove, I decided to follow him in my car. The thought of walking into the station alone made the hair on the back of my neck rise and, considering the gossip mill of Orchard Hollow having eyes everywhere, I figured a casual stroll in with Romero would be better in case anyone spotted me. I was mainly worried about Nancy catching a glimpse of my visit and giving her coven even more ammunition with which to mock me.

Sheriff Romero led the way, and we made the brisk walk from the back parking lot to the station. I clung to my sweater and tried not to shiver like a pigeon over a grate the entire way in. As we passed the small reception area, I made eye contact with the young police officer at the desk; he watched me while we passed, trying to put the pieces together. I assumed he heard about the sheriff's visit this morning and was wondering why I was there.

I was wondering the same thing myself.

"Right this way, Miss Addison," the sheriff said, pointing to a small room at the end of a dimly lit hallway.

I scooted past a row of chairs and walked in. The room was the size of a closet and housed only a table, two chairs, and a tiny window with bars across it. The walls were painted a vomit-colored shade of beige and the overhead fluorescent lights flickered every once in a while, giving the space an even more sinister appearance. *How many killers sat in this room,* I wondered.

Knowing Orchard Hollow, I guessed very few. Though I bet it got its fair share of drunks on the weekend. The few bars operating off Cliff Row drew in a less than favorable crowd, and I assumed most ended up here occasionally after the tequila shots and heated arguments took their turn.

The sheriff closed the door, and it creaked before locking.

"Take a seat," he said when he noticed me hovering over the table like a complete weirdo.

I did as instructed, the chair scraping across the stained cement floor as I sat down. When the sheriff took the chair opposite me and placed his hands on the table, my blood pressure hiked through the roof. Suddenly, my mouth felt dry like a desert, and I tried to swallow spit but failed, making a smacking sound with my lips that echoed down the station. Cringing, I crossed my arms, attempting to appear less nervous. As per usual, I failed miserably.

"You don't have to worry, Miss Addison," Sheriff Romero said. "We're simply having a chat."

"Oh," I whispered. "This is all a little out of my comfort zone. And Piper is fine."

"Alright, Piper. Now that we have more privacy, we can speak candidly. As I mentioned earlier, I am aware of the paranormal nature of some of this town's residents. In fact, I try to keep a rather open mind when it comes to the movements of those with your abilities."

He said the words *abilities* like it was ten times dipped in battery acid.

"So, I understand there is the law, and then there is paranormal law. Two very different things, you follow?"

I nodded.

"Which is why we are having a conversation right now and you are not in cuffs."

The saliva I was lacking before came back and I choked on it, covering my mouth with my hands as I coughed. "I had nothing to do with Daniel's death," I stated.

"Perhaps," the sheriff said. "How long have you known Mr. Tse?"

"A few years, I guess," I answered. "He moved here a while back, but I didn't really know him well. We were friendly when we ran into each other, and he was a regular of sorts in my cafe. Well, as regular as he could be, considering it's only been open a few days."

The sheriff took out the tiny notebook from his coat pocket and clicked his pen. He jotted down whatever I said that piqued his interest then creased his brow. "And you knew he was a warlock?"

"I did, yes."

"How? I was under the impression the paranormal gene did not activate in everyone who had it, so there is no way to know who has abilities and who doesn't."

The way he kept saying the word made me cringe, and I wondered if the sheriff wasn't as on board with paranormals as he wanted me to believe. I couldn't blame him; it was a lot for a human to process. I leaned back in the chair, the hard wood pressing into my rigid back. "That's true," I said. "And even those whose gene activated don't always have much power. Not unless their family has been gathering ley line energy throughout generations."

"This energy gets stored in regular items, correct?"

I pointed to my family's brooch on my chest. "Right. Every family has a reserve of magical energy. Once a person's gene activates, there is a ritual that is performed to feed some of their energy into whatever item the family chose years and years ago. With every new paranormal activation, the energy gets bigger, stronger, amplifying the collective magic of the family line."

"Why?" the sheriff asked.

It was such a simple question for such a complicated thing. In truth, I wasn't even all that sure I understood it myself. "I don't know all the details," I admitted. "The way my grandma explained it was that when the ritual first started among paranormals, it was a backup plan of sorts. A way to store magical energy in case something happened. I guess back in the day they felt a lot more threatened by humans, so they needed a way to have an advantage. A talisman that held the generational magic of an entire family line could be quite powerful."

"And there is only one?"

"Yes. Not every family has one, but those with the longest running magical lineage hold one. It usually gets passed to the firstborn in every generation, but the power of the talismans benefits the entire family. The magic in our blood mixed with ley line energy makes it like a conduit for paranormals."

The sheriff wrote the information down and underlined the words. "What happens when it gets destroyed?"

"Some people say nothing, others say that it will destroy the paranormal who holds it and everyone in their family still alive. It's a gray area, I suppose."

"What do you think happens?"

My belly pressed to the hard table edge as I scratched my arm. "I think it's somewhere between the two. I don't believe the person will die right there and then, but I think it will weaken them enough that they will no longer have any magic left. Or if they do, it will be considerably less than they would with the talisman in hand. Which, sometimes could mean complete destruction." I thought back to the vampire gran got rid of whose age, as the stories go, caught up with him in the blink of an eye with his familial magic gone. If gran truly did what everyone believed, it must have been a gruesome sight to watch; someone aging rapidly before dying. "In most cases, though, all it would do is make a paranormal garbage at magic."

Or in my case, it could happen even with a family talisman on hand.

I kept that part of my theory to myself and cast a questioning eye at Sheriff Romero. "You don't think Daniel's death was accidental, do you? And that his family's talisman may have had something to do with it?"

"Excellent deduction." The sheriff harrumphed under his thick mustache.

Score one for late night cop shows!

"If I were you, I wouldn't say another word, darling," Stella said. I jumped in my seat, swirling around to face her. In the interrogation room's corner, Stella leaned on one shoulder, her long legs crossed and her eyes darting between me and the sheriff. "One thing my husband taught me is to never trust the law."

"Wasn't your husband a convicted embezzler?"

"Excuse me?" the sheriff asked. He looked in Stella's direction but, of course, all he saw was an empty wall.

I swallowed hard. Looking unhinged would not win me any favors here, and I didn't want the sheriff thinking I had lost my mind. I could see it now. Crazy raccoon-hoarding witch kills warlock to steal his magic. Nancy Steeles and her coven would have a field day with the news if word got out I was a suspect in a possible homicide. I needed to get my act together and fast before I ended up on the wrong side of the bars in the police station. Tucking my hair behind my ears, with two unruly strands refusing to cooperate, I straightened my shoulders. "Have you found anything that might indicate someone did this to Daniel?"

"I am not at liberty to say anything yet," Romero answered. "However, considering your position in the paranormal community, I can tell you the coroner did not see anything unusual at the scene, which tells me that if someone hurt Mr. Tse, they didn't use magic to do it. In fact, we may have discovered evidence of drug use. It could explain the fall he suffered."

"You think Daniel got high and, what? Hit his head and bled out?" I asked, adding, "It would explain all the blood." My stomach swirled at the memory of Harry's tiny foot marks on the tile.

"I don't think anything yet," the sheriff corrected. "I have some theories and this is one of them, but we won't know for certain until the coroner runs a toxicology report. I will say that the wound on Mr. Tse's head was likely the cause of death, and the marks we found on his arms are consistent with repeated drug use."

My arm still itched like crazy, and I bit down on my tongue to keep my fingers at bay. "Not that I don't appreciate the info, but why are you telling me all this?"

"Because I need you to understand the gravity of the situation, Miss Addison. Your grandmother was a big supporter of peace between the paranormals in Orchard Hollow and a friend. I would hope you to hold a similar position."

"I-I do!" I stuttered. "Of course, I do!"

"While I am glad to hear it, it doesn't change the fact that Mr. Tse's body was found behind your place of business, you were the last phone call he made, and there is a known rivalry between warlocks and witches lasting generations," the sheriff said. "I want you to have all the information out of respect for Olivia, but I still have a job to do. And as it stands, I must keep an unbiased opinion until we have confirmation of Mr. Tse's cause and time of death."

Stella scoffed, and I fought tooth and nail not to snap at her. When I didn't acknowledge her existence, she said, "I told you, can't trust the law. He'll have you locked up before you can say hocus pocus."

"We don't say—" I crossed my arms and focused on the sheriff. "What does all of that mean for me?"

"It means I need you to stay in town until I say otherwise, and that the cafe is to remain closed for the time being."

With that, the sheriff stood and motioned for the door. I followed him out, walking silently down a hallway that seemed so much longer now than it did on the way in. Behind me, Stella muttered to herself and blew raspberries at the sheriff's back, a childish act

I tuned out. As I walked, all I could think of was what Stella said about not trusting the police. Not that I agreed with her, quite the opposite. But what were the chances Sheriff Romero would solve this on his own if magic *was* involved? And while there was no confirmation of it yet, Daniel's death did seem suspicious. I had a hard time believing that he was a drug addict. He struck me as a mellow individual who didn't care for much excitement. Granted, I didn't know him well, but still. The sheriff said repeated drug use, and that did not sound like the Daniel I knew.

So why did he have marks on him proving otherwise?

And if the sheriff was right, why did he make sure I was the last person he talked to? Why ask to meet me at all?

I couldn't help but feel that something was missing in this massive, gruesome puzzle; a crucial piece the Orchard Hollow police department might overlook. Mentally slapping myself, I refocused my attention on the present and stepped out of the police department into the fresh air of the morning. Who did I think I was? Some witch detective who could outsmart the police after watching a depressing amount of television nightly?

Not only did I not have the energy or the ability to find out what happened to Daniel, but I would likely make matters even worse if I butted my nose where it didn't belong. Instead of getting hung up on Stella's insane ideas, I had much more important things to think on—how on earth was I going to pay my bills now that Bean Me Up was indefinitely closed?

CHAPTER
8

T he rest of the day went by in a blur. The thought of returning to the cafe made me gag, so I spent the remainder of the morning and some of the afternoon wandering the shops of Cliff Row; window shopping since I couldn't afford anything. I considered popping into the diner, a short walk down from the main street, but in the end, headed home for lunch. Microwaveable noodles were all the comfort food I needed, and I already had the cupboards stocked up with enough ramen to feed an army.

When it came to dining, cheap and easy were always first on my list. I loved to cook but my cooking went the same way magic did—it was very messy and often left a foul taste in your mouth.

Gran was the cook in the family.

I salivated remembering her extra gooey risotto and, as I walked up the driveway to the front porch of the farmhouse, immediately regretted not going to the diner. Though I supposed given the morning I had, I wouldn't be able to taste anything anyway, so spending money on a delicious meal would be a colossal waste.

Taking the first two steps, I stood stone still and stared at the large brown envelope lying by the door. I looked around to see Charlie, the local mailman, but he was nowhere in sight. Stepping closer to the envelope, I nudged it with my foot before bending down to pick it up. It was strange to see a package arrive. Most things I ordered online were for the cafe and shipped directly there. Other than due bills and mom's postcards, I almost never received mail.

I turned the envelope over in my hands. It was heavier than a regular letter would be, and there was a slight bulge on one side. *Probably for gran.*

My eyes widened as I read the return address and a knot formed in my stomach. The envelope came from Daniel and was posted on Wednesday, the day before I found him in the alley.

"What in the..."

With unsteady hands, I ripped open the top and

peeked inside. There was a stack of papers and a shiny object on the bottom. I thought back to the phone call and tried to remember if Daniel mentioned sending it, but nothing came to mind. Dropping my bag on the porch, I walked toward the bench and sat down, the envelope in my lap. Carefully, I pulled out the paper stack. My lips parted as I flipped through it.

The contents made even less sense than Daniel's phone call.

There were several newspaper clippings from a local paper dated three years ago outlining a death which took place in the Rose Hollow Hotel. I skimmed them briefly, recognizing the name of the woman whose life ended in one of the rooms. Rosemary Hayes. As hard as I tried, I couldn't place a face to the name, though I vaguely remembered what happened. The town was in a frenzy for weeks after, since, like murders, unexplained deaths were not exactly common here.

I picked up one clipping and read.

"Rosemary Hayes, a local of Orchard Hollow, was found in room 312 of the Rose Hollow Hotel early this morning. While the police are yet to post an official statement, we have confirmation that Ms. Hayes died of a heart-attack at approximately three in the morning. There was no prior history of health compli-

cations. A service is being held for close friends and family at the Orchard Hollow Funeral Home and all those wishing to attend are instructed to contact Christopher Hayes, brother of the deceased. We wish to offer our greatest condolences to the family in this time of grief."

My teeth chattered, and I put the article down, looking through the rest. They were all similar in vain; a brief outline of what happened and not much in the way of information. If gran was here, I could have asked if she knew Rosemary since she usually had information on the town's business. Not that gran was a gossip, but people came to her for advice and spilled way more than was necessary. Gran used to say that her greatest gift was not magic, but her ability to listen to others without judgment. It was a gift I wished to have.

After reading all the articles, I focused my attention on the next piece of paper in the pile. This one was typed on thick, expensive paper. My rubbery knees knocked when I realized what it was.

Somehow, Daniel had gotten a hold of the autopsy report for Rosemary Hayes's case.

I squeezed my thighs together and read it. The coroner's handwriting was worse than a five-year-old's and I could only make out every third word. From what I strung together, they ruled the death natural and confirmed what the first article wrote: Rosemary died of a heart-attack. I tried to read the other notes in the report, but it was a hot mess of scribbles and dots, so I gave up, resting it onto the pile of newspaper clippings on my lap.

Then I fished into the envelope.

My fingers touched something cold and hard, and I fought the urge to yank them back. A tingling sensation ran down my spine and I felt the magic inside me rise to the surface. It was so rare for me to feel this way that I almost cried out. Circling my palm around the shiny object I saw earlier; I gripped it hard and pulled it out in one fell swoop. As soon as it was before me, I understood the reaction I had.

In my palm lay a crystal pendant. It was purple and, from the looks of it, made from pure amethyst. A thick chain dangled off my fingers, the clasp broken. The stone was quite large, though that wasn't the thing about it that made it special. This pendant was, without a doubt, magical. Why did Daniel send me a magical talisman?

I let the pendant drop while holding the thick brass chain and watched it dangle from side to side.

"Is this your family's magic?"

I checked the envelope again to see if there was an answer, but I already emptied it out. No mention of who the pendant belonged to. I pressed a finger to the stone, hoping to get a glimpse of a clue but whatever effect it had on me before was long gone. Either that or my crap magic refused to cooperate.

If it belonged to Daniel, why did he get rid of it? No one in their right mind threw away a family talisman. And why me, of all people?

Confusion laced through me, and I hated that my plans to relax after a grueling day were now replaced with worry and panic. Pressure built behind my temples, and I tossed the pendant back into the envelope and grabbed the stack of papers, ready to get them out of my sight. As I did, the coroner's report dropped from the pile and floated to the ground, landing face down on the porch. I knelt to pick it up, noticing a few more scribbles on the back of the yellowing paper.

The writing differed from the front and seemed to have been etched in a hurry.

If you get this, it's too late. -D.

My fingers gripped the edge of the paper and the sweat collecting on my palms wetted its sides. Knuckles white, I reread the words over and over, dread settling in the base of my chest. "Did you write this message for me?"

None of it made sense and I couldn't for the life of

me understand why Daniel entrusted me with this strange package days before he died. The only thing I could think of was if Sheriff Romero got wind of it, things would go from bad to worse in a flash. What else did Daniel do tying me to him? What other secrets did he hold and why was I involved in any of it?

Tears blurred my vision, and I blinked them away, refusing to succumb to the pressure. I looked at my phone and the time it read. Four thirty in the afternoon. Going to the police station to hand over the envelope made me cringe, so I decided to give myself the night to think things over. Tomorrow morning, I would tell Romero what I found and make sure he knew I am as clueless as he was with this case.

I studied the return address on the envelope, a crazy idea taking shape.

"Don't trust the law," I repeated Stella's words.

Maybe my less than stable familiar had a point. Before I gave Romero the envelope, I needed answers. Specifically, I wanted to know what else Daniel might have been hiding that led the police my way. It was an insane plan, but one that has now taken full-time residence in my brain. I glanced at my phone again, then at the sun shining high in the sky.

Tonight, when the sun sets, I needed to visit Daniel's apartment. I still had no clue what I was going there for or how I would get in, but one thing was for certain, by the morning, I would know why I was in the middle of all of this.

More importantly, I would get ahead of the crap-shoot that landed on my doorstep and clear my name before the sheriff got any more ideas about how involved I was in Daniel's death.

CHAPTER 9

Daniel's apartment building was an old, low rise at the edge of town. It sat close to the cliffs and had an amazing view of the water, which meant the wind whipping my hair around was akin to a small hurricane. I zipped up my jacket and scurried along the side of the building, feeling like a cat burglar. In truth, I resembled a lost creep that was way out of her comfort zone. With the mountains on one side and a sea view on the other, it was easy to see that this place was for the posh and proper, both of which were things I was not.

I brushed my hair down with my hand and opened one of the large glass doors leading to the lobby. My eyes narrowed on the digital display that lit up when I walked in, displaying the word *welcome* in bold, large letters. I tapped the display to bring up a list of last names and buzzer codes and scrolled down until I saw Daniel's name.

Foolishly, I pressed the numbers then cleared them immediately, realizing that wherever Daniel's cellphone was, it was ringing right now.

I scowled, hoping I didn't make matters worse for myself.

This was a dumb idea, I thought.

Before I could turn around, the lobby door swung open, and an older man stepped out. He nodded a curt hello and held the door for me, waiting. I looked around, making sure it was me he gestured to. When it became obvious I wasn't a resident—because heaven forbid I didn't make an interaction awkward for once—the man let go of the door.

"Waiting for someone?" he asked. I noticed his foot nudged in the frame, in case I wasn't a serial killer.

I smiled as wide as my mouth would let me. "A friend. She'll be down soon, I'm sure. Taking forever to fix her hair."

The way the lie rolled off my tongue made me feel all kinds of icky inside, but I tried not to let it bother me. I didn't want him calling the cops on my sorry behind because that would only lead to more questions and a scenario I one hundred percent did not want to find myself in. I was sure I would get cuffed and hauled to the station, so when the man opened the door wide again and said "Might as well wait inside," I all but dove for the lobby.

Thanking him on my way in, I waited for the door to close and for his footsteps to recede. For good measure, I looked around the lobby for a good two minutes before bolting for the elevator. As fast as humanly possible, I pressed Daniel's floor, then tapped the door close button more times than was necessary.

The elevator ride was as slow a ride as one could imagine, considering the age of the building. When it finally reached the fifth floor, the door rattled before sliding open and the entire elevator shook violently. It was straight out of a horror movie, and I half expected for a chainsaw-bearing lunatic to come barreling toward me. Instead, I was greeted with a gigantic, gold-framed mirror and a fresh bouquet perched atop an antique console table. Below the mirror, a gold plaque spelled out directions for suite numbers and I turned right, speeding toward Daniel's apartment.

"Not good," I whispered to myself as I stared at Daniel's door.

There was yellow police tape across the center and when I jiggled the handle, I wasn't surprised to discover the door locked. My head swiveled side to side to check if anyone was around before I ducked down to eye level with the keyhole.

"What are you even doing?"

I checked the hallway again, then reached inside my bag, pulling out a hairpin I stored at the bottom of my purse. Not that I was prepared to pick locks at a moment's notice, more that my purse was a hot mess express train headed nowhere fast. I'd be shocked if I didn't find Harry living in there one day.

Sweat beaded on my forehead as I jammed the pin into the lock and twisted.

Nothing happened.

Obviously, because this wasn't a movie, and I wasn't some suave lock-picking mastermind. I tugged at my ear and tried to think of what to do next. I could search for lock-picking on the internet but having that in my history seemed like a bad idea. There was only one other option, and I was certain I'd have been better off with the hairpin. This called for magic.

I sighed and reached back into the bag, praying I didn't leave gran's witch-on-the-go kit at home. "Aha!" I yelled out a little too loud when my fingers grazed the velvet pouch. I yanked it out, checking the ingredients. All I needed were a few acorns, some moon water and good old Addison magic. I had two of those things.

Crushing the acorns with my foot, I poured out

the moon water and mixed until I got a paste the consistency of rough porridge. I dropped the hairpin into the grimy mixture and made sure it was plenty covered before sticking it back inside the lock. My fingers pinched the end of the pin, the hard metal digging into my skin as I closed my eyes and called for my magic. If I was gran, or mom, or even Nancy Steeles, I would have already been inside Daniel's apartment.

Unfortunately, I was me and it took at least five minutes before I gathered enough magic to feed into the spell. The pin vibrated in my hold and as I twisted it again, I heard a click inside the lock. My eyes bulged, and I reached a shaking hand to the handle, turning it open.

The door swung into the apartment, and I fell back on my butt, shocked that my magic was useful for once. "Take that, Stella," I whispered into the dark apartment.

Picking my sorry self off the floor with little grace, I snuck into the dark and quiet of Daniel's home. As far as first impressions went, the warlock's apartment was like every other apartment I've been in. It wasn't until I turned the flashlight on my phone on that I realized how impressive it was. The entire place was one enormous open area with a hallway off to the right of the living space, which I assumed led to the bedroom.

The first thing that caught my eye was the gargantuan television mounted on the wall and the leather couch that could sit ten people comfortably. Opposite the couch, a modern cement coffee table held a stack of design books that looked like they had never been touched. The spines were in perfect condition and a direct opposite to my books at home that resembled ancient relics because of how often I read them. To the left of the couch was a sprawling kitchen with marble covering all surfaces and a vast island with brass finishes filling the center of the floor. Much like the books, the kitchen didn't seem to be an area that was used often.

Daniel's apartment looked as though it was staged for a magazine shoot and not a place one lived in.

I considered taking my shoes off out of respect for the delicate home but opted out when I realized I did not plan on sticking around for long. Taking the first step into a bad idea, I walked through the apartment, careful to shift my balance from my heels to my toes so as not to make any noise. If the police had been here as the tape on the door suggested, they left everything the same way they found it—in pristine condition.

A few more steps in and I was standing in the kitchen. My fingers grazed the cold marble, and I opened a few cupboards to peek inside. Nothing stood out as out of the ordinary except for the fact that Daniel's kitchen was quite bare. It seemed the warlock either spent little time here or he lived a minimal lifestyle, both of which struck me as odd. This place was expensive. We're talking hire-an-interior-decorator expensive. Why bother dumping so much cash into an apartment you're not going to use?

I closed the cupboards and checked the refrigerator, finding very much the same empty shelves there.

"Super strange," I whispered.

"No kidding."

My heart leapt into my throat, and I bit my tongue as I twisted around. The taste of iron filled my mouth, and I gagged on its metallic flavor. Behind me, Stella shimmered, then reappeared again. "Calm yourself, it's only me."

"Can you please, for the love of everything good, stop doing that?" I whisper-shrieked. "What are you even doing here?"

Stella shrugged; her body more transparent now than it had been this morning. *She must be having a rough day.* "You're joking," she said incredulously. "This is the most exciting thing you've done since I met you and you expect me to sit it out? No, thank you."

"Go home. I'm not even sure what I'm doing here and you're only going to distract me."

"Absolutely not," Stella said. "Nice work with the lock, by the way."

I knew what she was doing and while I wanted to pretend it didn't influence me, I'd have been lying. Compliments from Stella were few and far in between, so if she thought she would get her way by buttering me up, she was right to think it. My traitor mouth spoke before I could hold myself back. "Fine. But stay out of my way. Go check the bedroom while I finish up in here."

Eyes gleaming, she gave me a salute. "Sure thing, boss! What are we looking for?"

"I have no idea."

"Understood. Check the bedroom and look for nothing. On it."

With that, she vanished from my sight, and I loosened a breath. My gaze locked on a small console table under one of the three windows on the opposite side of the apartment and I walked over briskly, my hand reaching for a stack of papers there. There were two bills that weren't due for a few weeks and tickets to an opera in King City scheduled for next weekend. I looked at the tickets, noting there were two. "Who were you taking to a show, Daniel?"

My fingers skimmed through the papers and stopped when I saw the Rose Hollow Hotel logo in the top left corner of one page. I pulled it out, reading it slowly. It was a printout of an email sent to Daniel three weeks prior and when I read the contents of it, my stomach flipped.

"Daniel. I don't know who you think you are, but I will not stand by while you sabotage everything I worked for. You do not deserve this promotion and I'm going to prove it. You're going down, warlock. Mark my words!!!"

There was no signature at the tail of the email, but there was a return address at the top of the page. "Craven?" I studied the email address again and there was no mistaking it; it came from a Rose Hollow Hotel server and was registered to someone with the last name Craven. Only one person worked at the hotel with that last name. "Cilia."

Of course, it was Cilia Craven because life was just that wonderful. There were a good number of witches in town, but only a few that got under my skin. Nancy was one, and her coven mates were the others. Cilia was not only a coven member, but she was also Nancy's shadow. Where Nancy was, you could be sure you'd find Cilia trailing along and hanging onto her every word. It was sad to watch. It was even sadder when the two of them got together in their attempts to throw shade my way and made it that much harder to ignore them. I always wagered Nancy and Cilia never matured past high school and while the rest of us moved on with our lives, they were still stuck in the my-crew-is-better-than-your-crew stage.

I growled under my breath. If anyone would hold a grudge over something as petty as a promotion, it was Cilia. I knew Nancy egged her on in the background and made her even more angry with Daniel. I didn't even realize Daniel had received a promotion at the hotel until this very moment, nor that he and Cilia were on the outs over it.

Could Cilia have been mad enough to hurt Daniel?

I found that hard to believe.

"Hey! Sherlock Holmes!" Stella yelled out from Daniel's bedroom. "You might want to come over here."

Stacking the papers back in the order in which I found them, I rubbed my temples and followed the sound of her voice. On the way, I passed a door that, when I opened it, led to a very nice-looking bathroom complete with a clawfoot tub. You knew you had money when you made the conscious choice to have a clawfoot tub. The one we had at the farmhouse was old and decrepit and I would give anything to have it removed and replaced with a sensible shower, but here was Daniel, spending money to have one installed. Must have been nice to have those freedoms.

I closed the door to the bathroom and walked down the hall to the only other room in the apartment. The bedroom suite was, no surprise, stunning. For starters, the bed was bigger than my entire bedroom at home. It was also so high that I wondered if Daniel needed a step ladder to climb into it every night and made it a point to check for one. Turned out he didn't, so I guess I was simply that short. As I passed the bed, I ran a finger over the duvet and shuddered. It was the softest thing I'd touched in my life. The wall behind the bed was designed to form a wall-sized headboard that looked to be as soft as the sheets. There was a small seating area opposite the royal bed and two French doors opened to a walk-in closet fit for a king.

The closet was where I found Stella, standing with her arms crossed and her translucent foot tapping away. She pointed to an open dresser drawer. "Look inside."

I peered into the drawer and gasped. There, next to a pristinely folded stack of undershirts, lay a small pouch I recognized all too well. I didn't even need to check the contents to know that it was a hex pouch, one that most witches could put together with little effort. A hand sewn rune was roughly stitched into the fabric; three crossing lines with an upside-down crescent moon at their center. I looked from the pouch to Stella, then back again. "Why did Daniel have a hex pouch?"

"To hex someone," Stella said. "Obviously."

"Or was he hexed?"

I thought back to the email from Cilia and frowned. If I was being honest, I didn't want to believe Nancy's coven mate would stoop that low; though, knowing those witches, I wouldn't put it past them. I reached for the hex pouch and stopped myself. *Do not touch a hex, idiot.* My fingers itched to pick it up, and I shoved my hands in my back pockets to keep them at bay. "I bet those witches had something to do with this," I told Stella.

"What witches?"

"Never mind," I said. "Let's get out of here. I'll fill you in at home."

We started for the front door when my attention caught something on the floor. Close to the bedroom lay a small carpet with two silver dishes, one filled with water and the other empty. I bent down and picked up the empty dish, reading the inscription etched into the metal. "Margaret the Third."

"Who?" Stella asked.

I put the dish down. "Daniel's dog. Did you see a dog around here?"

The ghost shook her head and looked around.

"Me either. Very odd."

"Could someone else have it? Or maybe the police took it."

My thoughts ran a mile a minute, and my breath came out short as I continued the trek to the front. "Maybe." Before leaving, I went back into the kitchen and opened all the cupboards. Motioning for Stella to get closer, I nodded toward the big bag of dog food in one cupboard. "Don't you think if they took the dog, they'd take her food?"

"I don't know," Stella said. She opened her mouth with a fake yawn. "Well, this was about as fun as a trip to the dollar store. Good luck with the rest and I'll see you at home."

With that, she disappeared, leaving me alone in the apartment once more. I stared at the dog food for another few minutes, trying to figure out why someone would take Daniel's dog, but not anything to feed her with. If Daniel had a dog sitter, I was sure they'd take care of the animal, considering how important she was to the warlock. And if it was the police who took her... I shook the thought away. Why did the police need a spoiled brat of a dog? If anything, they'd ship her off to a shelter.

I made a mental note to check the animal shelter in the morning to ease my spinning mind and walked to the front. Before I left, I cast a glance at the stack of papers on the console table where Cilia's threatening email hid in the pile.

"Why was she so angry with you?" I asked the empty room.

The next question I kept to myself, refusing to give it power. Was Cilia angry enough to kill? If she hurt the warlock, it still didn't explain the envelope I received or the talisman. Unless the talisman was Cilia's and Daniel stole it?

But why?

It seemed the visit to the warlock's apartment only sparked more questions, and I still found nothing to help clear my name. "What if—No! Don't even think about it!"

I reached for the door handle.

"Don't think about what?" Stella asked behind me.

My mind must have been spinning furiously because this time, I didn't have a mini heart-attack when she snuck up on me. "I thought you went home."

"I did. Turns out it's quite a bore there as well," she explained. "What is it you shouldn't think about?"

Lips in a thin line, I looked at the console table again. "Wondering about the dog," I told her. "And the hex pouch. And Cilia."

"Who's Cilia?"

"One of Nancy's coven mates. Looks like she was pretty ticked off with Daniel for some promotion he got. I was wondering if she could have been mad enough to take it one step further."

Stella's face paled, or as pale as it could get for a ghost. "Witches will be witches, darling." She turned around and started to vanish again, but before she did, she said something absolutely crazy. "If you're that worried about it, why not ask her yourself?"

As my wild familiar disappeared, her words lingered in the air where she once stood, and for the first time, I didn't think her unhinged. I hated to admit it, but Stella had a point. There was one clear way to answer all my questions and find out how I got roped into this awful situation.

I had to question Cilia, and I had to do it before the police. If I was right and she was to blame for Daniel's death, I knew the witch would pin the entire thing on me, if only for the chance to gain favor with Nancy.

This was exactly why I didn't have a coven.

You couldn't trust a witch, not in Orchard Hollow.

CHAPTER 10

The night dragged on, and I slept a total of four hours, give or take, most of which were interrupted with Stella's random musings on how Cilia could have murdered Daniel. At one point, I vaguely recall throwing my pillow at her and getting told off by a furious ghost for my rude behavior. When Stella finally left me alone, I stared at the moonlight reflecting on the bedroom ceiling and tried to talk myself into some courage for the morning ahead.

Now, standing over the kitchen counter and sipping from an extra-large mug of piping hot mocha, I realized I was not the best cheerleader.

I was shaking in my boots.

"Maybe it's best you come clean to the sheriff," Stella suggested.

I took another sip, my tongue burning with delicious goodness, and knifed my eyes to her. "Didn't you tell me not to trust the police?"

"That was before I realized you're a worse detective than you are a witch," my familiar replied cheekily.

Don't snap at the rich dead woman. I put down the mug and licked the trail of whipped cream off my top lip. "Never mind that. I'm going to tell the sheriff about the envelope and everything else I know," I said. "But I need to make sure nothing else comes up that pins me to this mess before I do that."

Stella cocked her head to the side in a way that told me she didn't believe me. Her long body floated to the living room, and she made it a point to run a finger over the fireplace mantle, lifting it up to her face to inspect the dust gathering there. It took Stella months to learn how to interact with the physical world and it still baffled me when she used the skill to get under my skin. After two years of dealing with her shenanigans, I was quite accustomed to the backhanded insults Stella tossed my way and instead of getting upset, I treated them as a barometer for how the snobby ghost was feeling. Extra attitude meant Stella was in a good mood, so I took it for what it was.

"Where did you go last night, anyway?" I asked.

"Oh, you know, here and there."

That was as much of an answer as I was going to get out of her. For someone who constantly stuck her nose into my business, Stella was a vault with her comings and goings. I often wondered if she hid things to get a rise out of me or if the ghost simply drifted off into nothingness when I wasn't around. It was a self-absorbed stance to take, but there was very little I knew about the afterlife or why I could see Stella in the first place. Why her and not any other ghost? Stella assured me she wasn't the only one trapped in the realm of the living time and time again and yet I couldn't quite believe her. If there were others, you'd have thought I'd see them.

Unless the ability to see Stella was another half-baked witch power. If I was like my great-great grandmother, surely, I could commune with the dead. As luck would have it, I could only commune with a frustrating dead aristocrat who made my life more difficult than it needed to be.

Not bothering to get into it with her this morning, I let Stella's answer slide and turned my attention back to the coffee. My only friend in the farmhouse.

"I should head out soon," I said. "If I want to catch Cilia off guard, I need to be at the hotel early."

Stella eyed the mantel despairingly. "Are you sure

I can't interest you in staying here to clean this filthy house instead?"

I flicked a piece of toast off the counter and into the sink. "Careful," I warned. "It's sounding like you might be worried about me."

"Can you blame me?" Stella asked. Her eyes darkened, and she pouted her lips, making them appear even larger. Was it possible for a ghost to have work done? Because Stella was looking fresher today than yesterday. For a moment, emotion swelled in my chest at the thought of her caring for my well-being. Right until she said, "If this witch does you in, I might not be here anymore."

I rolled my eyes, polished off the last drop of mocha, and headed for the door. The weather had cooled overnight, and I had to bundle up in my warmest fall sweater and tweed coat to stay warm. Though my nerves may have played a part in the shivers that ran up and down my body as I walked from the front porch to the car. At my back, the trees rustled in the wind, and I could feel the energy of the ley lines coursing through the air.

How I wished gran was here to help me through this. She would know what to do.

Willing myself to climb into the beetle, I shut the door with a slam and started the engine. It roared to life with the power of a lawnmower and before I could chicken out, I backed the car out and made my way into town. Ready or not, I had to do this.

The Rose Hollow Hotel cast a wide shadow over the sidewalk as I stumbled out of the beetle and walked in. The grandiose colonial style building took up a good portion of Cliff Row and when I stepped through the front doors, I tried not to turn around to check on Bean Me Up across the street. Seeing the cafe closed would only spark more doubts in my mind, so I kept my steps quick and my back rigid as I hurried into the hotel lobby and to the reception desk.

At this early hour, the hotel was so quiet I could see why some thought it haunted. The thick, ornate carpet lining the mahogany floors camouflaged my steps and the only sound in the distance was that of the doors closing behind me. I walked past the small seating area made up of two antique sofas and a hefty wood coffee table. There was a slim side table to the left of one soda with pamphlets on site-seeing in Orchard Hollow, most of which I assumed had been dropped off by local businesses.

I made a mental note to print a few off for the cafe

and leave them here if Cilia didn't have me arrested by the end of our conversation.

Next to the sitting area, I spotted a bronze elevator door with an abandoned luggage cart next to it. On the other side of the lobby, a long hallway veered off to the left, and I heard light voices somewhere beyond it. Rooms filled with guests getting ready to start their day, no doubt.

I tip-toed to the reception desk and waited. When no one came, I pressed the small silver bell on the counter and cringed as the sound reverberated through the lobby. It took only a few minutes for Cilia to appear. Her shoulder-length hair was curled into pristine messy waves, and she wore a bright red shade of lipstick, making her gaunt cheekbones appear even sharper. She dashed to the counter, her mouth thinning when she spotted me.

"Piper," she said, not bothering with a hello. "What are you doing here?"

Talk about service...

My finger was still on the bell, so when I pulled it away, I accidentally hit it again. Cilia groaned. I shrugged. Then we stared at each other for way too long. *This is your cue to talk. Now or never.* I crossed my arms and took a step away from the reception counter. "Hi, Cilia. I was hoping we could chat for a minute."

Cilia looked at the watch on her wrist and scowled. "What is this about? I have a busy morning. With Daniel gone—" her words cut short, and her eyes burned into me. "Why are you here, Piper?"

"Well, since you brought up Daniel, he's kind of the reason I'm here."

"I'm not sure I follow."

The look Cilia gave me implied that either she didn't understand why I was there or, if she did, she was a better actress than I gave her credit for. I'd assumed her to be Nancy's minion, for lack of a better word, but if my suspicion was correct and she was capable of murder, lying wouldn't be that far off. Maybe I should have listened to Stella and gone to the sheriff instead.

Too late now, I told myself, drawing my attention back to Cilia. "Look, you're crazy busy here and I won't waste your time. If you could help me out and answer one question, I'll be out of your way."

"I don't have time for this," she said and started to walk away.

Watching her retreating, I yelled, "I know about the email!"

Cilia's body froze. Her foot hovered an inch off the ground and if this was a cartoon, there'd be exclamation points flashing over her head right now. My words struck a chord, and the thought both excited and chilled me to the bone. As Cilia turned around, I took my phone out of my bag. If she tried anything, no way did I have the magic to thwart her, so the best I could do was a 911 call since I doubted anyone would hear me scream in the lobby.

Walking slowly, Cilia stopped a few feet away from me as though I was the one she should fear and not vice versa. "What email?"

"You know what email," I said. "The one you sent Daniel about his promotion threatening to come after him."

The witch swallowed hard, and I suddenly had a matching lump in my own throat. "He told you about that?" she asked. Cocking her hip, she eyed me with a newfound appreciation I hadn't seen from her before. "I didn't realize you two were that close."

I kept my eyes wide open. Apparently, when I had nothing to say, my go-to was a staring contest. I cursed myself out in my head and tried to get the conversation back on track. "Why were you so angry about his promotion?"

"Are you serious?" Celia asked, quirking a thin brow. "I worked in this hotel for almost five years. Five years, Piper! That's a long time to work somewhere. It's not like I didn't have other places I could have gone but I stuck it out, despite it being a lower position, because I knew eventually, Isabella would need a manager. This place got popular too fast for its own good and her plan to be a hands-off owner wouldn't last long."

"Because of the ghost stories," I mused.

Cilia nodded. "Yes, because of those. So, I waited it out until Isabella figured it out and wanted someone to manage the place when she wasn't around."

"And I guess she did?"

"Oh, she did alright," Cilia said. "Except she never even posted it. You'd think she'd want someone who knew the hotel inside and out to take the job, but no. You know what she did instead?"

I shook my head.

"She brought Daniel in. Literally out of nowhere! One day I'm minding my business, trying to figure out the best way to approach her and the next, I have a new boss. Some guy she pulled off the street who doesn't even have experience running a hotel." She bit her bottom lip. "Didn't."

Before I could speak, Cilia continued her rant. "You know he dumped his best friend in a business they started to work here, right? Who does that? Yeah, I was pissed. Daniel didn't deserve that position, and I did. I wanted to make sure he knew it and I wanted him to understand that I don't care what Isabella decided. No way was I going to take orders from a warlock."

My jaw slacked.

"You knew Daniel was a warlock?" I asked. Daniel didn't strike me as someone who advertised his magic; I only knew of it because he was on good terms with gran. Strange that Cilia would know, of all people.

"Um, yeah," she said. "I think he let it slip one time. Probably a power move to set me in place."

Everything in Cilia's story checked out until that. Sure, Daniel was a warlock, but he wasn't a bad guy. I could not see him use his paranormal position to influence Cilia, and I definitely couldn't see him throwing a friend under the bus for a job. This wasn't adding up. I pulled at the edges of Cilia's words, trying desperately to fit the pieces together, but they wouldn't click into place. I was missing an integral part of a very intricate puzzle.

Placing the phone back in my bag, I set my gaze on Cilia. "Do you know the name of his business partner?" I asked. Following up with, "I can't remember it and I'm sure Daniel would have wanted me to pay a visit."

She looked me up and down, trying to gauge how someone like me could have been close to a warlock. As far as the paranormal society went, I kept to myself so I could understand her confusion. No doubt when I left here, Cilia would give Nancy Steeles a call and the gossip would be all over town by lunchtime. I wondered if the lies about my relationship with Daniel would come to bite me in the butt later.

Too late now.

"Charlie," Cilia said. "Savaun, I think. I don't remember."

She looked at her watch again and I took it as my cue to leave. Before I got out of Cilia's way, I faced her head on. "One last question," I said. "Did you ever end up talking to Daniel about the email?"

I was given a look of pure disdain that Cilia quickly masked with a wicked smile. She wanted me out of her hair, to call Nancy no doubt, and was growing tired of my questions. I couldn't blame her. I wasn't even sure where I was going with this pathetic attempt at an interrogation. Cilia backed away from me and said, "He never mentioned it. I bet I scared him off and then..." she paused. "Why are you asking all these questions?"

"I'm trying to figure out what happened to my friend," I said. It was only half a lie. "It all went down so suddenly; I'm trying to wrap my head around it. Do you remember seeing him on Wednesday night? After he finished up here?"

The suspicious look Cilia gave me made me take a few more steps toward the door. For someone playing detective, I was not at all prepared to stand my ground.

"I was off Wednesday. Spent the night at the Drunk Elephant with some friends."

Great. If Cilia was at the local bar on the night Daniel was killed, I'd never be able to confirm it. The Drunk Elephant filled up to the brim on most evenings and I doubted Eli, the owner and bartender, could account for every person who walked through the door. Plus, the friends Cilia mentioned were her coven mates and there was no way in fresh hell any of them would talk to me let alone rat her out if she was lying.

Which I didn't know was the case.

In our entire conversation, she said nothing that made it sound like she wanted to hurt Daniel. She was angry, sure, but her anger was superficial. And if I was being honest, I'd have reacted the same way if everything I worked hard for got taken away by someone I didn't think deserved it. It was looking like the email Cilia sent was a dead end, but as I said my goodbyes and left the hotel, I didn't walk out empty handed. I had another name.

Charlie Savaun.

Standing in front of the hotel, I pulled my phone out and searched for Charlie's name online. It took only a minute to track him. There was no one by that name in Orchard Hollow but my search pulled up a real-estate agent in Rockaway Ridge, a neighboring town. And by the looks of it, the agency had an office a half hour drive from where I stood.

I climbed into my car and pulled out of the parking spot, heading down Cliff Row toward the turn off out of town. As I parked at the stop sign, guilt gnawed at the lining of my stomach. To my right, a short drive over, was the police station and the place I should be heading. To my left, Rockaway Ridge.

Body stiff, I clicked on the turn signal and stepped on the gas, driving left toward my next destination.

CHAPTER 11

Rockaway Ridge was, for lack of a better term, Orchard Hollow's bland sister. While both towns had the same mountains tucking them away from the rest of the world and shared the same coastline, Rockaway Ridge lacked the charm of my hometown. Perhaps it was the nostalgia of home, but I could not imagine living here.

I veered the car down what I assumed was the central street in town and scrunched my nose at the view. There were no cobblestones to greet me as I drove in, no welcome sign above and most of the businesses appeared to have either been bankrupt or barely standing. To sum up, this place was a depressing stain on the map.

Checking my phone, I slowed down and counted off the numbers on the buildings until I located Charlie's real estate business. From the opposite side of the street, it looked like it had seen better days. The windows were so filthy I couldn't see through the glass and the sign above spelling out the name missed several letters.

"Savau and Tse Rea State," I read out. "Yikes."

I slammed the car door shut and walked across the street, avoiding the heap of garbage on the sidewalk. To my left, two women chatted next to a street side patio, and they glared at me questioningly when I passed. I guessed Rockaway Ridge did not get many visitors. Shocker.

When I approached the door to the real estate firm, I toyed with the idea of turning around, still uncertain why I drove here. But I came out all this way, so what could be the harm in checking it out? I wanted to know if there was any truth to Cilia's words and if there was, perhaps Charlie could point me in the right direction. Perhaps he knew why Daniel threw me into the dumpster fire that was his life.

Trying the handle, I found the door shut, even though the sign on the front implied it should be open. I pressed my nose to the glass, trying not to gag at the grime my face collected. The place was dark, but I noticed a faint light at the far end of the cramped area.

There was one table along the back wall and two leather chairs near the front that have seen better days. *Who in their right mind would use this agency to find a home?*

I thought back to earlier in the year when I secured the lease on Bean Me Up and the pristine condition of the real estate agency back home. Not only did I feel like I walked out of a five-star business when done, but they sent me home with the lease and a bottle of champagne to celebrate. One glance around this place told me the champagne fountain dried up a while ago.

Reluctantly, I knocked on the glass and waited.

And waited.

It took some time before I heard footsteps shuffling inside, followed by the shape of a burly man approaching. He wore a thick sweater and wrinkled brown slacks. The man's short hair was a solid mix of brown and gray, and his thick beard looked like it could use a proper shave. He fit right in with the rest of the office. When he noticed me at the door, he clicked the latch and pulled it half open. "Hi there. Can I help you?"

"Mr. Savaun?" I asked. "Charlie Savaun?"

"That's me," the man responded with a smile. "If you're here about a property, you should know the agency is closed. I can recommend another agent in the area if you prefer."

I was about to go into staring contest mode again, so I cleared my throat and tried to appear less desperate. "Actually, I'm here because of someone we both know," I said, then added, "knew."

It took Charlie less than a second to catch my drift. His eyes reddened and for the first time, I noticed the puffy circles under them. "You knew Daniel?"

"I did. Not as well as you, I believe, but still."

Charlie's lips parted, then closed; he took a step to the side, opening the door wider. As I stepped into the grimy space the hairs on the back of my neck stood straight, and I realized I should have been more on guard. What did Cilia say about him and Daniel? The warlock dumped this guy to work at the hotel and, by the sad state of the real estate office, I'd say it had quite an effect. What if Charlie and Daniel got into an argument over Daniel's decision to leave? What if Charlie took it a step further?

My hands fisted, and I stopped short, keeping myself as close to the door as possible. *I should have gone to the police with this,* I thought.

As if reading my discomfort, Charlie walked further away, giving me space. He sat in one of the leather chairs—that screeched for dear life as he did—and leaned his elbows on his thighs. Looking up at me, the man appeared broken and the lack of sleep on his face was quite evident now. "You'll have to excuse my appearance," he said. "I haven't been able to sleep since I found out about Daniel. Are you from Orchard Hollow? Do you know what happened to him?"

I thought I was supposed to ask the questions.

"I don't know much," I said. Kind of true. "I was hoping you might help me figure out why someone would want to hurt Daniel."

If it was possible for a man to shatter like glass, I'd have been sweeping Charlie into a dustpan. His posture stooped, and he ran his hands through his beard over and over, fingers clawing at the nest there. "So, it's true? Daniel was... he was..."

"Killed," I said. "I believe so. The police won't share any information, and I'm trying to piece it together for myself."

"Why?"

Because your friend roped me into his death. I walked over to the empty chair near Charlie and sat down. "Daniel and I weren't close, but he was always nice to me. I can't imagine someone wanting to hurt him. And in Orchard Hollow, of all places. It would ease my mind to know what happened and," I took a deep breath in, "I guess I feel like I owe it to him. I don't have a lot of friends."

I'm not sure why telling this man that I was a complete loser was pertinent, but it seemed to have done the trick. Charlie's face brightened, and he leaned back, appearing to be more at ease than before.

"Well, I'm not sure how much help I can be," he said. "Daniel and I haven't spoken in months. Not since he left our business here out of the blue."

"To work at the Rose Hollow Hotel," I said.

"Uh-huh."

"Did he say why he did it?"

Charlie looked out the window and thought for a moment. The thin strip of light piercing through the film of dirt brushed over his brow and when he creased it, the lines looked dark and deep, aging him. "That was the thing," he said. "Daniel never told me why. He called me one day and told me he was leaving and for me to do what I pleased with the agency."

"And that wasn't normal for him?"

"Absolutely not. Daniel knew I sank my life savings into opening this place with him. Hell, it was his idea! We talked about starting a real estate business since we graduated from college, so for him to up and leave was completely uncharacteristic."

I looked around the office and said, "Could it be he needed the money and the hotel offered it?"

"I doubt it," Charlie said. "Not sure how well you knew Daniel, but he never needed money. He inherited a good chunk of cash when his father passed away. Enough to set him up for life. This place existed because Daniel took a chance on us and helped me invest in it."

Thinking back to Daniel's apartment, everything made sense. The opulent decor, the nonchalant way Daniel carried himself; it all pointed to someone who did not have to struggle daily. I took my chance while Charlie was in a sharing mood. "Did you stop talking because of it?"

His chin dipped, and he looked to his feet. "Yes. And every day I wish I wasn't so hung up on myself," Charlie explained. "I should have put my pride aside and called him. The guy was my closest friend, family, since high school. I can't believe I ruined our friendship over money. I mean, sure, Daniel's move destroyed me, but I should have known better."

My ears perked up, and I held my breath.

"Destroyed you how?" I asked.

Charlie scoffed and motioned around the office. "Look around. Without Daniel here, I couldn't make this place run on my own. Daniel was the one out there getting clients. He was good with people, put them at ease. After he left, I tried to make it work, but I didn't have what it took to close deals. It got to a point where it was keeping the agency or paying the mortgage. I gave up everything to open this place and without it, I was done for."

"And Daniel knew this?" I found it hard to

believe someone would let their best friend—or family, as Charlie implied—get ruined. No matter how much I wished to, I couldn't blame Charlie for cutting the warlock off. It was a garbage move on Daniel's part.

"Look," Charlie said. "I know what you're thinking. But trust me, Daniel must have had his reasons. The inheritance dried up; I don't know. Whatever it was, it wasn't worth ruining years of friendship over. And now..." His eyes wetted, and he rubbed them with the back of his hands. "Like I said before, I don't think I can help you out much. I didn't know anyone who might have wanted to hurt him. The only person he ever had an issue with was Seb, and I doubt he did it."

"Seb?"

"Sebastian. His cousin," Charlie said. "When Daniel's dad died, he got the better end of the family estate and Seb wasn't too happy about it. From what I remember, Seb thought he deserved to be in on the main action and butted himself into the family business, one Daniel never wanted a part of. The two of them couldn't even be in the same room during the holidays because Seb was unbearable. Anyway, when Theodore died, he left the vineyard to Daniel and he up and sold it from under Seb. Man, did they have it out then. But trust me, that guy doesn't have it in him to do anything except complain. He's frustrating, but he's not a killer."

Maybe. Maybe not. If Daniel's cousin was a warlock too, he'd be capable of a lot more than Charlie imagined. I narrowed my eyes at him, wondering if he was privy to those family secrets. "Did you ever notice Daniel acting strange?" I asked.

"Strange how?"

"I'm not sure," I lied. "Like he was keeping secrets."

"Not really. But we haven't spoken in a while, so if he had something to hide, it could have been after we stopped talking. Daniel wasn't one to share his feelings, though I knew him as well as anyone else."

For a moment, I saw his eyes dart to the brooch on my sweater, then glance away. A glimmer of discomfort flashed over his face, and it made me question if perhaps Daniel shared more with his friend than Charlie was letting on. Did Charlie know about paranormals? Did he know about the pendant Daniel sent me and what it meant?

I pulled out my phone and scrolled to the photo of the pendant I took the night before, showing it to Charlie. "Have you seen this before?"

"Nope," he said. "What is it? Looks expensive."

"Never mind," I said, putting the phone away. As I stood up to leave, I looked down at Charlie and asked,

"Do you know why Daniel might be interested in an old case at the hotel from years ago?"

My statement rattled Charlie, and I could see the wheels in his head turning as he tried to figure out what I was asking. His brows crept low over his eyes and his thick lips pressed together, almost entirely hidden under the weight of his beard. This was not the face of a man hiding the truth. "I don't think I knew him all that well anymore," he said. "I planned to call him, you know. After I got back from a job interview in King City. But then when I returned, I got a voice-mail from Seb telling me what happened."

I wasn't sure if the statement was for my sake or Charlie's, so I stayed quiet.

"I should get things going here," he said, pointing to a stack of boxes leaning against one wall. "Turns out I got the job. Start next month."

"Congratulations," I said. "You're moving to the city?"

"Looks like it. Crappy way to leave a town, I'll tell you that."

He stood up and walked me to the door, his eyes on the floor the entire time. I didn't know what I accomplished by talking to him; I managed to make a sad man even sadder. Fantastic. Score one for the team. I let out a muffled breath and stepped into the street, turning to face Charlie. "Thanks for talking to me," I said. "I'm sorry about Daniel. I'm sure he knew how much he meant to you."

"I appreciate it. And do me a favor? If you get to the bottom of this before the police do, give me a call. The number is still the same." He handed me a business card with the name Savaun and Tse Real Estate and a phone number under the logo. I took it, shoving it into my bag so I didn't waste any time standing around. I had the feeling that the conversation I had with Charlie stirred him up, and while my intentions were good, I may have caused more damage in the process.

What was that saying about good intentions? I was on that well paved road right now; I could feel it.

Waving goodbye, I got into my car and closed the door, glaring at the street before me. Charlie seemed to think Daniel's cousin didn't have it in him to kill, but I wasn't so sure. Two warlocks in a feud? It could get ugly. If Sebastian *was* a warlock, as I theorized. Thinking of magic made me recall the other strange thing I found in Daniel's apartment: the hex bag. Gran never dealt in hex magic, so there wasn't much I knew about them, but there was one place that would have answers.

The thought of going to Brooks Books and seeing Joe made my stomach flip, and I pushed the nerves aside, telling myself this was not the time to milk a schoolgirl crush. The only thing Joe Brooks had for me was access to books on the paranormal. It definitely wasn't his chiseled jaw. No way.

I gave my thigh a hard smack and turned on the ignition, speeding away toward Orchard Hollow. I had two stops to make to keep my curiosity from driving me up the wall, and I dreaded both equally. Before I faced Joe and, without a doubt, made a fool of myself, I needed to speak to Sheriff Romero. It was time to tell him what I'd been up to and hope he didn't take it as a sign I was trying to cover my tracks. Here's to hoping I didn't land myself in jail before I saw Joe again.

With images of an orange jumpsuit crowding my mind, I made the tedious drive back home, fingers white knuckling the steering wheel the entire way.

CHAPTER 12

If there was an award for the most awkward entrance into a police station, I'd have been shaking a presenter's hand to receive it. When I walked into the station, it was at the same time as an officer walking out. As he swung the door open, it slammed into my shoulder, whirling me around hard enough to splatter into the brick wall of the building. The officer hurried out to make sure I was fine, and I recognized him as the young man I saw at the desk when I was here with Romero earlier.

He must have realized who I was because as soon as it was clear that I was just dandy, he backed off. "Hello, ma'am," he said.

When did I become a ma'am? I didn't think I

looked like a ma'am, but here I was, being ma'amed to next Thursday by someone who was almost half my age. I dusted myself off and tried to regain some composure. "Hi there. Is Sheriff Romero inside?"

"He is," the young officer said. "Anything I can help with? I believe he's on a call right now."

I considered telling him everything I came here to say about the envelope, Cilia, and what Charlie revealed about Daniel's financial situation. In the end, I decided it was best to speak to Romero as I was dealing with him before and, well, I could be more forthcoming about certain things. Things of the magical variety.

"Ma'am?" the officer asked since I had clearly zoned out.

For the love of!

"I'll wait inside until he's done if that's alright."

The officer tipped his hat and walked off, leaving me to attempt stepping into the station again. This time, I double checked the path was accident free and when I opened the door, I scurried in and headed straight for the reception desk. With the young officer gone, a woman took his place. She seemed quite busy and was typing ferociously when I approached. Her eyes met mine briefly, and she smiled before continuing what she was doing. I assumed that meant I needed to wait.

When the woman finished the world's longest writing streak, she motioned for me to come closer. "How can I help you today?" she asked, not blinking.

"I was hoping to speak with the sheriff," I answered. "I have some information regarding Daniel Tse I believe he'd want."

The woman's head tilted to the side like a retriever, and she eyed me suspiciously. "The sheriff is otherwise engaged right now. If you'd like, I can—"

"I can talk to her now, Marie!" the sheriff's voice boomed from down the hallway. "Send her through."

At his instruction, the woman said nothing else and only gestured toward the sound of Romero's voice. When I passed, she turned back to the screen and continued to clank away on the keyboard. *Is she writing a novel over there?* I bit my lower lip and hurried down the hall before Romero changed his mind. The first door to my right was wide open and when I neared it, the sheriff yelled out, "In here!"

I turned into the room, pleasantly surprised to find a small kitchen and not another concrete box meant for criminals.

"What can I do for you, Miss Addison?" the sheriff asked, dumping half a carton of cream into his coffee. When he noticed me staring, he added, "Can I pour you a cup?"

I for sure did not want whatever goop he was

peddling. "I'm okay," I said. "I was hoping to talk to you about Daniel. There are some things that—"

Romero held a hand up and I sealed my jaw shut. "It's a good thing you stopped by. I meant to call you later today so you're saving me the trouble."

"Oh? Is everything alright?"

"As alright as a case such as this can be," the sheriff said. "I wanted to let you know you can open the cafe back up."

"But Daniel?" I asked, baffled. "And the investigation..."

"The case is closed. We got the coroner's report back, and it was as I suspected. It seems your friend was under the influence and suffered a fall in the alley, causing him to hit his head pretty bad on the dumpster. It's an unfortunate event, but that's all it is."

What was he on about? Under the influence? An unfortunate event? None of those things corresponded with the web of secrets Daniel's life had been. The way the sheriff spoke made it sound like Daniel's death was an open and shut case, and I knew in my gut it wasn't. There were too many strange things surrounding Daniel for it to be nothing more than an accident. Unless I was pulling on strings and looking for a mystery where there wasn't one. My head pounded, and I tried not to let it show. Was I so desperate for excitement I fabricated a murder to give myself something to do?

I wasn't that pathetic.

At least, I didn't think I was.

"Are you sure it was an accident?" I asked. "Daniel sent me—"

I rolled the words over in my mouth, then swallowed them. What was the point of telling the sheriff about the envelope? Daniel had an accident and died. The coroner confirmed it. A questionable envelope filled with even more questionable items did not make it otherwise. All it did was prove Daniel was not in his right mind, and high as a kite most of the time. The more I thought about it, the more the sheriff's conclusion made sense. If Daniel was prone to drug use, he likely wasn't thinking clearly when he sent me the envelope. I mean, even his best friend didn't know about it.

Lips shut, I stared at Romero. I was looking a gift horse in the mouth, and I almost slapped it silly. The case was closed, Daniel's death explained; I could get back to getting the cafe back up and running. It was an early birthday present, and I had come this close to messing it up.

I didn't need to get involved. I shouldn't have been involved in the first place.

"Miss Addison?" the sheriff asked.

"Sorry. I'm relieved it's all over. And thank you for letting me know."

Romero smiled for the first time since that morning in the alley. "Of course," he said. "It's a shame it happened, but I'm sure you're eager to get back to business."

Returning his smile, I started for the exit. "Do you know if there's going to be a service?"

"I believe Sebastian Tse is handling the funeral plans. I'd reach out to him for information."

"His cousin?"

"Correct," Romero said. "Quite the gracious gesture if you ask me. From what I gathered when speaking with him, the two were not on the best of terms."

So, you did do your homework... I bid the sheriff goodbye and left him to enjoy his mug of sadness in peace. Sneaking past the reception desk, I scooted out of the police station and climbed into the beetle, the pressure on my shoulders releasing. With the mish-mash of Daniel's untimely death out of the way and me no longer under the police's eyes, I was free to get back to what truly mattered: the stupid espresso machine and trying to get my life back on track.

Two hours of searching on the internet finally paid off, and I secured another machine for an affordable cost. It was scheduled to be delivered in two days, which meant I had some time on my hands to figure out how to reopen with a bang.

Sitting at one of the small tables of Bean Me Up, I did my best to design a few flyers for the cafe. My art skills were not great, but I managed to put together a decent looking advertisement with a coupon for a free refill to anyone who purchased a latte on the first day Bean Me Up was to reopen. The plan was to drop it off at every business on Cliff Row that would have me and pray it worked. I was certain most wouldn't mind. People helped each other in our town, but there was one place I knew would take some convincing. I peered through the front cafe windows. Across the street, the Rose Hollow Hotel stared back at me, mocking me with its grandness.

It would be great if I got lucky and Cilia wasn't around when I came begging for help.

I thought about reaching out to Isabella Beaumont, but that would have been uncalled for. The woman lost her manager in a horrible accident, and I couldn't picture her taking my asking to use her hotel as a marketing ploy well. That and I never actually spoke to Isabella outside of a few vague instances which all involved me speaking and her looking through me.

No matter, I'd figure it out.

I saved the flyer to a flash drive and dumped it in my purse, planning to get a few printed off down in the library on my way home. As I closed my laptop, I heard a scurry of small feet followed by loud cursing from the office. I jumped up and bolted through the back door, readying for what I already knew would be an epic disaster.

I was *so* right.

In the middle of the office, Stella took a wide stance, her hands in fists and up at her sides. She was almost entirely transparent and I could see right through her grayish body, all the way to the desk atop which Harry Houdini rose on his hind legs and hissed at the ghost. There was something wedged in his mouth, and I tried to inch closer to decipher what it was.

"Put that down, you vile, insolent creature!" Stella bellowed.

I walked around her to stand between them, my hands up. "What is going on this time?"

Stella hissed. The raccoon hissed back.

I groaned.

"Seriously, what is up with you two?"

My familiar pointed a see-through finger at Harry and said, "He stole it right out of your drawer."

My head swiveled from her to the raccoon, and I worked to understand what had Stella up in a tizzy. It wasn't anything new for Harry Houdini to steal from the cafe. In fact, it was so common that on days when he didn't get his grabby paws on one of my belongings, I wondered if the little guy was okay. I turned back to Stella. "Stole what?"

"The necklace," she said.

"What neck..." My eyes rounded and when I looked at Harry again, I realized what it was he held in his teeth. The rascal had opened my desk drawer and grabbed the pendant Daniel sent. I had completely forgotten I brought the envelope here. Taking one careful step after another, I neared Harry. "Now, listen here, buddy. I'm going to reach my hand out and you're going to drop the pendant, got it?"

My palm twisted, and I pushed my hand closer to Harry's mouth. His eyes grew feral, and he chittered through his clenched teeth, then hissed at Stella for good measure.

"Oh, absolutely not!" she shrieked. "I will not have a dirty trash gremlin speak to me that way!"

I wasn't sure who was crazier: Stella, the raccoon, or me for being in the middle of this circus. Ignoring her freak out, I kept inching closer to Harry, hand still out. "Come on," I whispered. "You can do it. You can—"

Harry dropped on all fours and jumped off the desk. He landed on his feet clumsily, then rolled to the side, his bulging behind knocking over a bin of coffee grounds and spilling them all over the floor. Not thinking, I dove for the raccoon like a linebacker. I catapulted through the air, landing half on top of Harry and half in the beans. My knees hit the floor with a thud, and I yelped in pain, but it didn't faze me. I was victorious.

The raccoon twisted beneath me, and I got a good whiff of whatever garbage he ate before ransacking my office. With one arm locked around him, I reached over and grabbed hold of the chain. Careful not to get bitten—no one had time for a rabies case—I yanked at the metal, wrestling with Harry until he finally had enough. The raccoon spat the pendant out and it fell on the floor, bouncing a little when it did. I climbed off him and watched him run his little feet in place until he got enough traction to hightail it out of the office. His furry back slithered through the crack in the back door and he was off in the dust, disappearing.

I really needed to start checking that door.

When I turned around to face Stella, she was sitting with her legs crossed on the edge of the desk.

"You're most welcome," she said, and vanished almost as fast as Harry.

I rolled my eyes. My chin dipped, and I looked at the pendant cradled in my hand, then at the river of coffee beans on the floor. Harry Houdini sure had an easy time stealing the shiny thing. My vision lasered in on the stone and my heart gave a jolt as an idea popped into my head.

What if Daniel stole the necklace?

A family's magical talisman was nothing to joke about and if Daniel lifted it off someone, it would be cause enough for them to come after him. I knew what the sheriff said, but what if he was wrong? What if Daniel got himself into a sticky situation like Harry Houdini often did? Except this time, it wasn't me with a broom on the other end.

If my theory was right, then Daniel would probably need help to protect himself from whoever was after him. "Putting a hex on someone would be pretty useful," I told myself. "Get them before they get you."

My fingers closed around the amethyst, and I took a deep breath in. Even if it was an accident, it didn't explain the pendant, and somehow, deep down, I felt it all connected. Could a warlock use a hex on his own without the help of a witch? The hex bag was in Daniel's closet, so he must have had plans for it. I didn't know anything about that side of witch magic.

It was starting to look like my original plans were still in order.

Without hesitation, I grabbed my coat, brushed my hair out with my fingers, and headed for the front door. It was time to pay Joe Brooks and his bookstore a visit.

CHAPTER 13

Brooks Books was one of those bookshops that wouldn't last a day in the city, but here in Orchard Hollow, it fit right in. Tucked away on the corner of Cliff Row and a narrow side street, the sign for the shop poked out of the building's side; a decorative wrought-iron emblem of a book with the name Brooks in cursive letters below it. As I neared the shop, my heart sank further into my boots with each step. I hadn't visited the bookshop as often as other paranormals and the idea of mingling with the magical inhabitants of the town left a sour taste in my mouth. It was a constant reminder of my own short-comings, though this time, it wasn't my self-esteem that was causing me turmoil. Seeing Joe again did not sit well with me.

Mainly because of my unfortunate luck with men.

The last guy I dated was a big-time financial advisor in King City with a demanding job, not unlike what I pictured of Joe's legal career. It wouldn't have been all bad—considering my need for personal space —had the rodent who shall not be named been a decent person. But of course, this was someone I picked out, so he was far from it. Five months into what I thought was a committed relationship, I made an impromptu visit to the city for a surprise romantic weekend and promptly found the rodent in bed with another woman.

Turned out being a financial advisor wasn't the only job the sleaze bag had that weekend. As I found out later, there were quite a few *jobs* he was getting into while I was back home, clueless to his cheating ways.

Needless to say, I swore off men after that. At least those I didn't vet first with a fine-toothed comb.

That was two years ago.

The bookshop sign got larger as I approached, and I noticed my traitorous feet picking up speed. My stomach twisted into knots, and I battled the urge to cram my entire fist into my mouth so I could bite all my nails in one go. I was a few feet away when the door opened and the small bell above it rang out. Out stepped a tall brunette in a white coat. Her hair was tied into a pristine low chignon and when she noticed me staring, she smiled widely. "Hello," the woman said.

"Hi, Ember," I said, hurrying up, so she didn't get stuck holding the door for long. "How are you?"

Ember looked at her watch, then tucked a brown paper bag with whatever book she purchased under her arm. "Oh, you know. Busy as usual."

"I won't keep you then," I said and snuck inside the shop.

I watched her walk away through the large window with the shop's named etched on the front. As she crossed the street, she checked her watch again and rushed away until I could no longer spot her. Ember was constantly in some sort of hurry, which wasn't all that surprising considering she owned the only pharmacy in all of Orchard Hollow. You wouldn't think a pharmacy would get much traction, but for some reason, ours did. Come to think of it, I didn't think I'd ever seen Ember without her lab coat on; either the woman worked round the clock, or she wanted people to think it. Ember was a strange breed and while I didn't know her well, I knew gran held her in high regards. Though that likely had something to do with her being the only female werewolf in our town. Like vampires, werewolves kept their paranormal identities hush hush amongst the magical crowd, much more so than witches did, but a female werewolf wasn't a secret you could easily hide. They were rare—a magical unicorn of sorts—so Ember's secret was bound to make its rounds around the rumor mill. As did her recent separation from her husband, but I chose to stay out of it. I had no intention of becoming the next Nancy Steeles, gossiper extraordinaire.

Thinking about secrets drew me back to why I was here, and I peeled my gaze from the window and took in the bookshop. It was exactly as I remembered it. Small and crammed with books to the brim. It smelled of old paper and dust and as I inhaled, flashbacks of visiting here with gran overpowered me. I walked down the compact space between two large bookcases and read out the labels. *Manifesting and the Moon. Blood Magic. Ley Lines: Histories and Uses.* There was no order to how the books were arranged, but those of us privy to the underlying nature of the shop knew what to look for.

When I passed the first row of bookcases, the shop widened, and I walked into an open area with a round table in the center and several wood chairs tucked in. From here, five other aisles veered off into different directions, each one containing similar bookcases with even more tomes on the paranormal. In the center of one aisle, I spotted a young couple that didn't seem to be local. The man had a book in his hands and flipped through it, confused. Beside him, a woman read the spines on the shelf with a crinkled nose.

Tourists.

I hurried past them and turned into the aisle I knew had most of the volumes intended for witches. As I did, my shoulder slammed into a shelf and it wobbled, causing a book to pop out and tumble down. I reached to catch it, my palm colliding with what was definitely not the book.

"Ouch!" Joe groaned as I slapped him across the forehead. He rubbed his head, eyes flashing to me. "If we keep meeting this way, I might think you have it out for me."

I reached for the book on the floor, then remembered the last time we did this and stayed put. Joe double checked I wasn't going for it, and when the coast was clear, picked it up. He tucked it back on the shelf and turned to me. "Piper, right?"

"That's me," I said.

"Looking for anything in particular, or are you popping in to check up on me?"

Joe's lips curled at the edges, and I bit the inside of my cheek to keep from making a fool of myself. It didn't work because what I said was, "Oh, just checking you out." My eyes bulged and heat rose from my neck to my cheeks. "Checking the shop out," I corrected.

If Joe saw my embarrassment, he chose not to comment on it. *Point one to Joe. Negative forty-seven points to Piper.* He looked around the shelves and rubbed the back of his head. "Surprisingly, this place was a turnkey operation. My uncle seemed to have left everything in perfect order and ready to go. It was almost like he knew I'd be taking over."

"Call it serendipity," I said. "How are you settling into Orchard Hollow?"

"Fairly well. I still get turned around here and there, but I'm getting the hang of the place. Everyone seems friendly."

I briefly wondered if he met Nancy yet because she'd be more friendly than was necessary. "It's great here," I said. "But I'm not a good judge. I've lived nowhere else."

"Trust me," Joe said. "Other places are overrated. You have it good here. Nice people, beautiful views, and I hear there's a new cafe that has the best caramel mochaccinos!"

Is he flirting? He can't be flirting. I haven't even brushed my hair today. Did I brush my teeth? I took one small step back because I couldn't for the life of me remember the answer. What was wrong with me these days? I forced a smile. "Oh, now I know you haven't gotten out much! The cafe is still closed. Though now I feel I have to add the mocha to the menu."

"Only if I get the credit for suggesting it," Joe teased. "And royalties."

"Mocha à la Joe?" I asked. "How about a muffin on the house instead?"

Joe grinned. "You drive a hard bargain, but I'll take it." He tucked his chin, pinning me with a serious expression. In the hollow of his eyes, I saw a darkness creep in. "How are you doing, though? I heard about what happened to the hotel manager."

"Word gets around fast," I murmured under my breath.

"Nothing like that. I was in line at the grocery store and overhead a conversation." He held his hands up. "Not trying to start any rumors, I promise."

"Let me guess," I mused. "Bleached blonde, tight mini dress, lipstick overkill?"

He nodded. *Nancy Steeles.* Who else would chat away about a man's murder as though it was the latest news in a gossip column? That woman was unbearable! For the first time, I was relieved my magic skills were so lame because I'd have hexed her butt right on the spot. My body tensed and I straightened up, looking at the shelf beside me. As lovely as it was chatting with Joe, I was here for a reason, and it wasn't to line up the next heartbreaker on my list of failed relationships.

Sucking in a sharp breath, I wrapped my cardigan tighter around me and said, "I should let you get back to work. I think there's a pretty confused couple in the tarot card aisle who needs help."

"What is it with all these books?" Joe asked, scratching his chin.

"Your uncle had a unique taste in literature," I lied.

Joe chuckled. "Unique is one way of putting it. But hey, don't change what isn't broken, right?" He started to walk away and stopped. "Keep me posted on those caramel mochaccinos. And don't think I won't be collecting the promised muffin when you open."

When he was out of sight, I let my shoulders sag and breathed out. Poor Joe had no clue how unique this bookshop was, and I felt awful for keeping him in the dark. His uncle never spilled the beans on the paranormal, and it sure wasn't my place to do so. Unlike Nancy, I knew when to keep my mouth shut. I almost envied Joe. There were many nights I wished to be clueless to the world of magic and to exist as a human. Things seemed much less complicated where magic wasn't involved.

Case in fact, Daniel.

I spent the better part of the next hour skimming as many books as I could find on hex magic and found nothing resembling the pouch in Daniel's closet. The symbol on the front didn't match the rune I discovered, and I began to think coming here was a moot point. Sure, it was nice to see Joe again, nicer than I cared to admit, but I was as empty handed as when I walked in. More so because now I wasn't sure what I saw at Daniel's was not a hex at all.

Then what?

I was about to give up when another book caught my eye. I ran my finger over the faded title on the spine. *Protection Spells and Charms.* It was worth a shot.

Ten pages into the book and I found what I was looking for. The symbol on the pouch stared back at me and I read the spell ingredients quickly before getting to the purpose. According to this book, the charm protected one's mind from being magically influenced. I reread the paragraph, my brain running a mile a minute. Did Daniel fear someone might use magic against him? More importantly, who was the witch who created the charm? It couldn't have been Cilia since I doubted she'd do anything to help Daniel, considering the tense relationship they had. I turned to the next page, but there was nothing there. Whatever this spell was, it wasn't a commonly used one.

Closing the book, I walked down the aisle, my hand grazing the shelves as I went. Somehow, I doubted any of the books here would offer more details than I already found. Was it possible Daniel needed the charm to protect himself against the person he stole the talisman from? No, that couldn't be it. With the talisman gone, the paranormal it belonged to wouldn't have much power. Certainly not enough to magically control Daniel.

Unless the theory I had earlier was correct: a family matter gone out of hand. Perhaps Sebastian wasn't as innocent as Charlie seemed to believe, and there was more to the feud. Money got to people, made them different, and if Daniel and Sebastian already had bad blood, could Daniel selling the vineyard have pushed his cousin over the edge? A protection charm would do wonders against a warlock's magic. But to fear your own family? Warlocks weren't as close knit as witches were, but I still couldn't imagine someone killing their own over an inheritance.

I was missing an integral part and I couldn't put my finger on it.

A magical talisman and a protection charm—what did they have in common?

My feet froze in their tracks as a thought emerged. That wasn't the only clue I had. I pulled out my phone and searched for Rosemary Hayes, remembering the clippings Daniel sent.

Most of the results were to do with her death and I skipped over these, not wanting to recount what I already knew. There were a few links to a local book club and when I clicked on those, I saw Rosemary's name as being one of the participants. No one else rang a bell and when I went down the rabbit hole of tracking down the other members, none raised any red flags. I continued to scroll, almost giving up when I came across a Facebook profile matching Rosemary's name. The woman was fairly active on social media, which was uncommon for Orchard Hollow; people here stayed off the radar and lived a quiet, simple life.

I clicked on the link for the profile and waited for it to load. When it did, my mouth dried up.

Most of the posts Rosemary made were about books she was reading for the book club I found earlier, and there were a few mentions of local craft fairs. It was all very normal and very quaint, except for one thing.

My eyes scanned the profile photograph over and over until I finally clicked on it, enlarging it on my phone's screen. In the photo, Rosemary sat in a lush, velvet chair with a stack of books on the small table beside her. She had the short hair I remembered seeing in previous photos and a long, flowing dress that spread around her on the chair. In her hands, another book lay cradled, and I couldn't make out the title of it from the size of the picture.

What I could make out very clearly was Rosemary's neckline and the large, shiny pendant hanging from it.

The same pendant I now had stashed in my desk drawer at Bean Me Up.

CHAPTER 14

Night covered Orchard Hollow and I watched the silhouette of trees on the horizon from the porch, my fingers clutching the pendant. My head swelled with questions and each time I thought I might have it figured out, a wall slammed down and knocked me back.

Why did Daniel have Rosemary's talisman? Did she give it to him before she died, or did he come by it in another, less amicable way? Did Sebastian despise Daniel enough to murder him? Was Rosemary the witch that created the protection charm for him?

The timing didn't add up for Rosemary to make the charm and from everything I'd found online since I got home, the two didn't know each other. As for

Sebastian, I still didn't know if his magic gene activated, so the theory of a warlock cousin hurting Daniel over an inheritance was far-fetched. Possible, but not rooted in any facts. The talisman... that was a mystery I couldn't even begin to guess on.

Then there was the most important question of all —was all this one big coincidence?

Somehow, I couldn't get myself to stop thinking about the cobweb of clues leading nowhere. Every stone I unturned only spurned more questions. At some point, I might have to give up and leave the matter of Daniel's death gone and buried. The police sure had.

Heavy breaths sounded from the other end of the porch, and I shoved the necklace in my cardigan pocket, clutching my chest as I turned. "Oh," I said, seeing the familiar face. "It's you."

"Don't look so upset about it," Stella answered. "I might get a complex."

I doubted anything could make Stella Rutherford think less of herself, especially not me. "You're looking paler than usual. Aren't you supposed to be celebrating?" the ghost asked.

I raised one eyebrow. "Celebrating what?"

"Your newfound freedom! You're off the hook for the warlock's unfortunate demise, no?" When I nodded, she shimmied closer and leaned against a wooden beam. Her jaw tightened as she studied my face, and a disgusted look coated her features when her eyes traveled down my body and over my outfit. "Why not put on something a little more elegant and go out for a change? See if the book nerd is available for a drink?"

A deep growl reverberated in my chest. "How do you know about Joe? I never mentioned him."

"Hello?" Stella waved over herself. "Ghost familiar over here. Knowing everything goes with the territory."

I didn't even want to think about what that meant. It appeared the threats Stella tossed around about watching me in my sleep may not have been threats at all and I tightened my cardigan, shuddering. To keep my dinner from coming back up, I took a big sip of the coffee I made earlier. A caramel mochaccino because now that Joe got it into my head, I couldn't stop thinking about the yummy drink. I had to hand it to him; Mocha à la Joe was freaking amazing. *I may need to add it to the menu after all.*

Ignoring Stella's prodding, I said, "I'm not in the mood for an outing. Too much to figure out."

"Are you still on about the warlock?" Stella exclaimed. "Honestly, Piper. Leave well enough alone and move on. He's dead and you're not. Start acting like it."

"I can't!" I shot back.

"Why ever not?"

My face heated and my thigh muscles tightened in my jeans. "I'm not sure. The entire thing is odd, and I guess I want to make sense of it. Solve the puzzle."

"The only puzzling thing I see is why you've been single for two years. It's time to dust off those panties; this Joe character sounds like he might be interested in you."

The way she said that made it clear that it shocked Stella to know anyone would show even a remote romantic interest in me. I didn't have it in me to tell her that Joe was only being friendly because he was new in town and not because he had ulterior motives that included the dusting off anyone's panties. The woman was reaching. But at least she wasn't insulting me for a change.

When I took too long to reply, Stella let out an annoyed sigh. "Ugh, fine! If it'll help get you out of this rut and into the book nerd's bed, I will go to the hotel tonight and see what I can find."

"Absolutely not!" I yelled. "It's too dangerous. There could be a killer on the loose, and I'm not comfortable with you snooping in a haunted hotel at night."

Stella held up a gray finger. "One. For the millionth time, it's not haunted. Two. What can the killer will do if I come across them? Murder my dead behind?"

She had a good point. Still, I stood by what I said; I did not want Stella involved until I knew what we were dealing with. While it was true that my ghost familiar could not be hurt by human means, I had the distinct feeling that we weren't dealing with a human assailant. If there *was* any foul play involved at all. I shook my head furiously at her. "Stella, please. Let this be the only time you listen to me and don't do anything foolish."

"Or..." was all she said before she vanished.

Oh, so help me! She was insufferable. I knew that right at this moment, Stella was already in the hotel and getting herself into trouble. Double-checking the pendant was still in my pocket, I grabbed my car keys and headed for the beetle. Crisp air slapped my cheeks, and I picked up the pace, slamming the door shut behind me. As I turned on the ignition, my phone rang. I stared at the screen, not recognizing the number. "Hello?"

"Piper Addison?"

"Yes, speaking."

There was a pause and some heavy breathing on the other end, then a click. I waited, checking the number again. When someone finally spoke, I recognized the voice immediately. "Hello, Miss Addison,"

Sheriff Romero said. "I need to you stop by the station as soon as you can."

"Why? What's going on?"

"I can't say much over the phone," the sheriff warned. "We had a new break in Mr. Tse's case, and I need to speak to you in person."

My jaw gaped. "I thought you said it was an accident?"

"Sooner rather than later, Miss Addison," the sheriff said, then he hung up.

I stared at the phone with an open mouth for a good ten seconds before tossing it on the passenger seat and pulling out of the driveway. High beams on, I drove the rolling road into town, my chest tight and the knot in my throat growing with each mile passed. When I passed the Rose Hollow Hotel, my expression fermented. *Sorry, Stella. You're on your own until I get this sorted.*

With how often I visited the police station, I should be on a rewards program. I'd have enough points for a round trip to an all-inclusive by now. Pushing my way through the doors, I tried not to make eye contact with the two men parked in the lobby chairs. Both sported fresh black eyes and one was cuffed to the chair handle, glaring nastily at the second. The smell of a boozy night wafted in the air, and I gagged in my mouth as I passed them, rushing to the front desk and away from the trouble makers. They didn't strike me as the rough sorts, simply two guys who had a few too many and got into it.

Standard for a Thursday night in Orchard Hollow.

Nearing the front desk, I noticed the same speedy fingers I met before manning the station. The woman looked at me and nodded to the hallway around the back, one I had grown much too familiar with. I smiled and trotted toward it, refusing to spend more time here than was necessary.

This time, I didn't need to look for Romero for long because he was standing in the doorway of a room I vividly remembered, a scowl on his face. He greeted me with a curt hello and stepped aside, letting me walk into the concrete box of doom. Not waiting for an invitation, I plopped down on the chair, straightened my back, and said, "Good to see you again, sheriff."

"It might not feel that way soon," Romero answered.

Dread spread through my body and for the first time since I walked in, I noticed the two plastic bags on the table. The word 'evidence' was stamped in red across each bag and I tried to make out the contents with little success. When Romero caught me staring, he pulled out a chair, sat down and slid the bags closer to himself, obscuring them from view. "We need to talk about the Tse case," he said. "And I expect complete honesty from you."

I gawked at him. "I'm confused. Is the case open again?"

"It seems that way."

"But you said it was an accident," I reminded him.

The sheriff's brows crept down, and the lines at the corners of his eyes deepened. "There's been a recent development, one that made me question my original findings."

"What development?" I asked as sweetly as I could muster. Deep down, I was shaking in the chair and held on for dear life. My fingers dug into the torn brown leather, and I tapped the underneath metal frame with my nails. Tap. Tap. Tap. The sound of my sanity departing.

Romero inhaled sharply and said, "We received an anonymous call forcing us to take another look at Mr. Tse's apartment. What we found there was," he looked for the right word, finally settling on, "disconcerting."

"I'm not sure I understand."

In a flash, the sheriff slid one bag toward me. It

stopped a few inches from the edge of the table, and I peered inside, my stomach tightening. It was the charm bag from Daniel's closet, the one Stella discovered while I was there. I reached for the bag, then stopped. "May I?" I asked. When Romero nodded, I brought the bag close to my face to examine it. In truth, I was trying to buy some time while I figured out the best way to approach this. Telling the sheriff I broke into Daniel's apartment was going to look bad; handcuffed-with-black-eye-lobby bad. Then again, keeping quiet would likely come back to ruin me later. I was trapped between a rock and a witch charm, and I could see no way out.

"A charm bag," I said, playing coy while my brain scoured for a solution. "You found this in Daniel's apartment?"

The sheriff nodded again. "I'm going to be frank with you, Miss Addison." We were no longer on a first name basis. "I didn't know what to make of this when I first saw it. I told my guys to bag it and not to think on it further because, as we both know, we can't have hints of the paranormal activity in this town getting out. After the search was done, I tried to find what I could on this thing and there wasn't much out there."

You and me both. I frowned. "What does this have to do with me?"

"Nothing," Romero said. "At first glance. I did

some digging into your past; or your family's past, I should say. Have you had contact with your mother recently?"

Here we go. I knew that mom's sordid dealings would catch up to me eventually. And I knew where the sheriff was going with this but decided to act dumb anyhow. No way was I going to talk myself into incarceration. "I haven't spoken to her since she left. She sends postcards once in a while, but I never answer. Gran didn't either."

"Interesting. I take it you know what your mother got herself into?"

My eyebrows slanted. "Black magic, you mean?" Romero nodded. "Yes, I knew. It was why gran and I cut her off. We are not the type of witches who want anything to do with black magic. Look, sheriff, what my mom does is on her. I haven't talked to her in ages, and I have no intention to in the future."

Hoping I made my point clear, I leaned into the chair, trying to appear as calm as possible. My bouncing leg under the table proved otherwise, but I was hoping Romero couldn't feel the vibration of my nerves on his side. The sheriff eyed me distrustfully, then murmured, "Hmm." I wasn't sure what to say and when he slid the second bag my way, my vocabulary dwindled down to nothing.

Sitting before me, tucked into the plastic of the

bag, was a small key. It was the same shape as one I had on the keyring in my purse, and I recognized the decorative sleeve on the top instantly. The words Bean Me Up stared back at me with a picture of an espresso bean shaped spaceship underneath. It was a spare key to the cafe I kept in the back office in case I lost mine. What was it doing in the evidence bag and how did Romero get his hands on it? This did not look good. Damn me for branding literally everything!

The urge to pick up the bag grew, and I fought it tooth and nail, refusing to let the pressure of the moment get to me. I looked at the key, then back to Romero. "Where did you find this?"

"Daniel's apartment," the sheriff said with a deadpan stare. "You must have dropped it."

"I-I..." *Talk, you blubbering idiot!* I couldn't. Confusion laced through me, and I struggled to open my mouth to put syllables together. What was going on here? I knew I didn't bring the spare key with me when I snuck into Daniel's home, so how did Romero find it there? Cold sweat licked the back of my neck, and I felt an icy trickle escape into my sweater. "I don't understand."

"That makes two of us," Romero said. "Want to tell me what you were doing in Mr. Tse's apartment? I seem to recall you telling me you weren't close?"

"We weren't! I swear."

Romero tapped a finger on the bag. "Then how?"

This was it. It was time to come clean about everything. The breaking and entering, the envelope Daniel sent, my pathetic attempt at playing detective. I had to lay it all out and hope the sheriff didn't count it against me. I bit the inside of my cheek. "I'm not lying when I say I don't know how that key got into Daniel's apartment. I always keep it in my office."

"What are you lying about, then?" The sheriff asked. "Because I know you're keeping things from me."

"You're right. I kept some things to myself, but only because you told me Daniel's death was an accident."

As I chewed the rest of my cheek, Romero grew impatient. "I don't have all night, Miss Addison," he warned. "If you have something to tell me, now's a good time."

"Sorry," I mumbled. "When you told me you closed the case, I was going to let it go. But it didn't feel right. I couldn't peg Daniel as someone who would get high and die in a freak accident. Especially since he was so eager to meet me that same morning. It wasn't adding up, and I wanted to figure this out."

"You understand that is our job, right?"

I swallowed a lump in my throat. "I do, but with the case closed, you wouldn't be following leads. And I didn't want to waste your time if I was blowing things out of proportion."

"Following leads? What leads, Miss Addison?" Romero fumed. "This isn't a television show. We have procedures in place for a reason and you playing cop is not helping anyone."

"I know that now."

The sheriff sighed and crossed his arms, pinning me with cold eyes. "Tell me everything. Start at the beginning."

I spilled my guts so fast I wasn't sure if Romero could follow me. One by one, I revealed everything that happened up until this evening. Cilia, Charlie, the protection charm. As I spoke, Romero's eyes narrowed further and further until they were tiny slits across his face. He nodded periodically, letting me catch my breath between sentences. When I finished, he asked, "Anything else?"

Rosemary's pendant burned a hole in my pocket, and I reached for it, about to put in on the table. My hand froze. For some reason, I couldn't part with the stupid ting. Sparks of electricity formed on the tips of my fingers, and I could feel the pull of magic from the amethyst course through me. I never had this reaction to someone else's talisman before. Sure, most paranormals didn't sport theirs out in the open. I wore gran's brooch here and there, but even when I did, I felt constantly on guard. But since I lived alone, wearing it was a better solution than leaving it unattended at home. I was one of the few who wore their talisman since I was one of the few loners in our town; everyone else had people they could entrust to safe keep their precious items.

To feel this strong a pull toward another witch's talisman was new to me and I couldn't understand why I was having the reaction. It was the same feeling I had when I first touched the stone but multiplied tenfold.

It had to be a sign.

Slowly, I lowered my hand, leaving the pendant nestled in the bottom of my cardigan pocket. Rosemary's death occurred years ago and bringing up another dead case right now was not going to do me any good. It would only cause more confusion for Romero.

I eyed the sheriff through wet lashes. "That's it. That's all I know so far," I said. "Am I in trouble?"

His lips thinned. "I need you to pay close attention to what I am about to say," the sheriff bit out. "This, all of this, isn't good. I want to believe that you don't know how your cafe's key got into a dead man's apartment, but it's hard to do so. The breaking and entering you admitted to doesn't help."

I bit my bottom lip until I pierced the skin and hissed under my breath.

"I'm beginning to think there's more to this case than I originally thought," Romero continued. "So, I will make you a deal. Stay out of it. No more sleuthing, no more chasing after leads, and for the love of everything good, no more sneaking into other people's homes. Can you do that for me?"

"Yes," I said. I almost saluted the man but kept my act together. "I can definitely do that. Does that mean you're reopening the case? That you no longer think it was an accident?"

"It means I am going to put some more thought into it," Romero answered.

"And I'm not under arrest?"

He shook his head. "You're free to go," he said. I jumped up, about to bolt for the door. "But don't leave town. Not until I say so. You are still very much a person of interest, and I can't guarantee our next meeting will be as civil."

With the warning in the air, Romero watched me leave the room and scurry down the hallway. As I walked by the two men in front, I didn't even notice their arguing, nor did I see the officer from the front desk run to interfere. The only thing I could think of was someone broke into my office, stole my key, and dumped it in

Daniel's apartment. Why? To frame me? They must have put it there after my visit because I didn't remember seeing it, and between me and Stella, we scoured the place pretty well. Then there was the anonymous tip Romero received. I was certain it was the same person.

Someone wanted me to go down for Daniel's murder and I didn't know why. What I knew was where to start to find out. There were two ways to get into Daniel's apartment. One could use magic as I did, which would draw a lot of attention if caught. I doubted the killer would risk it. The other was to use keys and waltz right in. And who might have keys to Daniel's apartment?

A family member.

Thoughts of Sebastian Tse rumbled through my brain, and I cast one last glance at the police station before getting into my car in the dark of night. Romero said no sleuthing, but that's not what I was about to do. *A simple conversation to offer my condolences for Sebastian's loss,* I lied to myself.

It was high time I paid the maybe-warlock cousin a visit.

CHAPTER 15

Getting Sebastian Tse to meet with me was simpler than I expected. All it took was one message sent to an email I found online and the promise of a free lunch at Cliffside Diner. Daniel's cousin seemed to be harder up for cash than me and jumped at the opportunity of a nice meal at zero the cost. Either that or he wanted to scope me out to see if he should add me to his list of victims. Sebastian was possibly the killer the cops were after, and I didn't want to take any risks. If spending money I should have been saving on a fancy lunch meant I got to keep breathing, I was willing to spend it.

After moving some funds around, I put on the nicest dress I owned, topped it off with a blazer, and made the short drive to Cliffside. As I walked by the large, gold-framed mirror in the bedroom, I gave myself a once over and smiled. I cleaned up well. Too bad Stella wasn't around to see it, so I could rub it in her face.

Worry settled in my gut when I thought of the nosy ghost. I hadn't seen her since last night and it wasn't like Stella not to show up in the morning to start my day wrong. Locking the door, I made a note to scope out the hotel after my meeting with Sebastian. There was a good chance Cilia would be working now, so I decided to wait on the visit until evening to avoid confrontation. That, and there would be fewer witnesses around if I had to use magic to save Stella's sorry behind.

Between her and Harry Houdini, I didn't know how I got anything done.

The drive to Cliffside Diner was beautiful, and no matter how long I lived in Orchard Hollow, I never got over the road leading up the mountains. The diner was located a hike away from Cliff Row and sat on a drop off point in the cliffs, nestled into the mountain top like some secret lair. It was the poshest place in town and often attracted a richer clientele than I was used to. I had only been to the diner a handful of times, but from what I remembered, the food was to die for, and the view was unlike anywhere else in town. The diner

—more of an upscale restaurant—was made almost entirely of glass. On one side, a mixture of trees and mountain range obscured the guests from view while on the other, the cliffs dropped away, and you could watch the never-ending sea as you ate your fifty-dollar steak. It was breathtaking.

I pulled up to the parking spot, careful not to nick the high-end car beside me when I rolled in. As I walked out, I straightened out my dress and frowned. Wrinkles covered the entire backside of the skirt from the worn-out leather of the beetle. I worked to pull my blazer down to cover them, but it was a pointless feat. *Shabby chic it is.*

Wrinkles and all, I marched up the paved walkway leading to the front doors and into the diner. It wasn't busy for a lunch hour, and I was greeted by a hostess wearing a pristine, white pantsuit within minutes of walking in. I didn't fail to notice that her suit did not have one wrinkle in it. The woman, a tall redhead with a gorgeous complexion of sun-kissed skin and freckles, led me to a table along the mountain view wall and left me to my own devices with three different menus. One for drinks, one for appetizers and one for main courses. The material of the menu was nicer than that of my blazer.

I settled on a cappuccino while I waited for Sebastian to arrive. The server who brought it dropped it on the table without making eye contact and let me know he'll be back to take my lunch order shortly. He didn't, and it relieved me to know I wouldn't have to send him away again since Sebastian ran annoyingly late. As I sipped my coffee, I wished for a dash of vanilla to coat the bitter taste of burned beans. For a restaurant where a meal cost more than filling an entire tank of gas, I sure hoped for better coffee.

I was reading the lunch menu for the third time when the chair in front of me pulled out. Looking up, I saw a man in his late forties with sharp, dark eyes and messy hair that hung down to his jaw. He had the same crooked nose as Daniel, so I had no trouble recognizing him.

"Sebastian?" I asked politely.

The man sat down and pulled his chair in, looking me over. "Nice to meet you," he said, reaching for the menu. One track mind. Sebastian scanned the meals and put the menu back on the table with a smile.

"Thank you for meeting me," I said. I looked around to flag down the server, but he was busy at another table. My throat was parched, and I battled the urge to take a sip of my coffee since Sebastian was yet to order. "Sorry, this was so last minute."

"No worries. You said you wanted to talk about my cousin?"

He scanned the diner and disappointment flashed

over his face when he realized he wouldn't be eating any time soon. I pushed my cappuccino to the edge of the table. "I wanted to offer my condolences for your loss," I said, "and to ask about the service. It came to my attention that you were the person to contact for that."

"Were you and my cousin close?"

Blast. I didn't want to lie to the man since he would see right through me. Family feud or not, I was certain Sebastian knew Daniel's closest friends and since we'd never met, it was easy to deduct I wasn't one of them. I really should have prepared better for this and not tried to wing it. Giving it a quick thought, I settled on a semi-truth, one I hoped would get me closer to finding out where Sebastian was the night Daniel died. "Not as close as we could have been," I said. "But he was always nice. Actually, he called me the night before, well, you know. I wish I spent more time getting to know him. Maybe things would have turned out differently."

Sebastian's face paled, and he gave me a once over. "That's odd," was all he said.

"What is?"

"Dan calling you. We spoke a few days before his accident, and he didn't mention any new friends."

My ears perked up at the idea of the two of them talking. I wondered if they argued, but before I could ask, the server came by to take Sebastian's order. He ordered the most expensive meal on the menu, Lobster Linguine, and a glass of middle-grade Merlot. The combination made me realize Sebastian was as out of place here as I was, bringing a slight comfort to my rising nerves. I opted for a simple burger and fries, which still cost more than a day's worth of groceries. When the server spun on his heels and left, I sipped the cappuccino and buried my gaze on Sebastian. "Did you know most of Daniel's friends?"

"Not most," he said. "But I would know if he mentioned you."

I let that strange comment go because I had no idea what he meant by it and pressed for more information on his whereabouts. "And that was the last time you two spoke?" I asked.

"It was. Why are you asking?"

Shifting in my seat, I leaned in closer. "Curiosity, I suppose. From what I heard, you two were not on the best of terms after Daniel's father passed away. I'm surprised to hear you were speaking at all."

A strange look passed over Sebastian's features. He was either confused, or angered, or both. "Geez," he wheezed out. "This town! Everyone is in everyone's business, huh?"

I shrugged.

"No, we were not on great terms," Sebastian said.

"And I'm sure you and everyone else in this hole know why. The way my cousin handled the vineyard was despicable, and it ruined an already sour relationship."

"How come you two never got along?"

Sebastian tugged on his ear, thinking. It took him a few moments to collect himself before speaking and when he did, I studied his face, watching for the lie. His features never altered and if he *was* lying, I'd never know it. "Look," he said. "I don't want to speak ill of the dead, but Dan was a pompous ass. He wanted no part of the vineyard, and I actually loved the place. It wasn't about money either. Dan had more than enough from his side of the family. But for me, it was more than that. The vineyard was a baby of mine; I worked there for years, and I knew how much it meant to Dan's dad. Theodore would never have wanted it sold. I tried to tell Dan that, but the bastard didn't care."

"He sold it? Just like that?"

"Yep," Sebastian answered. "No notice and no explanation. I'm pretty sure he did it to put me out on my ass."

"And did he?"

His lips pursed. "In a way. I mean, sure, I miss the money; but to be honest, I don't think I'll ever find another job I like more. So, yeah, me and Dan never got along. And if I'm being honest, I won't miss much about the guy."

Wow. And I thought my relationship with mom was garbage. No matter what my mother did, I'd still miss her if she was gone forever. Sebastian seemed almost happy to be rid of his cousin. Was he happy enough to have killed him? I wasn't getting that impression. Why admit to wanting someone gone if you're the one who killed them?

Our meals arrived, and I shoved a couple of fries in my mouth, gulping them down like a seagull.

"You said you knew some of Daniel's friends," I said between chews. "Anyone he was particularly close with?"

Sebastian chuckled. "Oh, I see what this is."

"I'm sorry?" I asked, confused.

"You had a thing for my cousin, didn't you?"

A rogue fry lodged itself in my throat and I coughed several times before it came loose. My eyes widened, and I looked at Sebastian like he had grown a second head. What was he going on about? A crush on Daniel was the least of my concerns, and I wasn't sure how the conversation got so sidetracked. "I can assure you that is not the case," I said.

"Sure, it is!" Sebastian exclaimed. "It makes so much sense now! You call me out of the blue and ask all these odd questions. Why else would you care?"

"That is not what's happening here."

Sebastian crammed a forkful of pasta in his open mouth and chewed it loudly. I swore I heard him laugh as he swallowed. "Look, lady," he said. "Whatever business you had with Dan; I can guarantee you were not his type." He laughed out loud this time, and it made my blood boil.

"I know Daniel was gay," I told him. "It's not like it was a secret."

"Oh, that's not why you didn't stand a shot."

I was beginning to see why Daniel and his cousin did not get along; the man was infuriating. Resting my chin on my hand, I forced a smile and tried to keep my jaw set. "Okay," I said. "I'll bite. Why is it you think I wouldn't have a chance with Daniel?"

The entire conversation was teetering on the ridiculous, but I was willing to play along. If anything, I was glad Sebastian was relaxed enough to be taking digs at my expense. At this rate, he would spill his beans before the bill came. His eyes crinkled, and he wiped a rogue tear, still laughing. "You're a witch," he said.

The chair I sat in turned liquid and I felt myself sink into it, further and further, until I hit the floor. The room spun and my chest squeezed until I couldn't breathe. I looked at my blazer, making sure gran's brooch was tucked under it where it wasn't visible.

Clambering to reach the cappuccino, I clutched the saucer with clammy hands and brought it to my mouth. Even caffeine couldn't help me. How did Sebastian know I was a witch? I never hinted at the fact, and it's not as if it was stamped on my forehead. I couldn't tell if he was a warlock, so there was no way he'd know I had magic unless someone told him. Unless Daniel told him.

Shaking, I put down the saucer down and forced myself to meet his eyes. "How did you know?"

"Oh, please," Sebastian said, waving me away. "Your family's magical line is not a secret among para-normals."

This was news to me. Neither I nor gran adver-tised our background, but now, within a week's time, both Sebastian and the sheriff seemed to be in on our magical abilities. Who else was privy to the informa-tion? I did not like knowing that my magic was out there for everyone to know. It was private and even someone as daft as Nancy Steeles wouldn't dare out a paranormal. I flicked a strand of loose hair off my face and crossed my arms. "I didn't realize we were so exposed."

"Really?" Sebastian asked. "You come from a powerful line of witches, Piper. You didn't think word would get around?"

"I guess not."

He frowned. "Well, there you have it. I wouldn't stress about it though; most people could care less. Especially since..." He paused.

"Since I suck at magic?" I asked, keeping my voice down.

"That and the fact that most paranormals are much too concerned with themselves to worry about the magical whereabouts of others." Then he added, "Unlike my bratty cousin."

Nausea coated my stomach, and I pushed it down, concentrating on Sebastian's words. He was right, of course. If people knew about my family's magic, there wasn't much I could do about it, and it wasn't as though my shoddy abilities would be an advantage to anyone in town. Gran's, but not mine. From the sounds of it, the one person Sebastian believed could run his mouth about it was dead. "What do you mean?" I asked. "I didn't take Daniel for a gossip."

"Not a gossip," Sebastian corrected. "Dan was old-fashioned with all things paranormal. Especially warlocks and witches. And he swung both ways, by the way, but he still wouldn't touch a witch if his life depended on it."

"Ah," I whispered, understanding daunting on me. Perhaps his life did depend on it. "Did you share his beliefs?"

Heat flushed Sebastian's gaunt cheeks, and he

looked at everything in the diner but me. I noticed a few drops of sweat behind his ears; ears that were now as red as the sauce on his nearly empty plate. *When did this guy have time to inhale his meal?!?* I took a bite of my burger, finding it bland and unseasoned. Though, I doubted anything would taste good to me now. Not after the bomb Daniel's cousin dropped in my lap. I gave Sebastian time to collect himself and when he couldn't, I pressed on. "What is it?"

"Listen," he said, leaning in. "This stays between the two of us, got it?"

I nodded my agreement.

"Dan and I didn't get along but it wasn't the vineyard that ruined everything. That part stunk but it wasn't what did our relationship in."

"What did?"

Leaning further, Sebastian gulped his wine and said, "I'm sure you already knew this if knew Dan, but he was a warlock. As am I."

I knew it! "What happened to you two?"

"As I said, Dan was old-fashioned. He didn't approve of warlocks and witches mingling," Sebastian repeated. "Especially when the mingling happened in his family."

My jaw dropped open and I white-knuckled the side of the table. Under it, my feet did a little dance as the truth seeped out of Sebastian like a leaky faucet. "Are you saying you..."

"I'm dating a witch," he admitted. "Cilia Craven. Don't tell her I said anything, we haven't made it public yet even though it's been years."

Shut the front door! Cilia? This was better than a soap opera. I struggled to hide my smile, but my lips curled on their own and I grinned like an idiot. Sebastian breathed out heavily and continued, ignoring my childish behavior. "The night Dan died; I was with her. We were planning to talk to him the same week to see if we can figure out a way for all of us to stop bickering. That was why I called Dan a few days prior. It was such a dumb thing to argue over. And now," he sucked in a breath. "well, if I'm honest, I'm relieved. Dan made our lives miserable. Having to hide from him, worrying about what he might do if he saw us together; it was exhausting."

I pulled a fry off the plate and chewed it slowly. So, Cilia was lying about being at the bar that night. She was with Sebastian. Judging by what I heard, I could see why she wouldn't tell me. We weren't friends, and it sounded as though her relationship with Sebastian was complicated enough without me knowing. It also took Cilia off my list of witches who could have made Daniel the protection charm. No way was she helping the guy standing in the way of her happiness. *Wait, did Nancy and the coven know about this?* I was about to ask, then held off. Instead, I said, "Daniel had a charm in his house. A protection charm made by a witch. Know anything about it?"

I was expecting Sebastian to ask how I came to know that, but he did no such thing. "If Dan was messing around with witch magic, he must have been out of his mind. You know the sheriff said they found evidence Dan used drugs the night he died? There was so much I didn't know about my cousin, but trust me when I tell you, he would not ask a witch for help if he was drowning."

"Unless he thought he had no other options," I said.

"Yes, I suppose that's true," Sebastian agreed grudgingly. He looked around for the server and when he found him, motioned for the bill. *I guess we're done here.* "If you do want the details for the funeral, I can email them to you."

I reached into my purse and pulled out a pen and a paper napkin I found on the bottom. Clumsily, I wrote my email on it and slid it across the table. "I'd like that. And if you think of a reason Daniel needed protection, let me know."

The warlock pocketed the napkin and downed the last of his wine. When he spotted the server heading over with the bill, he stood up and buttoned up his coat. "I don't know why you're interested in Dan's life, but if you're dead set on digging, talk to his neighbor."

"Who is that?"

"I don't know his name," Sebastian admitted. "I only met the guy once. Lanky, rough looking fella. If Dan needed protection, it was from this freak."

"Why would he need protection from his neighbor?" I asked.

"The guy was crazy. Hated Dan's dog. When I was there to talk some sense into Dan about the vineyard, this psycho threatened to kill the dog if it kept barking. I mean, I don't blame him; the spoiled mutt deserved it." He ran a hand through his hair and fixed me with a serious look. "But that was ages ago, so I wouldn't put too much stalk into it."

With that, he said goodbye and left, promising to email me about the funeral arrangements when he had them ready. When the bill came, I tried not to let my discomfort show and paid it promptly before rushing out the doors and into my car. It was looking like Daniel's life was a spiderweb of drama, but nothing so far was setting off alarms. I doubted the neighbor would kill him over a loud dog and, as Sebastian mentioned, it happened too long ago to be important. Still, it was worth checking out.

I cringed, remembering the promise I made to the sheriff, then told myself I wasn't planning to do anything to get in his way. My asking questions was no different from Nancy running her mouth about everyone's business. At least, that's what I kept repeating in my mind as I started the car and pulled out of the parking lot. All I had to do was return to Daniel's apartment building and take a quick peek at the last names on the buzzer.

It wasn't illegal to pass by a building, and in my defense, I didn't plan on breaking in this time.

CHAPTER 16

W alking into Daniel's building was more uncomfortable than wearing a pair of pants two sizes too small. I looked around several times, making sure the coast was clear and there was no chance I might run into someone. I wasn't worried about people from town seeing me, more so about getting caught red-handed by Sheriff Romero. No matter how well I convinced myself that I wasn't doing anything wrong, it still felt like I was betraying my promise to him.

Head in the game, I urged, focusing my attention on the buzzer system.

Much like it did when I first visited, the screen lit up as soon as I neared it and the welcome message for the building popped up. I touched the start button and scrolled through the names. Unfortunately, apartment numbers were not listed, likely to prevent creeps from stalking the residents.

Creeps like me.

I frowned and scrolled down, reading out the last names. When I spotted Tse, my stomach flipped. It was surreal to read Daniel's name as though he was alive and well. Seeing it made me realize that if my hunch was right, Orchard Hollow wasn't as peaceful of a town as we all thought it was. Someone here was a cold-blooded killer, someone we all might know. I wondered how often I passed Daniel's assailant on the street without so much as a second glance.

Worse, did I serve them coffee?

Thinking of the cafe lit a fire under my butt and I turned back to the screen, pushing my thoughts away. There weren't any names I recognized, but I scrolled through so fast from fear of being discovered, that I might have missed one. My head was all over the place and I had to read the list a second time before giving up. In my hand, the to go bag from the diner holding what was left of my burger grew heavy and I felt it slip from my sweaty grip. Why did I even bring it with me? I was in such a hurry to get into the building, I must have snatched it without thinking. Nerves wracked my body and I switched hands, wiping my wet palm against my leggings.

"Need help finding someone?" a soft voice asked.

I whipped around to see an elderly woman standing behind me, her keys in hand. She wore a colorful cardigan that appeared to be hand-knitted and I didn't fail to notice the stacks of gold necklaces hanging over it. As my eyes traveled to her face, the large diamond earrings she wore caught the light and blinded me. I got out of her way, then thought better of it. "I have a delivery for apartment three twelve," I said, pointing to the take-out bag. "Can't seem to find the buzzer on the order."

In my mind, I patted myself on the back for the quick thinking. Shocking twist of events.

The woman nodded approvingly. "Ah, yes," she said and reached over me to tap on the screen. "Mr. Mint. Lovely fellow."

Why does that name sound familiar? The woman started to type in the numbers, but I crammed myself between her and the screen. "Thank you so much," I said.

Not bothering with small talk, she walked by me and, after a few attempts to find the right key, disappeared into the lobby. Since I wasn't planning to go anywhere near Daniel's apartment, I waited until she vanished from view and ducked out of the lobby.

Standing in front of the building, I scoured my memory for the name Mint. It was right on the tip of my tongue. I knew I heard it before, if only I could remember where.

Shadows cast on the sidewalk as I trudged away from the building and back toward my car. The sun was setting, and I could feel the chill in the air as evening reared its head. I checked the time, slowing my pace. There was no point of going home, not if I planned to return later to check on Stella in the hotel. I half expected her to pop up in the car when I got in to tell me off about the wrinkles in my dress and when she didn't, disappointment clutched my heart. That and worry. Stella never stayed away for so long. Since she wasn't a normal familiar, I couldn't expect her to be there whenever I needed her. But she was around when I least expected it and as much as I hated to admit it, I got used to arguing with her.

It was our thing.

I turned the engine on and grabbed the wheel. Now our thing was sneaking around hotels at night, I supposed.

The Rose Hollow Hotel was a spine-chilling sight this late in the evening. The front doors rose before me like a hungry mouth and the wrought-iron lamp posts on each side cast long shadows on the ground—fingers clawing at my feet. I walked in, letting go of a stifled breath when I saw an unfamiliar face at the front counter. The young man was no more than twenty and had the look of someone who tried to impress his boss at his first job. He straightened a black bowtie and buttoned up his silk jacket as I approached. "Welcome to the Rose Hollow Hotel," he said politely, checking for luggage that wasn't there. "Would you be needing a room for the night?"

"Oh," I bit out. "Not tonight, no. I own the cafe across the street and was wondering if there's a manager I can talk to about dropping off a few pamphlets."

I came prepared, holding up a stack of flyers I printed off while waiting for the evening. The young man, Tyler as his gold name tag read, leaned over the front counter to look at my outstretched hand. "There isn't anyone around to handle that now. You should come back tomorrow during the daytime."

Nodding, I flashed my teeth at him. "That would be fantastic! Any chance I can use your bathroom real quick?" When he looked at me quizzically, I added, "I already locked up the cafe and it's a hassle to get the security system turned off."

"Of course," Tyler agreed. "If you go down this hallway here and turn right at the end, you can't miss them."

After a quick thank you, I followed his directions and scurried to the hallway. Walking slower than was humanly possible, I waited until Tyler ducked out of sight, then changed directions, running for the staircase. The door opened and closed silently, and I thanked my lucky stars as I pressed my back to its glass pane. In front of me, the stairs rose high, spanning the floors of the hotel. I gripped the mahogany railing and climbed. Where I was going or what I was hoping to find was unknown, but I had to scope out every floor for sightings of Stella. Did the ghost decide she liked it better here than in the farmhouse? Wouldn't that be an occasion to celebrate?

Taking two steps at a time, I made it to the second floor in record time. I checked my watch, calculating how long it was acceptable to fake use a bathroom. The way I figured; I could probably milk a good ten minutes before Tyler started to worry.

Not a lot of time to find a trouble-making ghost in a possibly haunted hotel.

When I reached the door for the second floor, I opened it in the same manner I imagine Harry opening the back door of the cafe; slow as molasses. Much like the one downstairs, it unlocked without so much as a whisper. I slipped through into the upstairs hallway and teetered between walking and running back downstairs. There were voices in one room and a loud laugh, followed by a glass clinking on a table. In another room, sounds of a blow dryer buzzed down the hall and I checked my phone, noting the time. It was half-past eight, right about when most would head out for the night.

As quickly as I could and before I could run into anyone leaving their rooms, I took in the hallway's length. Dim bronze sconces lit the way to the rooms like a landing strip and the antique-looking carpet under my feet smelled freshly cleaned. There was a console table at the end of the hallway with a phone atop it, and next to it, the elevator doors. This floor wasn't as grand as I assumed it would be from the state of the lobby and only housed six rooms. I checked their numbers, mostly because I didn't know what I was looking for, and it seemed like something a detective might do in one of my shows. In the same shows, this would have been the time the lead had a major revelation and broke the case. Too bad this wasn't a hit on a streaming network, and I wasn't looking for normal clues.

I was looking for a ghost who refused to see logic.

"Stella," I whisper yelled into the hallway.

Crickets.

Frowning, I walked further down, all the way to the elevator doors. The decorative bronze reflected the light from the sconces, and it mesmerized me for a few seconds too many. I shook my head, turning back toward the stairs. "Stella!"

The voices from earlier got louder, and I heard the scuffle of feet in a room close to me, followed by the sound of a door handle turning. Speedily, I pushed the staircase door open and rushed inside, watching it close behind me. Chatter filled the hallway, a couple arguing over a place to eat, then softened, followed by the ding of the elevator and its doors swooshing closed. I slumped against the wall. Close call. My eyes traveled up the stairs and I reached for the railing, pulling myself away and toward the next floor. I was certain it would be as fruitless a task as the one I already checked; in fact, this entire evening was looking like a wild goose chase.

Why did I think I would waltz in and find Stella here? The ghost clearly didn't wish to be found.

Knots twisted my gut.

What if Stella wasn't gone by choice? What if this was the end of her otherworldly experience?

I could kick myself for not spending more time figuring out how the afterlife worked. There must be information in Brooks Books on the matter. Why didn't I look for it? Stella had become such a thorn in my side I assumed she would always be there, but what if that wasn't the case? This could have been it for my familiar and it didn't sit well with me. I imagined when the time came for Stella to leave, I'd be relieved; happy to have her judgmental self out of my life. Now, I didn't know what I felt. It wasn't relief though. If anything, I would say I was scared out of my mind to lose her.

Gross.

Picking up the pace, I double checked the time again, scowling. I took way too long for a bathroom break, and I knew I had to come up with a story when I got back to the lobby. No way Tyler, the overly enthusiastic employee, would believe I'd been peeing the entire time. Stomach flu perhaps? Feeling less and less excited about the evening, I decided to check one more floor, then hightail it out of there.

When I reached the third floor, it left much to be desired. The entire scene played out like it had on the floor below and I wondered down the empty, poorly lit hallway whispering Stella's name over and over. The ghost was not there. I turned, heading for the stairs, and my eyes caught sight of one door. Room 312. I shuddered. This was the room Rosemary Hayes died in. I studied the door and walked closer, listening.

Unlike the other few rooms I passed, there were no voices on the other side. Either the room was unoccupied or whoever stayed inside was very, very quiet. I took my chance, my nose brushing the dark-stained wood. "Stella!"

Nothing.

My fingers grazed the golden handle, and I pulled it away. *What are you doing? You can't barge into someone's room.* I frowned. *Especially without a key.*

I had half a mind to magic my way inside but thought better of it. The hallway wouldn't be deserted for long. How much time did I have until someone walked by and saw me? Or until Tyler came looking? Not long, I wagered. I held my palm to the door and sighed. "Stella," I tried one last time. A gnawing feeling crept through me, and I couldn't quite put my finger on what it was. It seemed to pull on me, beckoning me into the room to investigate. I wondered if Stella stood in the same spot I was in now. Somehow, it felt as though she might have.

It was a strange sensation and took me by surprise. Stella and I had never been intricately connected, as witches often are with their familiars. I didn't sense her when she arrived; quite the opposite. Often, Stella scared the life out of me with her comings and goings. I used to think that it was because she wasn't a normal familiar, but now that I stood here, feeling as though she was right next to me, I wondered if our connection was never strong because of walls we both put up. As much as I disliked it, Stella and I were alike. Both of us needing our independence.

Tonight, I wished to be a little less independent and a lot more needy.

Because I *needed* to find her.

Whatever the feeling was, it was short-lived and as I pulled away from the door, I found myself back where I started. No strange sensation of Stella's presence and only the loud beating of my nervous heart to keep me company.

The time was getting on and I didn't want to spend any more of it darkening the halls of the hotel with my presence. Pushing my worry for Stella aside, I rushed for the staircase and ran down to the lobby. I was halfway to the exit when a voice I dreaded sounded behind me. "Found the bathroom?" Tyler asked.

I turned, his narrowed eyes burning through me. "Um, yes," I said. "Got turned around."

"What did you say your name was?" Tyler asked. I noticed his hand on his cellphone.

My brain worked a mile a minute, and I tried to think of something to say that would get me out of this mess. Judging by Tyler's face, he was one minute away from calling the cops. My mouth opened, but no words came out. There wasn't a plausible excuse for why I was at the hotel and why I took so long to leave.

"There you are!"

Jarred, I turned to the door and saw Joe walk inside. He tapped his watch and said, "I've been waiting outside forever. Ready to go?"

Sheepishly, I smiled then turned back to Tyler. "Gotta go! Thanks for letting me use the bathroom!"

He yelled at my retreating back, but I was already out there, pulling Joe behind me. My breath grew ragged, and I slammed my forehead into the frame of the glass door when I exited. Still, I ran faster. Palms slick with sweat and clutching Joe's, I was halfway up the block when I realized no one was chasing after us. My legs had a mind of their own and ran a good few steps further, even after my brain told them to stop. When I finally halted, I was out of breath and full of flurry. I spun around to face Joe. Eyes lowering, I noticed I was still grasping his hand for dear life and heat rose to my neck and cheeks. I swallowed hard and grinned toothily. "Thanks for the rescue," I said. "Sorry to drag you out of there like a maniac."

"You're still dragging," Joe joked, nodding down to our joined fingers.

Of course, I am. Idiot. I let go of his hand like it was on fire. Teeth shining in the light of the street-lamps, I flashed my best I'm-not-strange-smile. Somewhere along the line, it turned into an I'm-an-axe-murderer smile, but I went with it.

"Well," Joe said, "what did you find on your mission?"

"Huh?" I asked.

"The sneaking into the hotel bit," he explained. "Find anything interesting?"

My labored breathing halted. How did Joe know to find me in the hotel and why did he assume I needed help getting out? I had so many questions. Uncurling my back, I sucked in another deep gulp of air and pinned Joe with an icy glare. "What were you doing at the hotel?"

He ran a hand through his hair, then shoved it into his jean's pocket. I tried hard not to look at his pants. "I figured you needed a hand," Joe said. "Unless the plan was to have the sheriff show up."

"There was no plan," I said.

"Sure, there wasn't." Joe winked and chuckled. "All I wanted was to help you get out of a tough spot. I'm sorry if I overstepped."

I considered his words. Joe showed up at the right moment and I needed the assist. Who knew what Tyler would do if he hadn't interrupted and, despite what Joe implied, I had no intention of spending the evening chatting up Sheriff Romero. I wanted to thank him for his help, but first, I needed some answers. "How did you know I'd be at the hotel?"

"I didn't," Joe said. "I saw you go in when I was drudging the sign back into the shop and closing up. Didn't see you come out for a while, so I thought I'd pop in and see if everything was alright. Was it?"

"In a way," I said with a shrug. "I wasn't sneaking in, by the way."

"Hmm."

"No, really! I came by to drop off flyers for the cafe reopening and had to use the bathroom. Took longer than expected." *Why? Just why, Piper?* I willed myself to stop talking, but it seemed my mouth had other plans. "Look, if you must know, I was following up on something that's been bothering me."

Joe's chin tilted up, and he pursed his lips. "Let me guess," he said. "The warlock."

How in the... Before I could ask how the word warlock made itself into Joe's vocabulary, he reached over and tapped gran's brooch peeking out of my cardigan. My eyes saucered and the back of my neck burned hot. "Turns out I share my uncle's unique interests in books," Joe said as though it explained anything.

"I'm going to need more than that," I pressed.

Joe smiled and my thighs clenched shut. "Do you have time for a coffee?"

I nodded, pointing to the cafe.

"The espresso machine won't be here until tomorrow, but I'm sure I can—"

The words vanished from my lips and my gaze floated past Joe and down the street, where Ember was locking up the pharmacy for the night. Her white coat flapped in the wind and when she shut the door with a slam, the corner of it caught inside. She tugged it hard, cursing under her breath before twisting the key and walking away. I watched her leave, my eyes circling the pharmacy's display windows.

"Piper?" Joe beckoned my attention.

I couldn't look at him, not when my brain was imploding with information. My mind traveled back to Daniel's apartment and the old woman I met there. As though a brick of memories slammed into my skull, I realized why Daniel's neighbor sounded familiar. Mint. I heard the name before. It was Ember's married name prior to her divorce.

Tristan Mint was her ex-husband.

Spying Ember's shadow disappear down the street, I squeezed my lips together. Mint wasn't only her ex-husband; he was Daniel's neighbor. And the next suspect on my list.

CHAPTER 17

I ced mocha was simply not as good with instant coffee. I took another sip of the drink and pretended it tasted better than it did and I didn't force Joe, who sat across from me at the table, to down a blasphemous cup of coffee. He didn't seem to mind, though I noticed he hadn't even tried a sip. I pointed to his glass. "It's terrible, isn't it?"

"No, no," Joe said. "I'm sure it's fine. I'm not much for coffee."

Excuse me, what? If there was ever a sign that I was crushing on the wrong man, this was it. *Who doesn't drink coffee?* Big city Joe with too much knowledge of the paranormal, that's who. I frowned.

"There's tea," I said with a shudder. "I can put a pot on for you."

Part of me wished Joe would refuse so I wouldn't have to get up and postpone the dreaded conversation I dragged him here for. Joe did no such thing. He grinned cheerfully, pushed his glass away and said, "That would be lovely."

Would it, now? Ew. Trying to let my disdain for his drink choice go, I stood up and walked toward the kettle on the back counter. I checked the tea selection the cafe stocked, settling on a simple Earl Gray, then waited for the water to boil. Spinning around to face Joe, I gauged his comfort level. He didn't act like someone who only recently found out magic existed. Joe was too calm, too relaxed. Most people would have been firing off questions. Some would have cried, but not Joe. He was as chill as ever and it made my brain hurt. Behind me, the kettle whistled, and I peeled my gaze off Joe long enough to pour a cup.

"Here you go," I said, pushing the saucer toward him. "It's hot."

"It's tea," Joe countered.

My eyes rolled skyward before I could stop them. "Care to explain how you know Daniel was a warlock? Or how you know about magic?"

A lesser man would have tried to charm his way through the conversation by now. Not that I was harsh, but I'd been told on multiple occasions I could be off-putting when I felt someone kept something from me. In my defense, it was because they usually did. And usually it involved another woman. Images of finding the rodent otherwise occupied by a busty brunette flashed before me and my fingers pressed on the glass in my hands, nearly shattering it. I looked back at Joe, finding him oblivious to my bad cop routine. When Joe answered, he did so matter-of-factly.

"My uncle shared everything he knew with me each time I visited since I was a child," he explained. "For most of my life, I grew up thinking he was not in his right mind and my parents did little to convince me otherwise. It was why I stopped coming to Orchard Hollow. Listening to his stories about the paranormal was exhausting."

I settled deeper into my chair, waiting for the rest of Joe's story.

"And then things in the city got hectic, and I was feeling the pressure of the job more and more. Right around the same time, I got news of Elijah's passing and the bookstore going up for sale. He left instructions in his will that unless someone in the family takes over, the shop was to be sold and the money from the sale to go to me."

My eyebrows quirked. "Why you?"

"Elijah didn't have children of his own and I guess he thought of me as a son of sorts. It made my having stayed away for so long even worse." Joe's eyes darkened, and he lowered them to look at his teacup. "I took it as a sign. Bought the store the same week and moved here, the town I vowed never to return to."

Not that I wasn't enjoying learning about what brought Joe to our small town, but I kind of wished he got to the point. The part where he realized everything his uncle told him the truth eluded me and I wanted to know how much Joe knew of magic. And of me. "You buy a book shop in a small town and move on a whim," I said, "and suddenly magic is believable?"

I wasn't buying it. Joe left things out. Important things.

"Magic was always believable," he said. "I simply chose not to believe it."

"What changed your mind?"

His eyes pinned me down and my tongue swelled in my mouth. "You did." He dipped a finger into the tea and swirled it, yet to take a sip. "You probably don't remember this, but I met you back when we were kids. It was before I labeled Elijah as a lunatic and before my parents drilled it into me that magic was a figment of my imagination. Uncle and I were walking down Cliff Row on the way to the shop, and I saw my first murder."

I flinched.

"It was a squirrel," Joe said. My spine relaxed immediately. "It jumped in front of a speeding truck and met its doom. I freaked out, naturally."

"Naturally," I echoed.

"I think I was only about five years old, and I remember letting go of Elijah's hand and running to it. I wanted to save it, make it better. I couldn't, of course. The poor thing was dead. But then..." he looked at me again, this time with even more intensity. "A tiny girl with bright red hair came running out of nowhere. She knelt beside the animal and while I was bawling, she seemed completely unaware of what we had witnessed. I saw her whisper and put her hands on the squirrel's broken body. Sparks flew from her fingers, and they were so quick, I thought I imagined them. I looked back at Elijah; all he did was nod. No one else saw what I saw."

I had no recollection of this memory, but I assumed the little girl in question was me. My brow creased. "What is it you think you saw?"

"I saw the squirrel get back up like nothing happened and hop away," Joe said. "I saw you bring it back to life."

Impossible. Resurrection was serious magic, black magic. How would a child know to practice it? Especially a child as bad at magic as me? I shook my head, refusing to accept what Joe said. "You must be mistaken," I said.

Joe must have sensed my panic because he smiled and reached into his pocket, pulling out a worn-out leather notebook, the edges frayed from years of use. As he placed it on the table, I leaned over, reaching for it. My fingertips grazed the leather and my head felt heavier than rocks. Somehow, this notebook mattered. I opened it, careful not to crease an already creased spine. All I saw were names. Some I recognized as people in town, while others were new to me. All had a symbol next to them and when I found gran's name, then mine and mom's, I realized what the symbols meant. These were paranormals. And each one was labeled with the type of magical person they were.

The panic I felt before multiplied and I shut the notebook, pushing it away. "Why do you have this?"

"Looks like Elijah was more than a simple book shop owner," he exclaimed. "I found this in his things after I bought the store. He kept a list of every paranormal in town."

"Why?"

"I'm not sure. But I will tell you that when I read it, everything made sense. Your name in there brought back the day with the squirrel and I figured combined with Elijah's stories, it must mean all of this—magic—is real." He tapped the side of his cup while I choked down iced coffee. "The warlock's name is in there, too. In case you were wondering."

I wasn't. Not until he said it. Grabbing the book again, I flipped through the pages until I found Daniel's name. Next it was Sebastian's, and both had warlock symbols beside them. A simple "W" in an upside-down triangle. Witches were noted in a similar fashion, but the triangle faced right side up. Werewolves got a circle, for the moon, I guessed; while vampires were categorized with their letter and a heart. Probably because they lacked those. I closed the book with an inhale. "Even if the story you told me is true, I don't remember it. And I'd recommend not going around talking about magic or you might get a reputation."

Joe chuckled. "I wasn't planning on it."

"What were you planning on?" I asked. "Now that you're in on the town's dirty little secret."

"That's another thing I'm not sure about. But I know I wanted you to know; it felt important to share it. And to offer my help with whatever it is you're tangled up in."

"I'm not tangled," I snapped a little too quickly. "Someone died behind my cafe, and I feel responsible."

"Why?" Joe asked.

This was my chance to lie and get him away from

me. I could tell him he's jumping to conclusions, and that I was a simple business owner trying to get her livelihood back up and running. I could even go as far as to pretend his uncle had a vivid imagination, but none of what he told Joe was real. These were all the things I should have done. Except, I didn't do any of them. It could have been the nonchalant way in which Joe spoke about magic—or because without Stella, I had no one else to talk to—but I didn't want to lie. So, I did the only thing I could think of at the moment. I told Joe everything.

I started with Harry discovering the body, a story which, as gruesome as it was, Joe found entertaining. Then I recounted the envelope Daniel sent and breaking into his apartment. I even told him about the snooping I'd been doing, despite Romero's warning. When I got to tonight and my reason for sneaking into the Rose Hollow Hotel, I was breathless. Joe, on the other hand, was as cool as a cucumber. He still didn't drink his tea, which grew cold by now, but his posture stooped, and he leaned in his chair in a way which told me he had no intention of running out the door.

Which was fantastic because it meant he wasn't about to have me arrested for everything I'd admitted to.

"That is quite the story," Joe said.

I fidgeted nervously, shoving my hands under my

thighs. "Who knew owning a cafe would come with a side order of murder?" I mumbled.

"And you're certain the sheriff has it wrong and Daniel didn't accidentally hurt himself?"

I nodded. "That is one thing I'm becoming surer of every day. Except I don't have any proof, thus the circus my life has become."

As if on cue, tiny claws clipping the ground sounded outside and I sighed, getting up to let Harry into the cafe. When I opened the door, he crammed his chubby body through and bolted straight for the office, where he would no doubt destroy what was left of the cookie stash. I closed the door and sat back down, noticing Joe's bewildered expression. "Don't ask," I said. "That was Harry."

"Right. Well, I should let you get some sleep."

When he got up to leave, my heart sank a little and disappointment reared its ugly head. Come tomorrow, Joe would pretend he didn't know me because who would want to associate with my nightmare of a life? One complete with a raccoon sidekick, no less. I stood to lock up after Joe and stumbled back when he turned abruptly. "See you tomorrow," he said. "Say seven in the morning?"

"For what?" I asked.

"Don't you want to scope out this Mint character? See what he knows?"

I must have heard wrong because no way did Joe suggest he join my circus. Could we both fit in the clown car? I held onto the wall for dear life since, if I let go, I'd fall straight to the floor. "Are you saying what I think you're saying?"

"Seven tomorrow," Joe repeated. "We have to get to Mint before he leaves for the day."

The drive to Daniel's apartment building, where I agreed to meet Joe the next morning, was a blur. Not only was it so early, it was still dark out, but I had forgotten my to-go coffee and was fretting the entire way there. As luck would have it, the beetle chose the coldest day in the year to break its heater, so by the time I parked, I was a human icicle. Before he left, I asked Joe to check for Tristan Mint's name in his uncle's record book and we were both relieved when he didn't find it. I don't think either of us wanted to deal with a paranormal on his own turf. Despite what Joe believed, I was not the competent witch he remembered from his childhood, so if Tristan had magic and used it, we'd meet the same fate the squirrel did except no one would be around to bring us back.

My head spun with possibilities, and I pushed them aside.

Chances were, all of this was one big coincidence, and I was wasting both mine and Joe's time by dragging him here. Granted, he dragged himself, so I didn't feel overly guilty about it.

Battling the wind, I made it to the lobby with some of my hair still somehow tied in a topknot. As I opened the door, I saw Joe already inside and he walked over to greet me, a paper cup in his hands.

"What's this?" I asked, accepting the cup.

"For the nerves I'm sure you have this morning."

I popped the lid and took a whiff, my eyes widening. "You brought me coffee."

"It's not as special as the one you make, I'm sure," Joe said apologetically. "I picked it up at a drive through on the way."

One sip was all it took for me to forget we were about to corner a man in his home. Paranormal or not, coffee was the real magic in this world. No one could convince me otherwise. I gripped the cup and followed Joe to the elevator. "How did you get inside?"

"I have my own magic," he joked. When I quirked an eyebrow, he said, "Someone was taking their dog out for a walk, so I got in with them."

Joe was way better at the whole detective game than I was, and I was glad he came today. Maybe spilling my guts to a complete stranger wasn't the worst idea. I briefly wondered what gran would have thought of my teaming up with a human to solve a crime I had no business solving. Mom would have been proud, which should have been the first sign I was sticking my nose where it didn't belong.

"Still with me?" Joe asked as the elevator door opened on Daniel's floor.

I smiled. "Let's do this."

Marching down the hallway reminded me of the last time I was here with Stella. My pulse quickened and my feet dragged when I thought of her. Stella was yet to return from wherever she disappeared to, and I didn't have any leads as to her whereabouts. Perhaps after we finished here, I could brainstorm a plan with Joe to find her. *Since when is this a team effort?* While it was nice not to be alone this morning, I couldn't assume Joe would be up for ghost hunting my familiar. He was nice enough to show up, and I couldn't loop him into yet another twisted mess in my life. Lately, it seemed as though everything I touched turned to disaster and I hoped this morning would be an exception.

Please don't let us get killed. Please don't let us get killed.

I repeated the phrase over and over all the way to Tristan Mint's door. Before I could change my mind and drag Joe out of there, he rapped his knuckles on the wood and flashed me a quick smile.

Please don't let us get killed.

The door swung open, and we were greeted by a tall, medium-built man in his late forties. His hair was combed and gelled to the side, and he wore a tailored suit the color of oceans. Spotting us, the man shut the door a few inches. "Can I help you two?"

I started to speak, but Joe beat me to it. He flashed a business card, and I tried to make out what it said, but it was so quick, I couldn't read one word. I assumed that was the point since Tristan Mint appeared to be as confused as me. "Sorry to bother you so early, sir," Joe said. "We represent the Tse estate and were hoping to ask his neighbors a few questions."

"What about?" Tristan asked, the door shutting more.

Refusing to back down, Joe's smile widened, and I noticed him steel his spine. He suddenly grew a few inches and was towering over Tristan, an intimidation tactic if I'd ever seen one. What kind of lawyer did Joe say he was in King City? I wondered if he was used to shaking out his tail feathers to get people to talk. Clearly in control, Joe stepped forward, letting Tristan Mint know we weren't leaving. "I'm sure you've heard the terrible news by now," he said. "The family is hoping to list the apartment next door, but in order to do that, quite a few renovations have to take place."

"I don't understand—"

"We're looking at a full gut job, if I'm being frank," Joe interrupted. "Old building such as this; noise carries. The family was worried about it affecting the neighbors and since they're trying to sell as quickly as possible, we told them we'd stop by, see if we can all come to an agreement."

Tristan's jaw set. "There's a building board," he said. "You should talk to them."

"That," Joe replied, "is what we're hoping to avoid. You know how these things can get. Between negotiations and permits, we'll be tied up in this mess for some time. The two of us were hoping we could get the direct neighbors to put in a good word. If you don't mind."

The door slid again as Tristan closed it further, his face flushing. "I really don't have time."

Acting before thinking, I stretched my leg and crammed my boot in the frame. The door slammed into me, and I hissed, acting as though I didn't possibly break my toes. Great. "A man is dead," I said.

My words must have registered with Tristan because he stopped pushing the door and the pressure on my boot lessened.

"I was very sorry to hear about Daniel," he said.

"But you should speak to the board. Like you said, this is an old building. There are rules in place."

"Any of those rules about dogs?" I asked, the words spilling from my lips before I could stop them. "The kind that bark uncontrollably?"

Face beet-red, Tristan crossed his arms and flared his nose. I hit a nerve. It turned out Sebastian wasn't exaggerating about Daniel's neighbor hating his dog; Tristan looked like his head might explode thinking of the mutt. I felt Joe's side brush against mine as he inched closer, and I struggled not to melt into the tile floor. "What does the dog have anything to do with this?" Tristan asked.

"Well, for starters, it's missing," I announced. Deciding to stick to Joe's original cover, I spun the tale further. "The family would like to find it prior to selling the place. It meant a lot to Mr. Tse. Do you remember seeing her around? We'd love to have some good news to deliver, since it seems the renovations will have to wait."

I was laying it on so thick, you could taste it in the air. Beside me, Joe stiffened, and I saw him fight a smile from the corner of my eye.

"Look, I need to run," Tristan said. "To be honest, and I'm sure this will make me sound awful, but that dog being gone has been great for the rest of us. I haven't heard it in over a week, and good riddance."

Over a week, huh? I did the math in my head and placed the dog's disappearance somewhere around the time Daniel died. Taking a chance, I asked, "Last Wednesday night, perhaps?"

"That sounds about right," Tristan said. "Yeah, actually, now that I think of it, that was it. My wife came by for drinks and the foul thing kept barking. I went over there to get it to shut up, but no one answered. That man let the stupid animal run the place. It was despicable."

Despicable enough to kill over? I doubted it. Tristan Mint was a dog-hating, rude man, but would someone kill a person over a dog barking? I replayed what he said in my head. Tristan mentioned Ember stopping by, but I was under the impression they were on the outs and going through a nasty divorce. Referring to her as his wife was also odd, all things considering. Perhaps the rumor mill had it wrong for once, and the two were mending their marriage and not ending it. What did this have to do with Daniel? Absolutely nothing, it seemed.

I took a step back and breathed out. "Did you notice anyone come by to visit Mr. Tse the same evening?"

"Not that I recall," Tristan said. "But as I said, I was otherwise occupied. And the dog was going nuts, so even if someone came by, I wouldn't have heard them. Not to speak ill of the dead, but that guy was a terrible neighbor. Selfish and self-absorbed. It was the hotel he worked in or that dog. Nothing else mattered to him. Obsessed if you ask me." He frowned. "I hope whoever they sell the place to is nicer."

Tristan shut the door in my face without saying goodbye. I looked at Joe, whispering, "Pretty sure Daniel wasn't the crappy neighbor around here."

We walked back to the elevator, deflated. Tristan may not have been my cup of coffee, but he said nothing to make me think he wanted Daniel gone. His dog was a different story. Could Tristan have hurt Margaret the Third? I shuddered. My brain worked on overtime, deconstructing every word of the brief conversation. The thing with Ember was questionable and the attitude unnecessary. Something else was gnawing at me and I couldn't put my finger on its pulse.

"Well, that was a bust," Joe said.

I pressed the button for the lobby and watched the elevator doors close. "Not necessarily," I replied. "Mint said Daniel was obsessed with two things, the dog and the hotel."

"And?"

"What could it be about the hotel to draw Daniel's attention so intensely? He dumped his best friend to work there, stepped over Cilia to get ahead even though she was dating his cousin, and for what? What was it that made the hotel so special?"

The doors opened, and we walked out, lingering in the lobby.

"Only one thing I can think of," Joe said.

Our eyes met, and I didn't have to ask him to know what he was referring to. There was only one thing to stand out about the Rose Hollow Hotel and it wasn't the fake hauntings it boasted online. This was more melancholy, closer to home. I recalled the night I came home to find Daniel's envelope on my porch and my blood froze. Rosemary Hayes's death.

The two were connected, and I was going to find out how.

CHAPTER 18

Boisterous laughter filled the cafe, and the doorbell rang every few minutes as people came in for their morning drinks. I waved hello to Sasha and his wife, then pressed the double espresso shot button and watched as the machine came to life. The scent of burning beans filled my nostrils, and I breathed it in, smiling.

Finally. Back in business.

A group of three women took a seat at one table and I hurried to pour milk into the latte I was making, setting it on the counter. "Double shot latte with skim!" I yelled out, walking to the table. "Morning. How can I help you?"

They placed their orders, and I wrote it down on

the small notepad I carried in my apron pocket, walking away. If business continued to boom, I'd have to look into hiring help. I glanced at the office door, Stella's absence weighing heavily on me. I wasn't sure how much longer I could wait before I admitted she might never come back. Leave it to me to be the only witch in the history of witches to lose their familiar.

The bell rang again, and I polished off three mochaccinos with a dollop of whipped cream and pushed the cups out of the way. Before turning my attention to the new, I placed two cranberry scones on a plate, crammed everything onto a tray, and carried it back to the women. They thanked me, devouring their drinks as I turned away. I heard one of them comment on the coziness of the cafe and my heart pitter pattered in my chest. It was nice to be on top for once.

Customers continued to pile in for another hour before the morning rush died away, giving me a moment to breathe. I wiped down the countertops, gathered abandoned mugs off the tables, and gave those a good cleaning as well. There were still a few people lingering, and it pleased me to see them enjoy the cafe enough to stay awhile. One couple, the Garrots, spent almost two hours reading their papers. They ordered two cappuccinos each and Mrs. Garrot had a blueberry muffin plus one to go. When they left, they told me they'd be spreading the word about

Bean Me Up around town and were glad to see me reopen.

Joyfully, I skipped around the cafe, sprucing it up for lunch hour, when I assumed the rush would pick back up. My happiness was short-lived because while I was restocking the croissant tray, the bell rang again and someone I did not expect to see this morning stepped inside.

"Hello again," Tristan Mint said. He hastened to the counter and scoured the blackboard menu behind it. My body stopped stock still. I was caught. "Single long espresso to go, please."

I rang in his order and prepped the cup. "Good to see you again, Mr. Mint." I scrambled for an excuse to explain why I was serving him coffee instead of sitting in my make-believe legal office I supposedly worked in. "About this morning—"

The man held up a hand like I was an unruly student. "Spare me the lies," he said. "I know you and your friend aren't lawyers."

My cheeks flushed. "We were only trying to find out what happened to Daniel. I'm sorry we misled you."

"Look, I'm going to be honest here. I thought about calling the police after you left, but given the circumstances, I let it go. I'd appreciate it if you didn't bother me again." I gaped at him, unable to move. "I'd also appreciate my drink sooner rather than later. My wife and I are meeting in a few minutes."

Leaping for the espresso machine, I made Tristan's drink in record time, handing it over and letting him know it was free. He glared at me with disgust before grabbing the cup and heading for the milk station. I watched him dump an obscene amount of sugar into the cup and swirled it around, shame circling through my veins. As he walked to the door, I yelled out, "Please let Ember know I said hello. And again, very sorry for this morning."

Tristan paused, his hand on the handle. I couldn't see his face from where I stood and wondered if I caught him off guard by mentioning Ember. Orchard Hollow was a small town, but it wasn't so small everyone knew each other. Case in point, Tristan and me. He said nothing, leaving me alone to brew over what a fool I made of myself. I decided when the day was over, I would walk over to Brooks Books to warn Joe in case Tristan stopped by later. His presence at the cafe was not coincidental, and I was certain he wanted to make a point. He was onto me, and I better steer clear.

Point received.

The rest of the day flew by in a flash. Customers came in and out until closing and I made more lattes than I could keep track of. As sour as my experience with Tristan had been, staying busy helped keep my mind from racing, and by the time I locked up for the evening, I could barely recall the encounter. I turned on the alarm and locked the door, then headed to the bookstore. As I turned, I ran headfirst into a wide chest. Joe's. Again. Of course.

"Oh, hi," I said, fixing my hair back. "I was just on my way to see you."

"Same here."

I cocked my head to the side. "I thought you weren't a coffee drinker?"

"Still not," he said. I hated that it bothered me so much. "But it looks like I won't have to pretend to be." Joe pointed to the closed sign hanging on the door.

"I can open again if you want to try a mocha."

He held his hands up defensively and shook his head, laughing. "No, no. I'm okay on that. A drink down the street instead?"

Every part of me wanted to say yes and spend the with Joe. Then there was a tiny, very annoying part urging me to stay away. As great as he seemed, Joe was a stranger; one who knew too many of my secrets. His showing up in town weeks before Daniel's murder, the sketchy notebook he found in his uncle's bookshop; it was all too closely tied together. What if Joe was the killer I was looking for?

I almost slapped myself right in the face. *You're*

not looking for anyone, I told myself. *The police are. Mind your own business.*

"So, about that drink?"

"Would love to, but I can't tonight," I lied. "I have some things to take care of at home and an early start tomorrow. Looks like you're in the minority and most people love their coffee."

"Another time then," Joe said. "When your witch schedule allows it."

Excuse you? I narrowed my eyes at him. "What does that mean?"

"Nothing weird. I assumed when you said things, you meant of the magical variety."

"And why did you assume that?"

Joe rubbed the back of his neck until it turned red and looked at me sheepishly. "I really meant nothing by it. Making a joke, is all."

Strange joke to make. I bid him goodnight and waited until he was out of sight to open the cafe door again. The alarm sounded, and I entered the code, checking to make sure Joe didn't double back when he heard the noise. I didn't fully trust him yet, and I had every right not to. Though he did say something that sparked an idea. I have been all over town tracking down people with a reason to hurt Daniel, but there was one thing I hadn't tried yet.

Magic.

Witch magic didn't work like it does in the movies. There was no wand to wave and no special words to utter to make it do your bidding. It was grueling work and often required physical sacrifices, mainly in the way of your energy being sucked out. Witches could refocus some of the energy drain and redirect it to items they used in their spells, unlike warlocks, but it was still a lot for a person to handle. Which was why I couldn't cast a spell to find Daniel's killer. If there was one. Magic was more delicate than that; a dance between the person casting and the outside world, a give and take. While I couldn't finger the person responsible, there was one thing I could do. I could use my magic to point me in the direction of the person who broke into the cafe's office to steal my key. The two instances had to be connected; no way would my backup key end up in Daniel's apartment for any other reason. If whoever took it was paranormal, they left their signature in the office. I could track that signature.

I wrinkled my nose. At least in theory. A proper witch that knew what she was doing could track the signature; I could muck around with spells and hope for the best.

Better safe than sorry.

Running faster than I have in my entire life, I bolted for the office. My hands moved quickly, and I cast a circle in the center of the room in record time. The stash of ingredients I kept in the cupboard had dwindled down after Harry broke half the bottles I stored there, but I had enough for a simple circle casting. Moon water at one point, a feather in another, a handful of earth I collected with gran ages ago, a lit candle, and a sprinkle of salt. I double checked that the back door was locked, then placed myself in the center, eyes closed. My thoughts settled and soon I could concentrate on the purpose of the spell. I made my intention clear, thinking of the spare key, and opened my eyes. Reaching for the feather, I placed it in my palm and poured my wishes into it. *Show me the thief among us.*

Nothing happened.

Breathing in, I willed for it again. *Show me the thief among us.*

Sparks flew from my fingers and singed the edges of the feather. The candle to my right fizzed out and a gust of wind blasted the room. The feather rose high in the air, floating with the current. Twirling. Twirling. Twirling. As though hitting a wall, it stopped and dropped, landing on my desk.

I groaned.

Surprise, surprise—it didn't work.

Knees creaking, I rose from the circle and went to pick up the feather to try again when I noticed the drawer under the desk. It stuck out a little like it had recently been closed. My hand reached toward it, gliding it open. As I did, the feather slid from the top of the desk and landed on the papers inside.

I gasped. It wasn't any pile of papers the feather perched on; it was the stack of magazine cut-outs Daniel sent recounting Rosemary's case. My teeth split open, and I ran my index fingers along the edges of the articles. "Did Rosemary break into my office?"

Slumping into the office chair, I shook my head. What was I even saying? Rosemary was dead. No way was she breaking into anything. And yet the feather pointed me to her. Why? Unless...

The thought entered my mind before I could stop it and once it did, there was no turning back. I may have been a garbage witch, but the spell worked. I knew it did. Whoever broke into the Bean Me Up office was connected to Rosemary. I pulled out the articles and laid them out on the desk. If there was any doubt in me before, it was long gone. "I need to find out more about Rosemary Hayes."

CHAPTER 19

There was no sleeping for me that night and I laid with eyes wide open until my body finally gave out. While I slept, I dreamt of Daniel. His eyes beckoned me toward him and when I walked closer, he vanished, leaving only fog behind. I tried to clear it with my hand, but it was so dense, I couldn't see a foot in front of me. I coughed, the world spinning around me, my hands waving maniacally to clear the space. My eyes widened and my throat ached from screaming his name. Finally, the fog cleared, and I found myself in the Rose Hollow Hotel. Staring at room 312. I pulled the handle; the door swinging in and slamming against the wall. Fear gripped my every bone. I pushed it aside and walked in. Beneath me, the floor gave out, and I was free falling. Hair in my eyes, my scream echoed in the darkness.

I woke up to a half-scream lying on sweat-soaked sheets.

Groaning, I dragged myself out of bed and looked out the bedroom window. The sun was rising and the field beyond the farmhouse looked eery in the shade of red. The shade of blood.

Shaking the dream off, I made a quick cup of coffee and got myself ready for the day. It was early enough I didn't need to hurry, but I hated the quiet of the house without Stella barging in on me. There were still a few hours until the cafe was to open, so I decided to make a stop by the sheriff's office to check in. I doubted he'd tell me much about Daniel's case, but it was a good excuse to ask a few questions lingering on my mind.

Questions about Rosemary Hayes.

Speeding into town—a law I never broke before—I parked in the lot behind the station and fought the morning wind to get inside. The police station was deserted, and it surprised me to find the front desk empty when I walked in. *One less performance to put on,* I told myself.

Elevator music boomed from a speaker in the lobby, and I wondered whose idea it was to play soft jazz in a police station. Did it help calm the criminals down, or was it someone's idea of a grim joke? My foot tapped against my will, and I swayed from side to side as the beat picked up. I was still in a trance when a throat cleared behind me.

I spun around.

"Hello, Miss Addison," Sheriff Romero said. "How can I help you?"

"Morning!" I said cheerfully and waved. "I was on my way to work and figured I'd stop by to see if there is any news on Daniel."

The sheriff looked me up and down. He wore a sheriff's hat today, and it sat low on his brow, like it was a smidge too large for his head. The brim cast a deep shadow over his eyes and when he looked at me, I shrank. "Did you, now?" the sheriff whispered. "Unfortunately, there is nothing I can share with you at this time. The investigation into Mr. Tse's death is ongoing. Once we have concrete information, we will share it with the town via the proper channels."

I assumed he meant a news conference of some sort, though it'd been ages since Orchard Hollow had one. Not since Rosemary's death and even then, it was a sad gathering, since the town only had one local paper and no one bothered to call the media outlets in King City.

"Actually," I said, "since I'm already here, do you

mind if I ask you about another case? One from a few years back?"

The sheriff's hat dipped lower, and he grumbled, "Which case would that be?"

"A death in the hotel. Rosemary Hayes."

I was met with a serious look pinning me in place. The sheriff wasn't impressed I was butting into yet another police matter, especially since this one was closed and what I wagered was an open and shut case. He brushed his mustache with his pinkie and looked to the door, making sure there was no one there needing his attention. I had the feeling the sheriff would have loved to be called away from my prying questions and when he wasn't, had no choice but to answer. "Why the sudden interest in this, Miss Addison? You're not stirring up trouble, are you?" He growled. "I need not remind you are still a person of interest in a current investigation."

"Trust me, I'm well aware," I said. "But I think we both know I had nothing to do with Daniel, though I understand you have a job to do."

My words must have appeased Romero because he raised his chin and that stupid hat rolled back a few inches, giving me a glimpse of his eyes. Creases formed at their corners, and he rubbed his temples, making the hat bob up and down comically. "What would you like to know?" he asked.

"From what I remember, Rosemary had a heart-attack in her room, right?"

The sheriff nodded. "That's correct. I wasn't first on the scene, but the deputy who was said it appeared she died of natural causes. Why are you asking about it now?"

"Daniel's death brought back memories of the hotel," I said. "This was one of them. I always wondered how someone so young could simply die out of the blue. No background of heart issues or anything."

This was such a blatant lie it surprised me I could keep a straight face. I never even met Rosemary, let alone be close enough to gauge the state of her health. Though I doubted Romero knew that. If the police cleared her death, there would be no further investigation into the case, so most stones in Rosemary's life would have remained unturned. My hunch turned out to be right because Romero said, "We can never gauge in these situations. I am sorry for your loss, Miss Addison."

"Thank you," I said, feeling all the more guilty for lying. "Did they ever figure out what caused the attack? If you don't mind me asking."

"There were no concrete signs of a major problem, but I do recall they found traces of medication in her blood stream which could have triggered heart failure."

Bells rang out in my mind. Rosemary's medication, Daniel's drug use. It was so familiar my head spun. I didn't believe for a second Daniel had a drug problem —was the same true for Rosemary supposed meds? I cleared my throat, wrapping my cardigan around me. "Any chance you can tell me what pills she took?"

"Oxycodone," Romero said. "Now, if you'll excuse me, I need to get back to work. And you need to stop drudging up the past and worry about your current situation instead, Miss Addison."

He pushed past me and disappeared down the hallway of doom leading to the interrogation rooms. I should have left right there and then, but my legs refused to cooperate. My tongue swelled in my mouth, Romero's words echoing through my entire body like a drumbeat. Oxycodone. Rosemary Hayes, the witch, took a poppy-based drug. Panic drilled through my bones, and I stumbled, catching my balance on the front counter. My nails dug into the wood veneer, and I blinked, trying to clear my spotty vision. How could a witch die from a drug she knew would cause her to have a severe reaction? Even without the heart-attack, Rosemary would have been in a great deal of pain from ingesting poppies.

The mere thought of it made me want to heave,

and most witches had a similar reaction. We could not be anywhere near the stuff. If one was unlucky enough to touch a poppy, the effects would be catastrophic. We're talking vomiting for days type of catastrophe.

And yet Rosemary had it in her system. How? How did she keep it down? If she wanted to ease her pain, I could think of a multitude of other drugs she could have taken that would have the same outcome with less trauma. Tendrils of hair fell into my face, and I rubbed my palms over my cheeks, ragged breaths shaking my entire being. Was it possible her death wasn't as natural as the police thought? That could only mean one thing.

I pressed a hand to my chest and held my breath. Rosemary Hayes was murdered in the Rose Hollow Hotel.

CHAPTER
20

"Enjoy your evening!"

"You too, Piper. See you in the morning."

I locked the door behind Sasha, who was fast becoming one of my most loyal customers. Flipping the sign on the door and dimming the lights, I scanned the cafe, relieved it wasn't in much disarray. A few plates to clear off and some pastries left from the day to put away, but otherwise, it looked like it would be an early night for me. I desperately needed one today.

The revelation I had at the police station hung in the air, and I had trouble putting it aside. Even the steady flow of customers didn't take my mind off what

I may have uncovered. Did the sheriff know Rosemary was a witch? I didn't think so. He wouldn't be so quick to label her death a natural heart-attack if he did, unless he didn't know the effect poppies had on witches. Or didn't put two and two together.

I didn't think Romero was that daft, so I settled on him not knowing of Rosemary's paranormal blood to make myself feel better about the situation. I should have told him. *And then what?* What did I expect the sheriff to do about a woman that's been dead for years, especially when he had a much fresher death to think about? If I could gather some evidence to bring to him, he might consider what I had to say, but until then, I shouldn't bother him with my theories. One of which was the reason I couldn't keep my head on straight all day.

I couldn't get the thought that Rosemary's death was the reason Daniel met his unlikely end. Working on autopilot, I wiped down the tables and refreshed the flowers in the vases, all the while thinking of Rosemary. Did Daniel discover what I had? That it wasn't a heart-attack at all? My body tensed. Did he know who killed her?

I walked over to the cafe's window and closed the blinds.

If my hunch was right and Daniel died because of

what he found out, I might be in danger of the same fate. How long until Daniel's killer came for me to keep me quiet?

"Who are you?" I whispered into the dimly lit cafe.

"Talking to yourself is not a good look."

The rag in my hand dropped to the floor, and I twisted on my heels, my knees knocking. "Stella!" I shrieked, running to the ghost. She took a step back, letting me know my excitement was in poor taste and not welcome. I supposed the time away did not change her one bit. "Where have you been? I've been worried sick."

My ghost familiar pursed her lips, crossed her arms, and meandered to the espresso machine. "Finally," she said. "One that works. I take it business has been well while I was away?"

She pointed to the dirty cups lining the counter.

"It has," I replied. "Surprisingly well. You'll never guess who came by? You know what? It doesn't matter. What happened to you? I thought you; you know..."

Stella made an explosion motion with her left hand. "Poof?"

"Yep," I said. "Where did you go? Why were you gone so long? Tell me everything!"

Oblivious to my harassment, Stella brushed her

hand over her tennis skirt, pulling it down her legs, and walked to the window. She peered outside despite the blinds being drawn, yawning. Her hair, in the same teased ponytail it was usually in, looked a little less put together, pieces of blonde hanging down the sides of her face. The polo shirt she wore was untucked, something Stella would never do. According to her, an untucked shirt was a close equivalent to rolling around in maneuver as far as fashion was concerned. I had no idea where she got these notions, but she stuck to them like glue, so I never argued. Though this time, it was hard to miss that the Stella that left and the Stella that returned were two wildly different people.

The ghost twirled the tip of her ponytail between her index and thumb. "Don't grovel for answers," she told me. "It's not a good look on you. Neither is that apron."

Okay, not so different after all.

"Will you stop messing around and tell me already? I'm dying to know."

"Interesting word choice, all things considering," Stella said. "If you absolutely must know, I went to the hotel."

Brilliant. I already knew that. I waited for her to go on and when she didn't, said, "And?"

"There was nothing there." Even more brilliant. "Except for room 312. That was an interesting one."

My ears burned to know more, and I closed the distance between Stella and me, beckoning her to spill the beans. Behind me, the sound of glass shattering made me jump, and I pulled my gaze off Stella to look at the office door. It was eerily quiet for a few minutes. Then the chitter of a sneaky raccoon filled the office. Urging myself not to stress over whatever Harry Houdini broke this time, I turned back to Stella. "I see things here haven't changed," she said.

"You don't know that half of it. Now, about room 312," I insisted. "That was the room Rosemary Hayes died in. I think she may have been—"

"Murdered," Stella finished my sentence. Her long lashes batted, and she pursed her lips, a tactic I assumed she used often on her husband when she was alive. "That woman did not go willingly into the night."

I took one more step inward, making sure I didn't invade Stella's personal space, or the ghost would let me have it and I couldn't risk getting her off topic. "How do you know that? I only now put the pieces together."

"My secrets are my own, Piper. Besides, that was not what kept me occupied the last few days."

Color me intrigued. "What *was*?"

Stella didn't answer and instead brushed by me with a little more sway in her step, her shoulder nearly passing through mine. She continued to walk all the way to the office door and when she reached it, she beckoned, "Coming?"

Following her like a rat following a flute, I dragged myself to the office and watched Stella breeze by the desk and stop at the back door. A door which was wide open. At its base stood Harry, his body rigid and his hind legs tucked in. The raccoon chittered and hissed, never moving from the spot he occupied. I looked at Stella. "What's with him?"

My ghost familiar didn't answer. She tipped her chin to the alley and motioned for me to come closer. The good little soldier I was obeyed instantly, curiosity carrying me forward. When I reached her, I dead-panned Harry, then turned my gaze to the alley.

Where a filth-covered Chihuahua shivered on the ground.

"Margaret the Third!" I exclaimed, scooping the poor creature into my arms. The warmth of my sweater didn't stop her shaking, and I concluded that shivering was Margaret's main way of existing. She was so small; I couldn't imagine her bothering Tristan. That awful man. But then Harry hissed again and pawed at my jeans to get to her, and the barking started. Sheltering Margaret the Third from Harry, and myself from Margaret the Third's tiny claws, I ran from the office, slamming the door shut behind me. Breathless, I slid down and sat the dog on the floor, waiting until she calmed down. My ears rang and when Stella made a snide comment about the mess my life was, I barely heard her. The one bonus of a Chihuahua's deafening high pitched bark.

Soon, the dog relaxed, sort of. I looked at Stella, my bones leaving my body. "Where did you find her? And how?"

"The how is irrelevant," my familiar said. "She was wandering in the woods. No collar, no direction. It was depressing."

Interesting. A part of me thought Stella may have saved the dog because it reminded her of the day she herself woke up in the woods all alone. Though unlike Stella, Margaret the Third was alive when she was discovered. I breathed out and stood, walking to the counter to grab a saucer from the cupboards below. Filling it with water, I put it down next to the dog and waited until she was done drinking before refilling. Then, I cut a plain croissant into tiny pieces and put it on a plate, sliding the meal her way. The tiny thing sniffed at it curiously, then started to eat. I noticed for a starving dog, Margaret sure wasn't impressed by what I offered. "This is probably the worst meal you've ever had," I said, remembering

Daniel treated the dog like a princess and not a tiny bark machine.

After polishing off the croissant and another bowl of water, Margaret the Third wandered over to where I dropped the rag, piled it up and plopped herself atop it. Her eyes closed in seconds, and she was out cold, tiny snores filling the air.

I took off my cardigan and draped it over the small thing, hoping it might keep her warm until I figured out what to do. "Incoming," Stella warned, pointing to the front door.

There was a knock outside and I jumped, startled. Who was coming here at this hour? The cafe was closed and, for the few lights still on, it didn't look like anyone was here. I peeked out the glass, wiping my wet brow. Unlocking, I opened the door and smiled. "Hi, Joe. What brings you by?"

"I saw the lights on and wanted to check in. Got a little worried since you're not usually here this late."

I didn't realize I had a schedule, specifically not one big city Joe noticed. "Oh, you know," I said, trying not to look at Stella, who was making obscene gestures toward our visitor. "Wanted to get ahead on tomorrow. All safe and sound, though."

"What is *that*?" Joe asked. He pointed past me. I didn't need to turn around to know he was gesturing the Margaret the Third, who continued to snore the evening away.

Rubbing my arms, I tried to laugh, but it caught in my throat, and I coughed up a lung instead. How attractive. "Well, you won't believe it. That's Margaret the Third."

"Daniel's dog? How?"

"Long story," I said. "The short version is that she was in the woods with no collar, and I don't think she got there on her own."

Joe's smile vanished. "You think someone tried to get rid of her? Tristan?"

"I don't think so. He can't be that nasty. No, I think it was worse."

"The killer?"

I nodded.

Fear cloaked Joe's face, and he stepped forward, his hands clutching my shoulders. Sparks rushed through my body and this time; it wasn't my magic malfunctioning. Joe squeezed my shoulders and said, "This is not good, Piper. Who knows why the killer wanted the dog gone? If this person knows you have her, they might come after you."

It was hard to concentrate on anything Joe said with him so close. I knew if I stayed here next to him, I'd say something stupid, but I also couldn't force myself to break free. *Please don't be the bad guy.* I fisted my hands and relaxed them again, attempting to get the blood circulating because I was pretty sure there was none pumping to my brain. Sucking in a sharp breath, I said the one thing I knew would break the tension between us. "That's not even the worst part," I whispered. "Let me tell you about a witch named Rosemary Hayes."

CHAPTER 21

After telling Joe my suspicions of Rosemary's death, we decided the best course of action was to find out everything we could about the witch. Well, Joe decided, and I agreed since I couldn't get him to let me snoop alone no matter what I tried. Which was how I wound up waiting for the last customer at Brooks Books to leave so the two of us could continue what looked to be a makeshift investigation into a possible homicide.

The young man browsing the Hauntings and Seances section of the bookstore did not appear to be a paranormal and, judging by the mishmash of books under his arm when he walked out, I could only assume he was a human boy in need of entertainment.

For as long as the shop was around, it attracted a crowd, both human and paranormal. The former treated the bookstore as a spectacle and a place to find out-of-the-box gifts for friends and family. Around Halloween, Brooks Books was especially popular because of the obscure selection of texts one could not find in any other bookstore. It was nice to see Joe on board with the strangeness of the place and not change it into something hipper. I even noticed he updated the paper bags for people's purchases—the one the boy walked out with was a deep purple shade with a cartoon ghost imprinted on the front. It was adorable.

I wiped dust off one shelf with the back of my sleeve and stayed in the shadows while Joe closed the store for the evening. As he dragged the sandwich board inside and tucked it behind the door, I looked away, refusing to drool over bulging muscle when I should concentrate on bigger things. Murderous things.

The front door locked, and Joe grunted, shifting the board over again. "Piper?"

I stepped out from the passage I occupied, a specter materializing.

"Thought you left," Joe said. "Ready to start?"

Nodding, I followed him through the vast open area in the center and to the rear of the shop, where a small desk housed an even smaller computer. Joe pulled up two chairs, flipped the laptop open, and waited until I sat down. "What are we looking for?"

"I don't know." I shrugged. "This was your idea. Where do you want to start?"

Joe typed in Rosemary's name into the search bar and pulled up new tabs for every one of her social media profiles. The witch was a busy woman and had her hand in almost every platform available. I couldn't even stay active on one while Rosemary posted daily, sometimes several times a day. Most of her profiles were public, so it was easy to track her movements in the last days of her life. While Joe read aloud, I took notes in a notebook he gave me with the same cute ghost on the front as the bag. I smiled. Good branding was a soft spot of mine. It was lovely to see Joe put this much effort into promoting the bookshop.

By the time we made our way through the last two weeks preceding Rosemary's death, we had a detailed timeline in place. In fact, it was so detailed I believed my theory even more.

"What are you thinking?" Joe asked.

My heart beating faster, I brushed my palm over the paper. "Does this look like the schedule of someone who was in any physical pain?"

"Not really."

"Look here," I said, pointing to a post Rosemary made the day she died. "She mentions a rock-climbing gym she's visiting the very next day. Why would she do that if she had pain bad enough to need heavy medication? And here," I pointed to the notebook in front me. "She had plans to go away for a week with her friends. Hiking in Costa Rica! It doesn't fit."

Joe nodded and pulled the laptop in, scrolling through Rosemary's Facebook profile. While he continued to scour the deepest corners of social media for clues, I studied the timeline. Rosemary lived a very full life. She had a good number of friends and seemed to be well regarded in town. I noticed a few posts from Nancy Steeles complimenting her on an outfit that looked straight out of a magazine. My toes curled. Rosemary Hayes was the witch I dreamed of being. She was very much like gran, solitary but social. It was a hard balance to achieve, especially if you didn't belong to a coven as Rosemary hadn't. I was jealous of a dead woman.

A new low, even for me.

"Interesting," Joe whispered, his face a few inches from the lit screen.

I put aside my pettiness and turned the screen to face me, zeroing in on what he was reading. "You're jealous and it shows. I can't believe I thought you were my friend. Don't fall for her act, people! Rosemary Hayes is evil, and she'll get what she deserves. Karma comes around!"

The message came from a Patty Nolan, not a name I recognized. I scrolled down. There were a few comments defending Rosemary and almost a hundred angry face emojis. Whoever Patty was, she did not expect the circle Rosemary had around her. I clicked on the profile image and Patty's personal page popped up. It wasn't public like Rosemary's, and all I could see were her photo highlights. Most were selfies with questionable filters added, but one caught my eye. It was a picture of Patty and Rosemary, dressed to the nines and hugging for dear life. I clicked it, reading the caption. "Happy Birthday to my best friend. You are the sister I never had, and I can't wait to celebrate with you!"

Joe and I exchanged cautious looks. "Wonder what happened with those two," he said.

"And why Patty thought it was a good idea to threaten her best friend on social media," I added. I continued to go down the rabbit hole of stalking Patty Nolan, though I had very little to show for my efforts in the end. After a few minutes, I slid the laptop away and glanced at Joe. A smile spread on his face and he held his phone out, the screen facing me. "What happened?"

He pushed the phone close to my face, and I stared at a picture of a quaint antique store. The display window was filled with knick-knacks and three decrepit chairs sat in front with a sign reading *Your Next DIY Project* leaning against them. My eyes traveled to the shop's name. "Second Life Antiques."

"Patty's store," Joe explained. "It's about a ten-minute drive from here and closes in a half hour."

I grinned. "What are you saying?"

"I'd been looking for a side table for that sofa," he pointed to a gorgeous, red velvet loveseat along one wall. "Care to help me pick one out?"

Joe wasn't kidding when he said the antique shop wasn't very far. It took us less than fifteen minutes to get there, park, and scope out the area. Despite the store closing soon, there were still a few people milling about. I noticed a woman put down a bronze horse with a missing leg, then pick it up again. Someone's trash, as they say.

The shop's sign had been turned around and the chairs we saw in the image online were gone. In their place stood a low iron bench that looked like it was ripped straight out of a fairy tale. The intricate design of the backing mesmerized me, and I found myself drawn to the roses and leaves spiraling up and down the bench. In the back of my mind, I hoped Patty wasn't the evil mastermind I made her out to be and I could return later to peruse the store. It really seemed to be a fantastic little antique shop.

Looking around, I noticed the narrow street the shop was tucked away in left space for several other businesses. Spotting a small bistro with the cutest patio out front, a convenience store, and a butcher; I marveled at the peculiar combination. Since the street was in the more residential part of Orchard Hollow, I assumed the businesses grew out of sheer convenience to offer residents a bit of everything without having to travel into the busier part of town. Though Cliff Row was a short drive away, I could see why some people would have liked to avoid it. Especially during tourist season, which lately seemed to take up a good portion of the year.

I followed Joe into the shop and started for the front counter, then stopped myself. There were two people checking out and the horse woman was still picking up items only to return them to their shelves. I tried to glimpse past the patrons at the counter and spot Patty; when I noticed the same short, curly hair from online, I relaxed. At least it wasn't someone else working tonight.

Nerves tickling the rear of my neck, I veered to the left, where a collection of vintage Christmas ornaments hung on display. We weren't even close to the holiday season, but I assumed a shop such as this sported Christmas decor all year round. Beside me, Joe bent over a small table made of marble. *Wow, he's seriously in character.* We both stayed where we were, pointing to items and discussing them until the last customer left. As the door closed, we dropped what we were doing and hurried to the front, where Patty greeted us pleasantly. "Welcome to Second Life Antiques. Are you two looking for anything specific?"

"I'm in the market for a side table," Joe said. "The marble piece you have over there is stunning."

Patty's thick-rimmed glasses slid down her long nose as she looked to where Joe was pointing. Her eyes locked on me, and she snickered. "You are a bold woman to let your husband do the decorating."

"Oh, we're not... I'm not... He's not..." I was beet red before Joe could catch on to what the shop owner implied. I shook my arms in a less than elegant manner and tried to correct course. "He needs the table for his business. We're not even dating."

"Try not to sound so upset over it," Joe teased.

He and Patty laughed.

I cried inside.

It took them a good few minutes to settle down and by that time, my cheeks regained their usual pale color and the stench of embarrassment barely wafted off me. Patty leaned over the counter, her finger pointing to another table Joe must have missed. "It has a matching coffee table," she said. "If you want both, I can let them go at a discount."

I piped in before we wasted any more time walking about tables no one actually needed. "Why don't you go check them out?" I suggested. "It might work better than what you already have."

One quirked eyebrow later and Joe walked to the slab of marble with legs the shop owner directed him to. I stayed and watched, pretending to find an old pair of sunglasses near Patty incredibly interesting. Sunglasses had never been my thing; then again neither had summer. Growing up in a town that was cold no matter the season, the few months of heat we got were excruciating. Call me weird, but I loved my sweater layers and slight sniffles for most of the year, thank you very much.

I twirled the sunglass case and leaned in to inspect one pair better. "Would you like to try them on?" Patty asked.

"Why not?" I asked. "You have the nicest things."

The shop owner undid a clasp and pulled out a pair of vintage Valentinos that were way too big for my face. She manifested a mirror from under the counter and pushed it closer to me, waiting for me to try on the ridiculous shades. Unsatisfied, she shook her head. "Those might be a bit too large."

You think? The glasses fell before I could even take them off and I caught them mid-air, handing them back to Patty. "I'm sure I'll find another pair next time," I said.

"First time at Second Life?" she asked.

"Yep! Beautiful shop. My friend wasn't kidding when she told us to check it out. You have an eye for antiques."

At this, the shop owner paused, proud ther store made an impression. "Who's your friend?"

Near to us, I heard Joe clamber around, but kept my eyes glued to Patty. *Here we go.* "Rosemary," I said. "Rosemary Hayes. Not sure if you knew her."

She knew her alright, and Patty spent no effort in hiding it. Her entire face crumbled at the mention of Rosemary, and she scrambled to get the sunglass case closed, flustered. The latch finally gave way, and she placed her hand atop the case for support. "You knew Rosey?"

"I did," I lied. "It's a shame what happened to her. She was such a lovely person."

I waited for Patty to tell me otherwise. And waited. And waited. She did no such thing. Her next move surprised me, and it must have surprised Joe because I heard him groan from behind me. The woman fell apart. One minute she was staring at me with doe eyes and the next those same eyes were blood red and leaking tears like a faucet opened. She hunched over the counter, her hair obscuring her face as she sobbed. I reached for her, stopping my hand an inch from her trembling form. *Don't touch strangers you think killed someone.* I couldn't help myself. My fingers squeezed Patty's shoulder, and she relaxed a little under my touch. As though emerging from a trance, she whipped her head up and wiped the tears off her cheeks with the back of her palms. She was once more the picture of calm. My hand was still hanging between us when she said, "I'm so sorry. I didn't mean to do that."

"It's okay," I whispered. "I take it you and Rosemary were close."

"At one point."

"I apologize for bringing her up. I didn't mean to upset you."

Patty wiped mascara smudges from under her eyes, leaving black marks resembling war paint all over her cheeks. I wanted to offer her a tissue, but not only did I not have one on me, I also didn't feel comfortable interrupting her when she was clearly going through something. After another minute of wiping, Patty stopped and looked at me. "It's not that," she said. "I was terrible to Rosey before she passed. I can't believe some things I said about her. And now it's too late to make things right and I..."

She trailed off, staring through the window of the shop blankly.

"I'm sure she knew you cared for her," I said, even though I had no clue if it was true. "People make mistakes."

"You don't understand. Rosey was a difficult person," the shop owner explained. "But she was my friend, and I shouldn't have let business get in the way."

This sounded awfully familiar. Wasn't business the same reason Daniel and Charlie fell out? What was it with people in this town and letting money impede relationships? Maybe that was how friend-ships worked and I never had a friend to test the theory. I sighed. "You shouldn't be so hard on your-self," I told Patty. "People fall out. It doesn't make you a bad person."

But killing Rosemary would. I sealed my lips shut.

"It was still no excuse," Patty said. "There would have been other investments to make, other hotels to buy."

My head spun so fast I nearly lost it. "What do you mean?"

"The Rose Hollow Hotel," Patty said. "I was in the process of purchasing it, but Rosey got in the way and made sure the deal never came to fruition. I think she may have wanted to buy it from under me; it was a very good deal, you see."

Did this woman say what I think she said? The hotel being up for sale was news to me. As far as I, and everyone else in town, knew the hotel belonged to Isabella Beaumont for years. I never heard her speak of wanting to sell it, especially not for a low price. Why would she want to? Despite the ghost stories, or because of them, it was a brilliant business. Unless she was over the hospitality trade for which I couldn't blame her. It wasn't for everyone. Still, to sell it and to sell it cheap was an odd way to go about things. I dusted invisible grime off the sleeve of my sweater and gazed at Patty's pouty face. "People make mistakes."

"Don't get me wrong," the shop owner said, "Rosey wasn't perfect. But she didn't deserve to die alone. I keep thinking if only I didn't go to that antique show in King City the same week, things would have turned out differently and Rosey would be here right now. But that's probably not true. You see, when she messed up the hotel deal, I felt betrayed. I had been there for her through everything and here she was, trying to take away what I really wanted. And I even kept my mouth shut about—" she clasped her hand to her mouth.

The damage was done, and my ears perked to hear

what Rosemary had to hide. Something bad enough for Patty not to have mentioned in her string of online slander of the woman. I leaned in close and whispered out of Joe's earshot, "It's okay, you can tell me. It might make you feel better to have it off your chest."

"I guess there's no point holding it in now," Patty said. "She's gone, and she's not coming back. Rosey had an affair, you see. With a married man." She made a face that told me she didn't approve. "And I was hush about it, even after I thought she pushed me out of the deal of a lifetime."

It appeared Patty wanted a medal for not running her mouth about her best friend's illicit affair, and it made my stomach roll. Perhaps the two were close at one point, but it was becoming clear that Rosemary falling out of the friendship may have been for the best. I tried not to let my repulsion show and kept my eyes on the gossiper. "You don't say," I whispered. "Anyone important?"

"He's not some celebrity if that's what you're after. Handsome, though. And quite charming. The wife, on the other hand," Patty said, "that's a woman you don't want to cross."

Out of the corner of my eye, I saw Joe stop what he was doing to inch closer to us, dying to overhear what Patty had to say. I couldn't even blame him because I was salivating for the next bit of information the woman's loose lips were about to let slide. Face as serious as I could muster, I widened my eyes in surprise. "Who was she?"

Seconds passed like years, and I tapped my nails against the counter, counting down until Patty spoke. For someone who had no trouble exposing all the sordid the details of hers and Rosemary's life, she sure took her time getting to the most important part. I dared to glance at Joe, who stood as motionless as a statue, Patty's words turning him to stone. I drew in a breath, and it got trapped in my lungs, turning liquid and drowning me while I stared at the shop keeper.

"Some big shot pharmacist in town," Patty said. "You don't want to mess with someone who has that much money. Especially when they know all sorts of ways to make a heart stop beating."

CHAPTER 22

"With a friend like that, who needs a dodgy accountant?" Stella asked.

I rubbed my head and fanned my toes out, dangling them closer to the fireplace. The heat spread through my fluffy socks, and I stretched on the sofa until I almost fell off. Forking another scoop of take-out Mac & Cheese from the restaurant near the antique shop, I groaned right in Stella's face. "That is not a saying."

"Well, it should be," she argued. "No one wants to wake up one morning to find their overseas account sucked dry."

There was no doubt in my mind that she was referring to her husband's accounts. The accountant in question was probably the guy I read about who fled the country after Stella's husband got booked for money laundering. I knew little of Stella's life before she showed up to be a downer in mine, but I did some research when we first realized she was my familiar and we were stuck together for the foreseeable future. What I found was not very reassuring. Despite Stella telling me time and time again that she had no hand in her husband's shady dealings, I still didn't feel comfortable talking about money with her. I wasn't sure why since even if Stella could leak my banking information to her criminal husband, there wasn't much there to steal.

Besides, Stella assured me her husband walked the straight and narrow after his short stint in the joint. Turned out when you're a retired banker with a questionable past, a night in the slammer was all you needed to get your head on straight.

That is, if Stella was telling the truth. Or if she even remembered anything about her life before she died.

Another thing I doubted.

Polishing off the last of my meal, I slid the plastic container across the coffee table and leaned my head back. "The more I dig into Rosemary's and Daniel's lives, the more I think their deaths were connected," I said. "And not at all accidental."

"You should be more worried about getting into book nerd's pants," Stella retorted.

Anger thrummed through me as I picked up a pillow and whipped it at her. Stella's body shimmered and vanished, reappearing next to the pillow on the floor with a scowl on her ghostly face. "All I'm saying is if you spent a little less time worrying about a bunch of dead folks and more about your dead social life, you might enjoy yourself for a change."

The next pillow sliced through her arm, and she winced. *Got you!*

"I'm not worried about them," I told her when she stopped flipping me off. "I'm trying to get to the bottom of what happened to two paranormals in our town. Not sure if you understand this, but if there's a killer out there wiping those with magic off the board, I'm in deep trouble."

"Oh, please! You do not have enough magic to even be noticed."

Ouch. My pride shriveled under the weight of her words, and I hated that she may have been right. Daniel was a seriously powerful warlock, and it seemed, from what I found out about Rosemary, she was also quite formidable in the art of magic. One thing they both had in common was they didn't hide their abilities from the paranormal community. Could they have been killed for it? Another thing they shared was the way they died—from drugs I was certain they did not willingly take.

If only I had a way to prove any of this.

I twirled a strand of hair around my finger and let it fall. "Do you think Ember could have done it?"

Stella looked away for a moment to think, then shrugged.

"They say poison is a woman's game," she said, as though she had some finger on the pulse of the criminal mind. "And a woman who has easy access to drugs and the knowledge on how to use them; well, color me impressed!"

"You don't really believe that? Ember? The pharmacist Ember?"

Stella shrugged again.

"What reason would she have for killing them?"

"For starters," Stella responds, "her husband was cheating on her with the witch. I'd have killed for a lot less when I was alive." I let that part go and waited for her to continue. "The public embarrassment alone is enough to push you over the edge And as you said, my guess is the warlock found out and had to be dealt with."

It all fit together, didn't it? Ember's access to the drugs, her paranormal bloodline, Tristan Mint's cheating. If I was a betting woman, I'd have said it fit too well, but I wasn't willing to wager on this. Not when there was a murderer on the loose and not with how close I placed myself to them in this situation. Close enough to be next on the list. My tired eyes snapped open, and I glued them to the fireplace, watching the flames dance in chaotic intervals. Finger in my mouth, I chewed off the last of my nail and grimaced. "Would you truly have killed someone for moving in on your husband?" I asked Stella.

"Honey, I'd have killed someone for winking at him," she said. "But that was never an issue. Stanley was as devoted as they came. It was one reason I married him."

I smiled. *The loads of cash were a close second.*

"It wasn't the money, you know," she continued, reading my thoughts. "Everyone thought so because of the age difference, but that wasn't it."

My smile deepened and my chest was suddenly warmer. "What was?"

"He saw me," was all Stella said.

The ghost's eyes drooped and the vacancy in them frightened me. Stella had the same look on her face when she wanted me to back off, and this time, it was worse. Perhaps it was because she was gone for so long, or the way her shoulders slumped when she talked about her husband; whatever it was, Stella Rutherford changed. The rich man's trophy wife looked as though she might have actually missed her husband now that she was dead. I wanted to ask her more questions, get to know her better, but those gates were shut for the evening. If Stella ever let me in, I'd know it. So, I focused on the two dead paranormals instead, because talking about them seemed somehow less tragic than discussing Stella's life.

"Do you think I should tell Romero what I have so far?" I asked.

At this, my familiar laughed so hard I winced. "Tell him what, darling? Your cute little theories about a woman scorned and a serial killer pharmacist?"

"I mean, when you put it that way, it sounds insane."

"Because it is," she said. "Which is what you'll be labeled as if you bring anything to the police without hard proof. I must tell you, being your familiar is not my best look, and I'd like it even less if I had to do it in a sanatorium."

Facepalming, I looked for another pillow to throw at her but came up short. "Geez! They will not send me to get examined for not having proof. You're unhinged."

"But will they listen to you?"

Probably not. "What—and I can't believe I'm asking this—would you do?"

Despite the hard time I gave my familiar and her obvious poor opinion of all things Piper, she had a good head on her shoulders for this type of thing. Probably from all that time she spent married to a criminal. Whatever it was, Stella was surprisingly great at bouncing ideas off and between her and Joe, I seemed to have found myself a good team of fake detectives. The thought of Joe made my toes curl in the fuzzy socks, and I clenched my teeth before a moan escaped. Seeing my face, Stella pursed her lips, and I counted to three, waiting for her to make some remark about my crush. Somehow, the ghost was extra good at reading my mind lately.

I was heavily relieved when she didn't and instead said, "You have to talk to the pharmacist."

"Really?" I asked. "It didn't go great when I talked to her husband."

"Ex-husband. It's only a matter of time."

I crossed my legs, sitting up higher on the sofa. "The impression Tristan gave me was the two were still together."

"All the more reason to speak to the wife," Stella said. "You need to find out if she knew about the affair. And if she did, why are they still together? Look at it this way: why bother killing a man's mistress, staying married to the weasel, and yet living in separate homes? It's Fish and Chips, honey."

"Huh?"

Stella rolled her eyes. "Smells fishy. Doesn't add

up. Keep up, please, Piper. I can't explain everything twice; I'm on my only afterlife here." Ten manicured nails flashed in my face as Stella waved her arms to make her point. She walked to the fireplace and gazed into the flames, grinning. The light reflecting off her ghostly face would have appeared sinister on most people, but on Stella, it added a warm glow to the gray. I liked it. It made her look more alive. Stella's grin dropped. "Do you want me to scope her place out?"

"No!" I yelled out before she even closed her inflated lips. "You will not do any more investigating. I thought something happened to you last time and I can't be up all night worrying about my familiar while also trying to solve two murders behind the sheriff's back. It's too much!"

Eyes still on the fire, I swore I saw the glimpse of genuine joy on Stella's face. It was gone as soon as it came and she whirled around, her tennis skirt floating like a cloud over her thighs. She pointed to the small dog bed beside the sofa where Margaret the Third shivered under two blankets, her half-eaten tuna tartare in a bowl at her tiny feet. "While you're in a go-getter mood," she said, "mind taking care of that? I don't do dogs."

I already explained to Stella that the dog's presence in the farmhouse was temporary and I was only caring for her while Sebastian got his condo to clear bringing a pet home. It surprised me he wanted to keep her. When I called to tell him I found Daniel's dog, right after I told the sheriff and he made it clear it was my problem, I expected to have the phone slammed in my ear. Yet Sebastian insisted on keeping the dog; it made me wonder if this was his way of making amends with his dead cousin. Whatever it was, I was glad Margaret the Third had somewhere to go that wasn't a shelter. Much gladder than Stella, who now shot knives with her eyes at the poor creature.

Ignoring her, I nestled into the warmth of the blanket and sank into the couch. I spent the rest of the evening planning my chat with Ember the following day and thinking about how I ended up with a spoiled Chihuahua, a stubborn ghost familiar and a troublesome raccoon.

Compared to those three, the murders I was trying to solve were a walk in the park.

CHAPTER 23

My fingers froze around the hot chocolate cup while I waited for Joe to wrap up. After my late-night planning session with Stella, I sent him a text asking if he wanted to accompany me to speak with Ember and he agreed immediately. It seemed Joe was as eager to discover the truth about Rosemary as I was. Though maybe not as interested as Stella, whom I had to beat off with a bat before she agreed not to follow me to the pharmacy.

What was it about this case that had my ghost up in knots?

I switched hands, blew hot air on my blue fingers, and peered into the bookstore. Joe was ringing a customer up when he saw me, his face contorting into an apologetic expression as he rushed, shoving a couple books into a paper bag. The bag tore, and he had to start over, leaving me to freeze outside a while longer. I probably should have waited indoors.

Glancing at the cafe, I noticed Sunny and Ray walk up to read the handwritten note I put up letting people know I'd return shortly. When they turned back around, I hid half my body behind Joe's sandwich board and pretended to look at the window. My breath fogged up the glass, but I kept my concentration, fake reading the titles of the books on display. The bookshop's bell dinged and the woman I saw at the register walked out, hurrying off down the street with her purchases. Joe appeared a minute later.

"Sorry to keep you waiting," he said. "It's busy today."

I handed him the cup of lukewarm chocolate and smiled. "It should slow down in a couple of weeks when the tourists leave. But then it's holiday season."

Joe eyed the cup. "What's this?"

"Hot chocolate. Or cold chocolate by now. So just chocolate."

Grimacing, I looked away from him and crossed the street toward the pharmacy. I wasn't sure what it was about Joe, but I could not even pretend to be socially adept with him around. Not that I was all that cool to begin with, though I could at least fake it with most people. Except Joe. This guy had my tongue in knots and my brain in a vise.

I cursed whoever made me this way and asked, "You sure you're up for this?"

"Definitely. Been thinking about it all night."

"You've been thinking about Ember all night?" *Don't act jealous. Don't act jealous.* It was too late and if I wanted to hide my envy, I was certain my face sold me out. Joe smirked and I died inside. "Um, anyway, about today. I'm not sure what the best approach is with Ember. She's hard to read."

A cross expression flashed over Joe's face, and he looked toward the pharmacy we were quick approaching. His eyes narrowed to slits, and his chest bobbed up and down with deep breaths. Was there something between Ember and him? I brushed the thought off before my mind could latch on and tear it to pieces; and I spent the rest of what was supposed to be a scouting mission picturing Ember and Joe together. *Jember.* Why did I invent a couple's name for them? Wonderful.

"It'll be fine," Joe said. I choked on my spit, Jember still lingering in my thoughts. "We'll be direct. Ask her about the affair and get the hell out of there."

Easier said than done. For all we knew, we'd be getting out of there in the back of a cruiser, and judging by how her ex-husband handled our questions, I worried Ember would go down much the same way. I cast a glance at Joe, my eyes too occupied to notice the encroaching sidewalk. My sneaker caught the edge, and I stumbled, limbs flailing in all the wrong directions to stop me from falling. I sucked in a breath and readied to faceplant on the asphalt right as Joe caught my elbow. Grip strong, he broke my fall while balancing the hot chocolate in his other hand.

I chuckled; embarrassment plastered all over my face. I was not a clumsy person, but with Joe, I did not differ from the poorly-cast girls in teenage dramas that needed a makeover to win the guy. It was pathetic. "Thanks," I said. "Quick reflexes."

Joe's eyes darted to the sidewalk. "I'd tripped over this stupid thing before."

He said it in a way that implied it was the sidewalk's fault I was a complete imbecile, and it made my flushed neck pale. I knew Joe was lying to make me feel better, and it worked. "They should really flatten out this entire block," I joked. "It's a safety hazard."

As Joe laughed, we neared the pharmacy and my heart pounded in my ears. Pulse thundering, I felt sweat pool under my sweater. What if Ember calls my bluff? What if she clams up? What if the pharmacy is busy and we look like complete creeps?

So many things could go wrong it made my head spin.

Before I could plummet down the dark hole of self-doubt, Joe opened the pharmacy door and gestured for me to get in. I stepped over the threshold. No backing out now.

Cold air slapped my face when I walked inside, and I followed the gust of wind to an overhead fan running in the middle of this icy season. *What kind of freak has a fan on right now?* I spotted Ember's messy bob behind the counter, saw she wore only a camisole under her lab coat, and groaned. Werewolves ran hotter than the rest of us, but this was ridiculous. No way would she be able to make out anything I said with my teeth chattering. It felt as though we had stepped out of Orchard Hollow and into Santa's lair in here, and not only from the frigid temperature. A bazillion Christmas ornaments hung off massive garlands on either side of the narrow pharmacy. Above the door, a sad looking mistletoe clung for dear life; I cringed at Ember's choice of decor. Why would anyone kiss in a pharmacy? *Come on in, folks! Get your dose of romance while waiting to pick up the cough medicine!* What a bizarre choice for a pharmacy.

I dashed down the aisle and avoided the Santa figurines Ember stashed on the shelves next to bottles of ointment and Band-Aid cartons.

Luckily, the pharmacy was empty save for Ember and when we walked up to the counter, she appeared to be excited to have someone to talk to. Putting down a box of tiny bottles that rattled with pills, she smiled at us, beckoning us closer. "Hi, you two."

I waved like a five-year-old. "Hey, Ember. This is—"

"Joseph Brooks," the pharmacist finished my sentence. "Elijah's nephew, right?"

Stiffening beside me, Joe nodded. I noticed his discomfort instantly. *Seriously, what was up with these two?* He straightened his shoulders and met Ember with a sharp look. "Joe is fine."

"Joe it is. What brings you two by?"

I almost lied and made up an ailment I needed help with. After quick consideration, I took Joe's original advice and got straight to the point. "We were hoping to ask you something," I said. "But it might seem strange."

"Hit me with it," Ember answered, still grinning. "You got me on a slow day."

The day was about to become a heck of a lot faster if our questions had anything to do with it. Throat full of rusty nails, I swallowed hard and tried to force myself to relax. Ember had been very pleasant, and not once did she act like she was better than me, even though she kind of was. A female werewolf carried a lot of weight in the paranormal community but that wasn't what made Ember stand out. She wasn't only a female werewolf; she was a woman with one of the most successful businesses in town. There was a chance the Mints had more money than Stella if that was possible.

Four concerned eyes laser focused on me, and I stumbled. *Less thinkie-thinkie, more talkie-talkie.* I was honestly done with myself today.

I tucked my unruly hair behind my ears, trying to match Ember's careless perfection. "Did you know Rosemary Hayes?"

"More importantly, did Tristan?" Joe added. The way he said Ember's ex-husband's name suggested history there, but I wasn't about to grill him when we were here to light a fire under someone else's butt. That was better saved for another time, and I hoped I didn't forget to ask Joe about his relationship with the Mints. Or in Ember's case, the Crowley-Mints.

Panicking, Ember fumbled with the box on the counter and for a second, I thought we had her. This was it. She was going to break like a toothpick and splinter in front of our eyes. I half considered pulling my phone out to record her confession for Romero, but a short moment later, was glad I didn't. Mostly because Ember laughed like a hyena right in our faces. "You have got to be kidding me!" she shrieked between strangled heaves. "Don't tell me he roped you into this. What an idiot!"

I peered at Joe's scrunched face in confusion. "Excuse me?"

"Tristan," Ember said. "Do you work for his lawyer?"

"I-I own a coffee shop," I stuttered. "Barely."

"No, I know that. I meant did his lawyer put you up to this?"

Understanding and me were in different time zones because I had no idea what this woman was trying to say. Why would Tristan's lawyer send us to ask questions about Rosemary? I scratched my chin and said, "I can truthfully say I am quite clueless at the moment."

If Stella was here, she'd add some smart commentary about how those moments were piling up. It was a good thing she wasn't, so Ember could explain what she meant without me looking like a buffoon.

"I assume since you're asking about Tristan's mistress, you're here trying to get me to say things I shouldn't," she said. "For the divorce settlement."

Insert double take here because I was pretty sure Tristan said the two were back on good terms. Didn't he mention a dinner recently? Flags the color of a horror clown's balloon went up in my head and I crammed them down, focusing on Ember. "Are you saying the divorce is still on? You're not getting back together with Tristan?"

She laughed again, this time for longer. When she trailed off, she wiped tears from her kohl-lined eyes. "Goodness, no! Why on earth would I stay with a man who cheated on me? A witch nonetheless." Her eyes darted to mine. "I'm sorry. She wasn't one of yours, was she?"

"No coven," I explained. "By choice."

I wasn't sure why I added the last part, but it felt important to emphasize. Ember must have agreed because she said, "I respect that. A woman of her own mind. Well done, Piper Addison!" I almost bowed. "Anyway, yes. To answer your question, the divorce is very much still on and it couldn't happen soon enough."

Those red flags blurred my vision, and I had to hold onto the counter for balance. The room spun and I crammed my finger into a bowl of Christmas candies but didn't care. Why did Tristan lie? I had to find out if what he said about having Ember over the night Daniel died was true, but before I could, Joe stepped closer and the smell of old books penetrated my nostrils. Did he always smell this good?

The man who wore the scent of stories cleared his throat and I snapped back to reality. "You're implying you're pleased your husband was cheating?" he asked.

"I'm ecstatic!" Ember said, shocking both of us. "Finding out about their sordid affair was the best thing to happen to me. I'm finally able to divorce the sleazebag and not lose all my hard-earned money in the process. The only reason I put up with his wandering eye for all these years was because he held all our assets over me. Assets I paid for with my salary, I'll have you know. After I found out about the witch, it was over. I called my lawyer the next day and served that scum of a husband the papers." She smiled. "Best day of my life. Except the bastard is dragging things out, no surprise there. According to the paperwork, he still owns half of everything."

"Oh," I muttered.

"Wait, if you're not here because of the divorce, why did you ask about Rosemary?"

Whatever answer I may have had, I forgot it. We were way off about Ember, and I couldn't think of a lie good enough to get us out without looking foolish. I wished Stella was here. She was great in a bind, and even better with spinning a tall tale. I looked at Joe, who seemed to be a lot less flustered than me. "There are some questions that arose about Rosemary Hayes' death. You had the motive to want her gone so we wanted to come to you before going to the police."

Well, that was that. I guess Joe decided to lay all our cards on the table no matter how improbable they seemed. Perhaps it was for the best. Less lying meant fewer ways I could embarrass myself later. I tried to smile but couldn't quite pull it off. "Not that we're going to the police," I said. "We're trying to find out what happened to her."

"She had a heart-attack," Ember said bluntly. "You're not suggesting I killed her, are you?"

Joe and I exchanged twin looks of worry and Ember let out another howling laugh. "I'm so sorry! It's funny someone would think a snake like Tristan might be worth going to extremes for. Trust me when I tell you, no one in their right mind is killing for Tristan Mint. And if that witch was alive today, I doubt she'd be with that flea of a man. Tristan always shows his true colors."

The front door opened, and I spun on my heel to see an older couple walk in. They held hands and the man guided the woman toward us, both admiring the holiday decor as they passed. I watched the woman point to one Santa and they laughed, sharing an inside joke none of us were privy too. My heart swelled seeing them. It was the type of bond only years spent together could forge and I hoped to one day have a life as beautiful.

You'd have to date first.

My happiness fluttered away, leaving me cold and empty. I tugged on Joe's sleeve, gesturing for us to leave so we didn't take up any more of Ember's time. Before we walked away, I had one more burning question I couldn't not ask. I moved closer to Ember and spread my fingers wide over the counter. "Did you and Tristan have dinner last Wednesday? At his apartment down on third?"

Seeing the couple must have put Ember in pharmacist mode because she somehow managed not to laugh this time, though I could see her fighting it tooth and nail. She leaned in, her eyes low and her voice hushed. "Not even if he paid me a million dollars would you catch me eating with that man again."

CHAPTER 24

My phone rang within minutes of us leaving the pharmacy. I fumbled with the keys, waved goodbye to Joe, and picked it up. For a brief interlude, the other line was dead. Then I heard elevator music slowly build up tempo. I knew that song. Hissing under my breath, I looked at the screen, the number I dreaded glaring back at me. There was a loud click, followed by another, and then a deep voice on the other end. "Hello, Miss Addison."

"Sheriff Romero, good to hear from you again."

It was the opposite of good to hear from the sheriff. I scratched the back of my neck, standing four feet from the pharmacy, and waited to hear why I was summoned by the police. My eyes darted up and down the as though I expected to find snipers hiding out in plain sight. Now more than ever, I missed gran so badly it hurt. I wanted advice on what to do from someone that wasn't prone to spurn action. Geez, even talking to mom would have been great right now. I missed my family, dysfunctional as it may have been.

Maybe I should join a coven after all.

On cue, sparks covered the tips of my fingers and died away. I laughed. What coven would want a witch whose biggest magic trick was a touch of electricity? I was as useful as a balloon rubbed on a cat's back.

"I'm glad I caught you," Romero said. I scowled hearing his unintentional pun. He sounded cheerful for someone who was about to tear me a new one. "I have some great news."

"Oh?"

My brows slanted, and I shifted my weight from one foot to the other, bouncing to stay warm. On the phone, Romero mumbled, and I heard the rustling of papers. "You can file this one," he said to someone that wasn't me. "Sorry about that. Where was I? Ah, yes. The good news. I'm declaring Mr. Tse's case an accident. Again."

"What?" I yelped. "But you said it was suspicious."

"It was, but after following up, it turned out my

original findings were correct. The death was accidental, and the case is officially closed. Which means you are free to leave town if you wish to do so."

He spoke like I had bags packed and ready to go. I had no intention of leaving town, hadn't in my entire life living here, and now less so than ever. Romero said he followed up, but how could that be true when there were so many unanswered questions? I thought back to our conversation with Ember and the lies Tristan spewed. I should tell the sheriff what I discovered.

Gasping for air, I knocked my knees together and clutched the phone tighter. "I think you're wrong," I said boldly. "And you need to reopen Rosemary's case. The two are connected, I know it!"

"I believe I made myself clear, Miss Addison. Have you been meddling in police business?"

I gulped. "No. Not exactly. I found out some things you need to know. About Rosemary. Sheriff, there is no way she could have died from—"

"That is enough," Romero grumbled. "I will not hear any more of this nonsense. This is a peaceful community, and I cannot have you throw the balance off by going around bothering innocent people to prove your wild accusations. I am going to say this for the last time," he warned. "Stay out of this. Get back to your life and stop causing trouble."

Pins pricked my skin, and I shook as the rage in me

clawed its way to the surface. I wasn't bothering anyone, and I wasn't throwing anything off balance. A woman died, was possibly murdered, and the sheriff wanted to close a blind eye and move on. How could he not see that tying a nice little bow on these murders was only going to cause more harm? How long until Rosemary and Daniel's killer struck again? Who was next? *Will Romero smarten up when he sees me on the coroner's slab?* Doubtful. I'd be another accidental death; a file stamped closed and put away where he needn't bother with it further. I wanted to scream. I wanted to march down to the police station and tell Romero off, threaten him to do his job before I talked to the media.

But that would not be the right play.

I took a deep, slow breath and tapped into my inner Stella. "Why, of course, sheriff," I said sweetly. "You will not hear a peep out of me about this again."

When Romero hung up without saying goodbye, I spun around and marched back to the pharmacy. *You won't hear from me again because I am going to do your job for you.*

Getting Ember to give me Tristan's phone number was easy-peasy. All I had to do was tell her the truth: I suspected her ex-husband took part in something terrible and I was going to prove it. Tristan ending up behind bars was all the convincing it took, and I was texting him to meet me in the cafe before I even unlocked the door. The lights over the front counter flickered as I flipped them on and I rushed to make a triple shot latte, desperate for a boost of caffeine.

While I waited for Tristan to arrive, I checked my online accounts and was happy to find that the last few days of steady business have taken me out of the red. I could afford to keep the cafe closed for another few hours to take care of this.

Guilt gnawed at me as I thought about Joe back at the bookstore. He would have wanted to be here. I couldn't risk it. The last time the two of us tried to trick Tristan into speaking did not go as planned, and I needed this to be a smooth conversation. I couldn't risk spooking Tristan off and I definitely couldn't risk him making a fuss over my badgering him. But he lied, and I wanted him to know I was onto him.

I watched the clock over the door impatiently, counting down the minutes to his arrival. Ticktock, ticktock. The sound of a tiny espresso bean making its rounds. The sound of my sanity departing.

Thirty minutes later, the door swung open at the

exact time Tristan set for us to meet. For a liar, he sure was punctual. I supposed even liars had redeeming qualities.

When Tristan spotted me sitting at one of the round tables, he scowled. He looked around the cafe, noting the lack of customers, and closed the distance between us. "What is this about?" he asked, hovering near the empty chair across from me.

"Please, sit," I said. "Can I get you a drink?"

"No, thanks. I won't be staying long," he bit out. *We'll see about that.* Despite not staying long, Tristan sat down and looked everywhere but at me.

A door squeaked behind me, its shriek piercing the air, and I clamped my jaw tightly, working hard not to curse out Harry Houdini as he snuck his way into the office again. I had enough to worry about without guessing what mischief the stubborn fuzzball was getting into. The clock was running. I had about a half hour before the evening rush and even less time before Stella showed up to scream at the raccoon. *Better move fast.*

Gulping down the latte, I faced Tristan head on. "I'll get straight to the point, then. I know you lied about having dinner with Ember the night Daniel died."

Tristan's smile dropped, and he ran his fingers through his overly gelled hair. *Got you!*

"I don't know what you think you know," he said, his words cutting out, "but I don't like where you're going with this."

"You're going to like what I say next even less."

Tendrils of rock-hard hair fell from their slimy hold and into Tristan's eyes. He brushed them aside, fidgeting in his seat. Beady eyes locked on me, and I held my chin high, letting him know I was not afraid. And I was not backing down. Unrolling my shoulders, I took another painfully slow drink and said, "I have the dog."

"What dog?"

I scoffed. "Margaret the Third. Daniel's dog. The one you drove out in the middle of nowhere and left for dead."

"You have some nerve!" Tristan exclaimed. I noticed he was not getting up to leave. "What is it you think you're doing here? This is none of your business. I should call the police right now and tell them you're stalking me!"

Smirking, I put the cup down with a bang. "You came to me, remember?"

"What a fool." Stella's voice cut through the cafe. I cast her a side glance, motioning for the ghost to stay quiet. She settled into a seat near to us, her chin in her hands and her mouth zipped shut.

"Why don't you tell me why you lied and what

you did that night, and *I* won't go to the police," I suggested. "There's no point hiding the truth. Ember will vouch that she wasn't with you on Wednesday night."

"I bet she will. She'll do anything not to pay what she owes me."

If I didn't dislike Tristan before, I hated him now. The man was an insufferable egomaniac. I could see why Ember would want to cut ties with this vile human being and why she'd be so relieved to be free of their marriage. What a woman like her saw in a guy like Tristan, I'd never know. What did Rosemary?

I looked at Stella, whose eyebrows were so high they were making their way to the back of her head. "Talk. Or I make a call," I threatened. "And while you're at it, tell me about Rosemary Hayes."

The scumbag's jaw tensed, and I watched him fight the urge to yell at me. I had him. I knew I had him. There was nothing Tristan could say that would make me understand why he lied about having dinner with Ember.

"Fine. It wasn't Ember I was with that evening. It was Isabella. We're trying to keep our relationship quiet because of the divorce, but since you made it your business to butt into mine, there you have it."

Except that.

"Did I hear that correctly?" Stella asked. *"Three* women found this frog appealing?"

I choked on a laugh and kept my eyes on Tristan, so I didn't look like a lunatic laughing with her invisible friend. "Isabella Beaumont? That's your alibi?"

"I don't need an alibi!" Tristan shrieked. Actually freaking shrieked. How suave. "I did nothing wrong. And if you tell Ember about my relationship with Isabella, I will sue you for slander."

As he rose to stand, I heard the office door open and tiny feet scrape across the tile floor. Stella pointed a finger, her large lips parting in a perfect O. From behind the counter, the footsteps got louder and picked up speed. Tristan, still towering over me and looking as angry as ever, stopped his glaring and looked toward the sound. His eyes flared, and he backed away, his long legs hitting the chair. "Ouch!" he yelped. "What the hell!"

I looked under the table and gasped. Harry Houdini had latched his sharp canines into Tristan's shoe and was shaking it like a bag of candy. I made a move to help but stopped myself. Let this charmer try to charm his way out of this one. I doubted Tristan could convince Harry Houdini to leave him alone, like he convinced those poor women to fall for his deceptions.

Tristan continued to shake his leg, but the

raccoon's grip would not falter. I knew there was no getting Harry to back down once he, quite literally, sunk his teeth into something. Learned that the hard way battling the monster for a box of freshly delivered muffins. Tristan, on the other hand, thought he stood a chance, so he kept shimmying around the cafe, bumping into chair after chair and yelling profanities the entire time.

Near to us, Stella laughed her butt off.

After a few minutes of the circus show, I felt bad for the cheater and had to step in. I rolled my eyes, reaching into my back pocket for a packet of mints. I shook the plastic box, the tiny mints rattling inside.

Harry's entire body froze. His dark eyes darted to the box, and he let go of Tristan's shoe instantly. Grabby paws reached for me; I shook the box again, then tossed it behind the front counter. That should keep the bugger occupied for a while. Sure enough, snarls and licks filled the air, and I laughed, sinking into the chair.

"I would have let him lose a leg," Stella said.

"I know," I answered.

Tristan's fuming face got redder, and he looked from me to where Stella sat. "Who are you talking to, you freak?" He inspected his shoe, gaped at me, and stormed out of the cafe, the door slamming behind him.

"You're welcome!" I called after him, but he was already long gone. I turned to Stella, grinning. "That was quite a show. Think he's telling the truth about Isabella?"

My familiar rubbed her chin. "I don't think that man would know the truth if it bit him in the shoe. Only one way to find out, though."

Behind the counter, the raccoon worked his way through the plastic box and to the minty prize awaiting him. Voices filled the street outside, and I grabbed my unfinished latte, emptying the cup into the sink and throwing my apron on as I readied for customers to come in. My mind raced with possibilities. As I used my leg to scoot Harry and his box of mints into the office and lock the door, I kept thinking about tomorrow. Stella's words ran circles in my head. There really was only one way to find out the truth about Isabella and Tristan. I had to speak to the hotel owner directly.

CHAPTER
25

Another car stood in the driveway when I pulled up to the farmhouse. I didn't recognize the license plate, and it was too dark to see inside. My shoulders tensed as I turned off the ignition and slammed the door of the beetle shut, walking up the gravel to the house. The porch light was on, signalling that someone was there.

Waiting for me.

I jammed my keys between my fingers like mom taught me to do when I turned sixteen. At the time, I laughed when she told me to constantly be aware of my surroundings when walking late at night. It wasn't until I was much older that I realized how important the lesson was. Even in a small town like Orchard Hollow, you could never be too careful.

I thought of the recent string of murders and goosebumps covered my arms and legs.

Especially here.

Keeping my stride light, I snuck by the black truck and rounded the side of the house. The porch planks creaked under the weight of someone moving and I froze. Keys slipping in my grimy grip, I repositioned my hold on them and flung my arm out. "Whoever you are, I have a weapon and I'm not afraid to use it!" I yelled into the night.

"Piper?"

I expelled a breath, stepping out from the shadows. "Joe? What are you doing here?"

The bookstore owner sat up straighter and his gaze flicked to the keys in my hands. One side of his full lips curled, and he looked at me, brows slanted. "A weapon, huh?"

"They could be magic keys," I said, swinging the glittery bow keychain around for emphasis.

Joe raised his arms. "I come in peace. Please don't cover me with sparkles."

Walking up the steps, I dropped a bag of unsold baked goods on the stoop and joined him on the bench. It was a small two-seater and Joe had to squeeze to one side so we could both fit. He tried to make himself comfortable, but I could tell he couldn't even move. I regretted sitting down immediately. Two seconds passed when neither of us spoke and we sat in silence, two sardines staring outward. Joe shifted his weight, his side pressing against mine. "Quite the view you got here."

"It really is," I agreed. "My favorite part of this place. It was gran's favorite too. Mom loved it too."

I sighed.

"What's wrong?"

"Nothing. I miss her, is all," I admitted. "I shouldn't because of what she did, but I still do. Such a sucker, I know."

Knees knocking, Joe rubbed his thighs and kept his focus on the dark field before us. "It's okay to miss her. And it's okay to want her back. She's your mom," he said. "My parents are not perfect, but I still love them. I think sometimes we forget parents are people too. They make mistakes and we have to accept that."

"Did your parents join a coven and started practicing dark magic?"

He shook his head. "Not exactly."

"Well, then they're still a million times better people than my mom." I sniffled, the wind wetting my eyes. "But I get it. Thank you."

When he said nothing, I thought we would spend the rest of the evening sitting side by side, uncomfortably close, in silence. It was strange how easy it was to be quiet around Joe. I knew I could tell him anything and he wouldn't judge, and yet it was as comforting to simply exist in the same space. No words needed. Above us, the moon sat low and the light from it reflected off the dew in the grass, making the field resemble a body of water. If I narrowed my eyes enough, I could almost pretend to be on an island somewhere overlooking an ocean. A beach vacation. With Joe. My body burned, and I crossed my legs, praying Joe didn't develop mind-reading skills like Stella seemed to have recently.

"Can I ask you something?" I asked. I waited until he nodded and said, "Do you have a history with Ember and Tristan?"

"Not Tristan, no," he answered. "First time I met him was in his apartment with you. I didn't even know he was Ember's ex until you mentioned it."

I rubbed my temples hard enough to leave a red mark. "What about Ember? How do you know her?"

"I know *of* her," Joe corrected. "Female werewolf, you know."

Feet scraping the wood floor, I wrapped my arms around my waist and looked at the moon. I wondered if it was hard for Ember to have all this attention on her because of who she was. Coming from someone who was invisible in the paranormal community, it was easy to take it for granted. I didn't think I could handle being in the spotlight as much as Ember. It would be a living nightmare.

Joe rustled beside me. "Any updates on our investigation?"

"As a matter of fact, there is," I said. I really, really enjoyed hearing Joe mention an *us*. Almost as much as I enjoyed him wanting to talk about the murders. I had issues. "Let me get some drinks on and I'll tell you all about it."

Two cups of coffee and one untouched tea later, and I filled Joe in on everything that happened with Tristan. When I got to the part where Harry made his appearance, Joe was in stitches. I had to admit, now that I was home, the entire spectacle was even funnier. Picturing Harry latched onto Tristan's leg made me break out laughing each time I thought of it. At one point, Joe and I were both hunched over, slapping our thighs in unison as I re-enacted Tristan's pompous face.

"And then he said he wasn't with Ember that

night, but with, and get this," I said, "with Isabella. Can you believe that? That clown is implying he's having a relationship with Isabella Beaumont! I'm not saying that she's a god but come on! I can't see her falling for his act."

I turned around to face Joe and realized he was no longer laughing. His eyes were the color of the night around us and his teeth clamped shut so tightly, I could see veins on the side of his jaw. Panic flowed through me. "Joe?"

He shook himself like he was trying to shake off a bad dream. Like Tristan shook off Harry.

"You can't talk to her, Piper," Joe said. "You need to stay away from that woman."

"I wasn't—"

"Don't lie. I know you well enough by now to know you won't be able to leave this alone. Please promise me you won't go to Isabella. At least not without me."

The night swallowed me whole, and I pressed my back into the bench, my body an icicle unable to thaw. Why did Joe not want me alone with Isabella? What was he keeping from me? It appeared that no one in this wretched town was what they seemed, not even the guy who recently arrived here. What was it about Orchard Hollow and secrets?

Alarm bells rang in my ears, and I clamped a palm over my mouth. How did Joe know Ember was a were-wolf when he found out about the paranormal days ago?

I bit the inside of my cheek. Hard. "How do you know Ember again?" I asked. "You didn't elaborate."

Beside me, the bench felt suddenly larger, and Joe was a million miles away. He leaned forward, his head hanging low, and his arms curled over his thighs. I couldn't see his eyes from this angle, but I knew they were the same dark shade they were before. The easy-going nature of our time together replaced by something else, something menacing. I shimmied to the side, trying to put as much distance between us as I could. "I wasn't entirely honest with you," Joe said.

Shocker.

"It's true I didn't know about the paranormal community for most of my life," he exclaimed. "But it's a lie that I found out about it when I came here. I already had a clear idea of magic when I bought the bookstore, and it was one reason I moved here. Ember was a good friend of my uncle's and I asked her to show me around."

"You came to Orchard Hollow to be closer to magic you didn't know about?"

Joe sighed. "I came here to be closer to my kind."

The bells were so loud now I couldn't hear myself breathe. My head spun and my body twitched beyond my control. I held onto the handle of the bench, using it as a lighthouse to keep me grounded. To guide me back home. If Joe wanted to be close to his kind, that meant he was a paranormal. I thought back to the type of magic Elijah Brooks' family was rumored to have had. Joe could only be one thing. "You're a vampire," I whispered.

Joe nodded, and my lungs emptied. My body ached to be away from here. Away from the porch and away from Joe. I didn't know any vampires and gran's message had always been clear: stay away from them. Nothing good came out of friendships with bloodsuckers. Instinctively, I rolled up my collar, hiding the veins in my neck. I saw Joe wince when he noticed, but I didn't care. I wanted him gone before I ended up being his late-night snack.

Lucky for me, he read the room. Or porch.

"I'll get going," Joe said. "I'm sorry I didn't tell you sooner. It's not something I like to advertise."

He stood up and started for the steps, turning to look at me over his shoulder. I hated that I still found him attractive, despite him probably eating witches like me for breakfast. "I know it's a lot to ask, but if you decide you want me around, I'd really enjoy continuing our friendship."

One wide step after the other, Joe was at the bottom of the steps and walking to his truck when I yelled out, "Hey! Why did you warn me about Isabella?"

"Because she's a vampire too," Joe said and disappeared into the night.

CHAPTER 26

Stella stayed with me all night. She said little aside from the occasional nod while I fumed over the information Joe dropped in my lap. Occasionally I could see her shuffling, wanting to offer an opinion and holding back; a gesture I assumed came hard to her. I needed someone to vent to, and Stella made herself completely available. I knew she had all the time in the world, being dead and all, but it was still nice to see her alter her behavior for my sake. I really wished I could hug her.

Around three in the morning, my eyelids drooped, and a yawn interrupted my whining. I let my head hit the pillow, closing my eyes while Stella sat at the edge of my bed. When I awoke, she was gone.

My anger was still there, though.

Breaking two eggs into a skillet, I set the heat to high and burnt them to a crisp while telling Joe off in my head. I crammed the meal from hell into my mouth, washed it down with yesterday's cranberry muffin, and downed an entire cup of flat white before rushing out the door. I had about an hour before the cafe opened, which gave me a brief interval in which I could tell Joe to go bite himself. Metaphorically, of course. No way was I going anywhere near that blood drinking liar.

But I did plan on figuring out what happened to Rosemary without him, and—in my mind—that was as good a payback as any.

Joe warned me to steer clear of Isabella, a warning I didn't take lightly now that I knew what she was, but there were other ways to get information. And one of those ways had a feisty attitude and was starting her shift at the hotel in fifteen minutes.

I put the beetle in reverse and tore out of the driveway, heading for the hotel. When I made it to Cliff Row, I was right on time. Cilia walked in minutes after I did. Her high heels clicked on the shiny floor, and she brushed lint off her leather leggings as she rounded the reception desk to tell the night concierge to beat it. The woman hurried off with a huff and the bags under her eyes told me she enjoyed working at the hotel as much as one enjoyed sitting on rusty nails. As she stormed through the front doors, Cilia tidied up the counter and said, "Why are you back here?"

So, she did notice me in the corner. The witch. I took two long strides to near the desk and crossed my arms. Last night's fury dripped off me and I ground my teeth into pulp, refusing to succumb to Cilia's arrogant display of power.

"I need information about the hotel," I said. "And you're going to give it to me."

"What I'm going to do is call the police," Cilia replied.

Her hand was already on the phone when I said, "Call them and I'm telling Nancy and the coven about Sebastian. Pretty sure your friends aren't as open minded as I am, so unless you want to be kicked out for dating a warlock, you better talk fast."

A scowl formed on her face, but her hand dropped from the phone and she forced a swallow. I took that as my cue to keep going. "What do you know about Isabella's private life?"

"You want to know who my boss is dating? How would I even know that?" Cilia exclaimed. Her face stayed stoic, but her posture spoke volumes. The witch fidgeted with the designer belt slung over her oversized sweater and her body swayed from side to side like she wanted to flee.

I pressed on. "Are Isabella and Tristan Mint a thing?"

Cilia's eyes widened and her hand dropped away from the belt, ripping a small rhinestone off. She tried to recover, but it was too late. We both knew she had what I sought. Leaning into the front desk, I curled my fingers over the side and shoved my face into hers. "Are they a thing?" I repeated.

"Yes! Geez!" she yelped. "Why do you even care? Do you have a crush on him?"

Bile rolled into my throat, and I was pretty sure I was green enough to be cast as a witch in Oz. "Gross, no. I need to know more about the two of them. It's important. Life or death important. Do you understand?"

She nodded.

"How long have they been seeing each other?"

Turning away from me, Cilia bent down and rummaged through her purse, pulling out her cellphone. She tapped on the screen, opening a calendar app and scrolled through it. As she read over the dates, my mouth gaped. Did this woman take notes on when her boss started seeing Tristan? And I thought I was obsessed. Cilia's mouth twisted, and she said, "A year, give or take."

"Okay..." I struggled to think of a way to let her save some dignity and not come off looking like a stalker. I couldn't. It seemed Cilia was much more devious than even Nancy Steeles and I wondered if I made a mistake getting on her bad side. Who knew what she noted in her calendar about my life? I twitched thinking of all the things I had gotten myself into the last few weeks that could be used against me. Glancing from Cilia to her phone, I asked, "Do you know if they were together last Wednesday? In the evening and through the night?"

"Definitely not."

"How can you be so sure?"

This time, Cilia pulled out a business card from under the counter and slid it my way. I reached for it, looking at the name on the card. It was a commercial brokerage firm in King City. The card was premium quality, printed on thick stock with gilded edges. This wasn't some low-key operation like the one Charlie and Daniel started. This place was the real thing. I eyed Cilia suspiciously. "A brokerage firm?"

"She's selling the hotel," Cilia explained. "Or trying to. Has been for a few years now. I guess there isn't a large market for haunted hotels, so she's been getting other businesses involved to dump the place. Isabella was in the city most of last week and through the weekend."

My mind raced, trying to remember the last time I saw her. No wonder Isabella was so keen on putting out the fire the viral post caused about the hotel's most recent fake haunting. If she was having trouble getting rid of the place, bad publicity would not help move it. I laid the card down and covered it with my palm. "Why would she want to sell the hotel? It's always busy here when the tourists arrive."

"Not busy enough, I guess. It's been slowing down the last few seasons and, to be honest, I don't know if Isabella can afford to keep sinking money into it." Cilia said. Her head dropped as she shrugged. "Look, I don't know what to tell you. Isabella was over this place. She wanted it gone, and she wanted it gone fast. If you came here to rub it in that I'll be unemployed soon, spare me. I already know I'm in deep. Now, if you'll excuse me, I have to get started on the day while I still have a job to do."

As she logged into the hotel's computer, I ran through what I found out. One: Isabella was attempting to dump the hotel and fast, which explained why she was going to let Patty have it for a lowball offer. Two: the hotel was going under. It was highly possible Rosemary found this out and stopped her best friend from making a colossal mistake in buying it. Three: Tristan lied his face off about being with Isabella the night Daniel died.

The last part made my skin crawl.

Memories of Tristan's self-righteous face flashed

through my system, and I hugged my sides, my stomach swirling. The man was a piece of work. Was there any truth to anything he said? My leg muscles tensed, and a hunch gnawed at the rear of my mind. I turned my attention to Cilia, still busy with whatever she was doing. "I need one last favor and then I'll leave you alone," I said. She rolled her eyes. "Can you tell me if Rosemary Hayes came in alone the night she died?"

The color drained from Cilia's face, and she stopped breathing. The veins in her neck pulsed as she swallowed hard, fear overtaking her.

I smiled. "You won't get into trouble," I said. "I'll keep anything you say to myself."

The tension between us heightened. Cilia's lips puffed out as she blew out air and her chest rose up and down, rippling her sweater. She tugged on its loose collar, her eyes rounding. She was going to cave. I held my breath, keeping myself as calm as possible and—

"Good morning, ladies."

The hairs on my arms rose. Knots formed at the base of my throat and my lungs refused to expand. I turned around, watching Isabella Beaumont walk through the front door. The morning sun shined bright behind her, casting a deep shadow across the floor. If I looked close enough, I could see it twist and reshape into something more sinister than a curvy woman. Isabella's hips swayed side to side and her four-inch stilettos tapped a beat my heart couldn't match.

She passed the front desk, her eyes following me as she walked. "Good to see you," she said.

"Piper," I reminded her again. *I know what you are.*

The hotel owner brushed by me, her shoulder a mere inch from mine, and waltzed up to Cilia behind the desk. "Can you bring last month's projections to my office, Miss Craven?" she commanded. "And any messages from last night."

Cilia nodded obediently, typing away. A second later, the printer under the desk came to life, and I heard papers slide out of the tray. Cilia bent down to retrieve them, taking much too long to do so. It seriously felt like she was down there for hours; long enough for Isabella to nod at me before walking toward the elevator. I watched her glance at her phone and disappear into the metal box, the doors sliding closed behind her.

When she was gone, Cilia popped back up. "I can't talk about this here," she said. She reached into an acrylic tray on the desk and pulled out a gold pen and a paper pad with the hotel's logo stamped on the top. Scribbling in a hurry, she handed me the paper. "Text me later tonight."

With that, she tossed the stack of papers she printed under her arm, grabbed her cellphone, rushing after Isabella. As the elevator opened, a young couple walked out hand in hand, their eyes glued to each other. The man whispered in the woman's ear, and she giggled, the sound of her joy echoing through the lobby. Brushing past them, Cilia cast me one last look and disappeared. I pocketed her note soon after, following the couple outside. They continued to laugh together all the way down the street, pointing at the different shops as they walked.

I looked across the road at Bean Me Up, a wavering smile on my lips. In my back pocket, Cilia's number grew heavy with expectation and the promise of answers. As I crossed the street to open the cafe, my mood brightened.

Take that, Joe Brooks, I thought. *I got what I needed, with or without you.*

CHAPTER 27

"**O**ne mocha with a twist, one double espresso, and two oatmeal cookies!" I yelled out.

Two women in the world's tightest yoga pants strolled to the back counter to pick up the order. They tried each other's drinks, then made a cheers motion with their cookies, taking giant bites of each. I had to look closely to make sure they chewed before they swallowed. The women caught me staring and giggled.

"We need our energy for the class," one said, pointing to the rolled-up mat strapped to her back. "Dice puts you through the wringer, but it's so worth it."

As they walked away, an annoyed huff sounded at

my ear and I side-glanced Stella. "You wish Dice put you through the wringer, Beatrice."

Following the women with my eyes, I wiped the steamer handle with a wet rag and turned it on to clear the hose. My back ached from standing so long; the cafe had been non-stop busy since I opened, and it was already half-past three. I haven't even had time to eat lunch. Scanning the packed tables, I turned to my familiar. "Do you know those two?"

"Unfortunately, yes," she bit out. "We took the same yoga class. They were constantly trying to outdo me to get Dice's attention. It was sad to watch, really."

I assumed Dice was the yoga instructor and from the description Stella painted, he must have been attractive for two women to fight over him. "Let me guess, Dice only had eyes for you."

"Darling, please," Stella said cheekily. "I am more limber than a circus performer. Of course, he only had eyes for me."

"And how did your husband feel about that?"

Stella winked. "Why would he care? He got the limber all to himself."

Gagging, I waved her off and continued to clean my station. Mugs covered every surface, plates stacked to unbelievable heights, and crumbs dusted the counter's surface. The cafe was a mess. I glanced at the tables and breathed out. At least it was all contained to behind the main counter. Chatter filled the cafe and my lips curled up. It was nice to have a pleasant moment amid all the chaos. Despite the obstacles, Bean Me Up was going to be fine and with it, so was I.

My phone vibrated in my apron, and I dropped the rag I held on the floor. I looked at the screen, my throat suddenly bone dry. "It's Joe," I told Stella.

"Wow, he's got it bad!"

Sliding the message off screen, I crammed it back in the apron, unamused. "He probably wants to lure me into a dark alley for a late-night snack."

"Oh, he wants a late-night—"

I brushed by her and hummed loudly so I wouldn't hear the rest of that sentence. Joe Brooks wasn't getting a late-night anything from me, snack or otherwise. This was the fourth time he tried to reach me today, and I was fed up. If gran was still alive, she'd have me block his number. Then burn my phone. She never talked about the vampire she killed, and I never asked, but it was an unspoken rule for me to steer clear of them if I knew what was good for me. Despite my recent activities, I was intent on listening to words of wisdom for once.

Checking that everyone was settled in and didn't require further service, I snuck into the office to let my temper cool down. The mere thought of Joe made my blood boil, and I hated that even though I had every right to be upset, his message made my heart race. *Stupid heart.* I took the phone out and threw it in the desk drawer, wanting it out of my reach before I did something stupid like text back a vampire. As I did, the gleam of a purple stone caught my eye. I reached a hand into the drawer and pulled out Rosemary's pendant, swaying it before me like a pendulum. "I'm going to find out what happened to you," I said.

Then I grabbed my phone again.

Fingers typing fast, I messaged the number Cilia jotted down on the notepad and waited for a response. Three dots flashed on the screen, followed by a message bubble.

"I'm going to get into some serious trouble if anyone knew I told you this," she typed.

I waited, but no other message came through. "Don't worry," I wrote back. "I won't speak of it to anyone. Promise. Smiley face emoji. Smiley face emoji. Smiley face emoji."

Embarrassed, I deleted the last three and pressed send.

It took Cilia a few minutes to respond and for a second I thought she changed her mind. When I read her message, I nearly fainted. My eyes ran over the letters time and time again, making sure I got it right.

"Rosemary checked in on her own," the text read. "But she wasn't alone for long. A man came to see her."

"Who?"

Those incessant dots flashed again, then disappeared. They reappeared a second later, and I waited, chewing on my fingernails. "Tristan Mint."

I knew it! The phone slid from my clammy grip and hit the table, bouncing off it and crashing to the floor. I yelped, diving after it maniacally. The screen cracked in one corner, and I growled, calculating how much it would cost to fix it. That wasn't important now. The phone still worked. I sucked in a sharp breath and typed, "Do you think he could have hurt her?"

"I don't know. But you should know I'm the one who found her. In the room."

A hot lump filled my throat and knots twisted my stomach. Poor Cilia. She wasn't the nicest person, but I still wouldn't wish that on anyone. I vividly remembered finding Daniel in the alley, and it was an image that would haunt me for the rest of my days. "I'm sorry," I wrote. "That must have been awful."

Cilia took a while to reply. I ate three of my nails while I waited.

"It was pretty terrible," she finally wrote. "There's one more thing."

I didn't know what to say, so I typed out three dots and left it at that.

"I don't think it she died of a heart-attack. At least not a normal one. When I found her, there were signs of a struggle. The room phone was on the floor and there was a broken glass on the nightstand and some blood on the wood. It all seemed very strange to me, but it's not like I was used to finding dead bodies."

You and me both. I put the phone on the desk and stared at it. My hair fell into my face and curtained off the rest of the room: my attention focused only on Cilia's message. Why did the police think Rosemary died of natural causes when Cilia had her doubts? I shook myself back to reality. "Are you sure?"

"One hundred percent," she replied. "The whole thing was off, but Isabella told me to leave it alone and let the cops do their job. That the hotel couldn't handle any more bad press. I couldn't risk getting fired, and she was already dead so..."

This woman was worse than I thought. Who walks away without pushing for the truth? Probably most people. I knew I wouldn't have, but then again, I wasn't Cilia. As dreadful as I found her behavior to be, I had to keep myself on track. "Where was Tristan when you found her?"

"No clue. Gone. I can't talk about this anymore."

I craved to force her to go to the police and tell

them the truth. Actually, what I wanted was to march across the street and slap her silly for keeping it hidden in the first place. What was it they said about small towns? That everyone knows everyone's business? Well, apparently not in Orchard Hollow. Here we locked up our business in a safe, tied it up with chains and dumped it in the sea. Was everyone in this town so conceited they couldn't step out of line for one second to help a person in need?

Note to self: don't get yourself into a situation you can't get out of. No one is coming to your rescue.

I had never felt more alone in my entire life.

Air whooshed behind me, my hair flying in all directions. I turned my head to find Stella peeking over my shoulder and reading the text thread. Her eyes widened and her mouth gaped as she read. Even Stella was shocked by Cilia's garbage actions. I returned to the phone in time to see another message pop up from the witch. "Lose this number, Piper. Never talk to me again."

Whirling around, I stomped to the office door and peered out. A few customers left, leaving only a couple sitting at the bar in the front window. It was the same couple I saw earlier today, and they were so entranced in conversation, I doubted they'd need anything. I slumped against the doorway. "Can you believe her?" I asked Stella.

"Definitely. I'm a little surprised she came clean."

"Me too," I admitted. "She didn't give us much, though. We know Tristan was with Rosemary the night she died and that she didn't go peacefully like the cops said. And Isabella helped cover it up to avoid the hotel getting wrapped up in a murder."

Saucer-eyed, I glared at Stella. "Do you think Daniel had the protection charm made for Isabella?"

"It's possible. If the warlock knew she was a vampire and he found out about the cover up."

"Okay," I whispered. "Okay, so Daniel knows Rosemary didn't die of a heart-attack and thinks Isabella had something to do with it. Could he have threatened to expose her? We know he had the charm made, but that's all the information we have."

"Too bad you can't see through the witch's eyes, huh? Find out what Cilia might be holding out on."

My hands stopped fidgeting. Thoughts racing, I caught them one by one until I had an idea in place. I couldn't see through Cilia's eyes, not unless she was here and let me experiment my condemned magic on her, but there was a pair of eyes I could see through. I walked toward Stella, arms out for a hug. "Stella Rutherford, you are a genius!"

Taking one long stride, she moved herself out of my path. "How many times do I have to tell you, darling? Flattery will get you everywhere."

Six doggy treats later followed by a bowl of chicken stew, and I finally had Margaret the Third calm enough to sit inside the circle. Following gran's instructions, I cast it near the fireplace and waited for the flames to get high enough to ripple the surrounding air. The living room smelled of wormwood and crushed dragon's blood; a spicy mix that made my eyes water. I petted the dog behind her ears, and she pulled away, snarling. *Don't bother the Chihuahua when she's snacking.*

I reread the spell from gran's notebook again, then cleared my mind, allowing for the energy of the burning incense to overtake me. Reaching toward the fire, I used the flames to light a black candle and sat it between me and Margaret.

"Are we sacrificing the beast?" Stella asked, amused.

"Shh!" I hissed. Margaret's one ear perked, but she continued to chow down. I had about three minutes before she devoured her stew and was done with me. "I need to concentrate if this is going to work."

"Fine, call me when you're finished whatever this is."

The ghost vanished, leaving me alone in the center of the floor with only a loud-chewing dog as company. It was much easier to pay attention to the spell without Stella's dumb jokes and I lit four more candles, setting them carefully around Margaret the Third. When the wax dripped down their sides, I spread a dab of scrying oil at the base of the candles, tracing a rune for each element. With my free hand, I pulled out Rosemary's pendant and Daniel's note and placed them in the circle. Satisfied with my arrangement, I moved to the last part of the spell. While Margaret ate, I drew a thin line of salt around her and repeated the same for myself. Between the two circles, I placed a sprig of rosemary and was ready to start.

One palm on the amethyst and one on the letter, I closed my eyes and pictured the night Daniel died. At first, I saw myself on the phone with him and my body stiffened as I remembered his voice. The letter warmed beneath my palm, the energy of the spell taking over. Sparks of electricity danced between my fingers, and I kept my breath steady for fear of losing my balance. Near to me, Margaret's loud snarls died away, and I felt myself drift into nothingness.

Heat covered my flesh, and I snapped my eyes open, fighting through it as the stone burned my skin. My lips parted. I gasped. I was no longer in the living room. My feet sank into the soft weave of expensive carpet, and I shuddered, suddenly feeling the urge to use the bathroom. I looked up, realizing I was much lower to the ground than I should have been.

It worked! I was in Margaret's head.

I wanted to jump for joy but feared that any unnecessary movement would break the spell and send my butt flying back to my own body. Transference spells were tricky. Once you locked into the person—or in my case canine—you were trying to scry through, you had better stay still. Any slight disturbance could cause the spell to fracture. I took a very slow breath and let Margaret do whatever it was she did on this night. We were in Daniel's bedroom, and she did not want to stay put. The tiny thing seemed keen on running in circles and I grew dizzy by the seventh pass, which was when a door swung open, and Margaret stopped in her tracks.

She turned, and I turned with her. Our eyes locked on Daniel entering the room, his arm out. Dangling from his fingers, the amethyst glimmered, and Margaret jumped up to snag it. Daniel said something, laughing, but it came out garbled. Whatever it was, Margaret seemed to understand and stopped her whining. She sat down and scratched her belly with her back leg while Daniel perched on the edge of the bed next to the nightstand. He reached into a drawer and pulled out a piece of paper, the same one I later received.

This is it! This is when he wrote to me.

After a few minutes, Daniel folded the paper and crammed it inside a large envelope. Tossing the pendant in, he sealed the edge and walked out. Margaret followed him like a hound. We made our way to the lobby where Daniel slid the envelope into the outgoing mail slot and headed back to the elevator. In the five minutes we traveled, Margaret received four treats and even I had to admit that they were delicious. No wonder she was excited when I bribed her with the same snacks.

The smell of Daniel's apartment upon our return made the dog ecstatic, and she went back to running circles on the couch while Daniel stacked papers into a pile. I tried to make out what they said, but Margaret's vantage point was dizzying and all I could see were pieces of text. When the furball stopped her madness, she settled next to her owner, and I could read.

The magazine cut-outs. Daniel made copies of everything he sent me. He even took a photo of the necklace and had it laid out right on top of the pile. *Why?*

My question didn't linger long because Daniel got up, grabbed the pile from the couch cushion, and headed for the door. Before he left, he patted his thigh and Margaret leaped up and skidded after him. We followed Daniel together, down the hall and to the second door over. Terror clawed its way up my body as Daniel raised a hand and tapped on the door. For a second, there was no answer, but then it opened, and Margaret stutter-stepped backward. My thoughts reeled with alarm, and I wanted to scream. *Don't go in there.* Daniel spoke again, more garbled noise I didn't understand. I didn't have to understand him. All I had to do was look up at the person he was speaking to, the last person who saw him alive.

Tristan Mint.

The warlock held up the papers, shoving the picture of the pendant into Tristan's face. Tristan buckled back, his face scrunching into a mixture of fear and anger. He opened the door wider as Daniel stepped inside. I tried to make Margaret turn around, but I had no control over the dog's body. All I could do was watch as she followed him into the next-door apartment and listen as the door closed behind us.

My back hit the floorboards, and I coughed, my breath escaping me. Above me, the farmhouse's beamed ceiling felt so much closer than it was, like the room was closing in on me. I gasped for air, falling into a fetal position. My body wasn't my own. I still felt like

I was back in Margaret's compact frame. Back in that building. Back in Tristan's path.

Woozy, I forced myself to get up. I petted behind Margaret's ear, and she whined, twirling a couple of times before laying down on the floor and closing her eyes. The poor little thing was constantly tired.

Continuing to pet her, I yelled out, "Stella! You here?"

"Obviously," she answered, reappearing in the kitchen. "Any luck?"

"It worked! It actually freaking worked!"

Stella worked her jaw. "You know what happened to the witch?"

"If my hunch is right, the same person who killed Daniel killed her too."

"And who would that be?"

I cast one last glance at the sleeping dog and snuffed out the candles. My head still spun from the spell, and I couldn't quite get my limbs to function, so I stayed seated, crawling around to break down the circle. As I swept the last of the salt up, I looked up at Stella and said, "The man he confronted the night he died. Tristan Mint, the liar and the cheat."

CHAPTER 28

P anic attacks were no joke and as I walked circles outside of Daniel's building, I was thinking I might have a heart-attack like Rosemary did. Except it wasn't a heart-attack that killed the witch, and I was more certain of it now than ever. Tristan was the last person to see Daniel alive. I recalled the vision I had witnessed through the Chihuahua's eyes and my pace quickened.

Daniel discovered what Tristan did and confronted him. I didn't see what happened next, but it wasn't difficult to imagine. Tristan invited Daniel in under the presence of an explanation. They argued. Tristan attacked Daniel to cover his tracks, killed him and planted evidence of drug use to throw off the police. Ember mentioned Tristan still having ownership of everything, which would include the pharmacy. It wasn't a stretch to assume he had keys to the place and access to all the illicit drugs his murdering heart could desire.

Before coming here, I called the pharmacy and begged Ember to do a last-minute check for any missing medication. It took her almost an hour to get back to me, but when she did, I knew I had Tristan pegged. His ex-wife sent a detailed email with a list of drugs, most of which I couldn't pronounce. Ember mentioned running a recent inventory and the current numbers of her stock did not match. She also ended the email letting me know that if this had anything to do with Tristan, she wanted the police to call her directly.

Fumes propelled from my ears, and I bit a hangnail.

I dug out my cellphone and clicked it open, ready to call the sheriff so I could watch as they rolled Tristan away in the back of a cruiser. As I dialed, another call came through and, in my fury, I accidentally answered it.

Crap. I brought the phone to my ear, blanching. "Hi, Joe."

"Piper, I'm glad I caught you," the bloodsucker answered. "Look, I need to explain—"

"I can't talk right now."

"Piper, please," he begged. "I know I dropped a bomb in your lap, but I feel I owe you a better explanation than the one I provided. Give me a chance. I can come by, and I promise I'll stay six feet away the entire time."

Except I might end up six feet under if I let you. I growled. "I'm not home and I really, really don't have time for this."

There was a long sigh and some labored breathing on the other line. "Where are you?"

"None of your business."

I thought he'd leave it alone, maybe even hang up and never bother me again, but it seemed once a vampire got it into his head, there was no getting rid of him. Joe breathed heavily again, and I could almost feel the heat of his breath in my ear. I pulled the phone away.

"You're about to walk into danger, aren't you?"

I sighed. "No, I'm not." I rubbed my temples, trying to find a way to get Joe off my case. Nothing came to mind. If I didn't tell him the truth, he'd keep calling, and I didn't want my phone put on blast while I waited for the police to get here. In fact, I didn't want to wait at all. I looked at the screen, a new and likely idiotic idea coming to mind. "Actually, if you want to make it up to me, I need you to call Sheriff Romero and tell him to come to Tristan Mint's apartment. I'll meet him there."

"Piper, don't—"

Click.

I hung up and stormed into the building, catching the door as a young girl with a very large greyhound walked out. Putting my phone on silent, I rushed to the elevator and tapped my foot the entire ride up. What was I doing? I had no idea. This was the dumbest act in the history of dumb acts, and yet I couldn't get myself to slow down. I wished to confront Tristan myself. I wanted him to know that I, the girl he treated like an imbecile, figured it all out.

To know I caught him.

The police station was only a five-minute drive away, so I didn't have to spend much time with the pompous buffoon.

What could possibly go wrong in five minutes?

Briskly, before I could chicken out, I rapped my knuckles on Tristan's door. While I waited, I covered gran's brooch with my palm, wishing it could share a bit of the family magic, or at least a slice of courage.

"Coming!" His voice sent chills down my spine, and when he opened the door, my temperature spiked. It looked that Tristan had much the same reaction to seeing me because he ground his teeth and said, "You."

"Yes, me." I threw my hands out. "Surprise!"

"What do you want?"

I didn't answer. Instead, I reached into my bag and fished out Rosemary's pendant, dangling it in front of his sleazy face. Tristan wobbled and his lips turned blue, the color rushing from his garish face. He looked like a black and white movie; pale and two-dimensional. He looked defeated. I threw the pendant in the air and caught it, taking one step into his apartment. "You want to do this out here or inside?"

Who was I even? Where did this devil-may-care Piper come from? If I thought I was a fool for coming up here, I was an even bigger fool for asking to go inside. Did I learn nothing from Daniel's experience with this monster? Apparently not, because when Tristan stepped aside to let me by, I walked right in.

Not bothering with formalities, I stomped through the narrow hallway and into his living space. The layout of the apartment was the same as Daniel's, so at least I knew where to run in case things went south. I looked around, noting the furnishings. They were nowhere close to the class of decor Daniel owned. Every piece of furniture was mismatched and there was a musty smell in the air; it reminded me of gran's trunks in the farmhouse which bore the stale scent of old things. Like someone sprayed the place in musk and month-old lemons. I turned up my nose and faced Tristan. "You should know the police are on their way," I said. "In case you get some ideas."

"Why would the police be on their way?"

I see we're still playing games. "Listen here," I said, steeling my voice. "I know everything. I know what happened to Rosemary. I know Daniel found out and confronted you, and I know you killed him and covered your tracks with drugs from your ex-wife's pharmacy."

Tristan chuckled. "If you know everything, why are you here and I'm not in cuffs?"

He had me there. This all would have gone much smoother if I wasn't so hot on my heels and waited for the sheriff. Except I was my mother's daughter, and I couldn't wait. I had to know now, and if I was being frank, I couldn't leave this to the cops. I lost all hope for the Orchard Hollow police department when they mucked up not one but two cases involving the murderer in front of me.

My body stiffened.

What was I doing confronting a killer? *Run, you moron. Turn around, say you made a mistake, and get out of here.* What I did instead was lean on the side of Tristan's couch and cross my arms. And what I said next made me abandon sanity altogether. "I want to know why. Just you and me. Tell me why."

"Whatever it is you think you know," Tristan said,

his lips peeling away from his lips, "I'll deny every-thing. You have no proof. You wouldn't be here waving some stupid necklace around if you did. Rose-mary had a heart-attack. Daniel was a drug user whose nasty habits caught up with him. And you are harassing an innocent man."

What a disgusting wart of a man. I took out my phone, pulled out Ember's email and crammed it in Tristan's face. "Except I also have this, and I'm pretty sure that string of drugs will match what they found in Daniel's system. It might not be much, but I'm betting it's enough to get Romero looking into you." I sneered. "Still think I'm harassing you?"

I expected another snide comment or for Tristan to send me packing. What I didn't expect was for him to yank the phone from my hand, drop it on the floor and smash it with his fake designer shoes. His smug smile made me want to throw up all over the cheap, tacky carpet I stood on. Mouth wide open, I stared at my phone, then up at Tristan. Did this man not under-stand how emails worked?

"You know I emailed a copy to Romero already, right?" I lied. "And if they ever let you out of prison, I'll be expecting a new phone."

Shockingly, the fear I felt downstairs was gone and replaced by an attitude I could only label as Parfume Stella. I liked the new Piper. Tristan, on the other hand, looked as though he wanted to set my hair on fire. He walked toward me, and I held up a hand. "Don't even try it. Tell me why, and I'll leave you to deal with the sheriff on your own."

I was bluffing, of course. No way was I going to miss seeing Tristan Mint getting arrested for the murders. And I definitely would not walk away from the chance to show Romero I wasn't a flake like my mother. I made a difference in this town, and he needed to treat me with respect in the future. Everyone did. Something stirred inside me and for a second, I confused it with confidence. Except, it was a very primal urge to flee because instead of explaining himself, Tristan lunged for me. His feral eyes blinked rapidly as he threw his arms out and reached for my throat. Slimy fingers grazed my neck, and I shoved my palms outward, acting on instinct. Electricity built within me and when my hands contacted Tristan's chest, I zapped his butt all the way to next Friday. He catapulted backward, his body slamming into the kitchen counter with a thud.

Tristan groaned and dropped to the floor like a bag of bricks. He rubbed his chest. His wild gaze locked on me. "What the hell was that?" he hissed out. "What are you?"

"Someone you shouldn't mess with," I replied. I

held up a hand, relieved the sparks still danced over my fingers. "Now, talk or we do this again."

Tristan flinched but stayed silent.

"I'd do what she says, buddy," Joe said from the doorway.

I whirled on my heels, hiding my arms behind my back. When I remembered Joe already knew I was a witch, I let them fall at my sides. He wasn't one to judge. Joe was much, much worse. My traitorous heart slammed in my chest, and I bit the inside of my cheek, willing myself to get it together. "What are you doing here? Where's Romero?"

"On his way," Joe said. "I wanted to make sure you were okay, but clearly you don't need my help."

"Clearly," I bit out. Then turned to Tristan with my fingers flashing like a sideshow performer. "Why did you kill Rosemary?"

The slimeball made a move to run, but Joe was on him in a flash, his large boot pressing down on the scumbag's fingers until I heard a crack. "Ow!" Tristan yelled. He swatted at Joe's shoe, having little success in removing it. When he realized there was no escape, he slumped against the counter, his legs collapsing under him. Glancing at the dining table and around the room, he sighed. "It was an accident," he whispered. "I didn't mean to hurt her. We broke it off a few days before and I wanted to convince her not to tell Ember."

"Was she going to?"

I couldn't picture Rosemary as the type of person who would stoop so low, but I didn't know her. And as Tristan proved today, people in our town were capable of pretty much anything. Literally anything. Sometimes, I wished I left with mom if only to be somewhere else for a change.

Tristan nodded, proving me wrong. "I couldn't risk Ember finding out."

"Maybe you shouldn't have cheated on her then," I sniped. "Repeatedly."

"Probably." Tristan shrugged. I balled my hands into tight fists. One more wrong move from this ghoul, and I would lose it. "Things got out of hand. She fell and hit her head on the nightstand. When she got up, she was so out of it; kept telling me she's calling the cops. I panicked. Rosemary passed out, and I got the hell out of there."

"But you came back. You drugged her and it caused a heart-attack."

He nodded, lowering his chin. "I didn't mean for it to go that far. I wanted her to calm down so we could talk it out in the morning."

I didn't believe that for second. No one drugs a person to have a lovely little chat. Tristan wanted to hurt Rosemary, and he did. "And Daniel? He figured it out, and you killed him," I said. "What I don't understand is if Daniel came here to confront you, how did he end up in the alley behind Bean Me Up? And how did you get your gross hands on my spare key?"

Nose flaring, Tristan looked up at me and Joe pressed his boot down harder. I wasn't sure if he worried Tristan might freak or if he simply enjoyed hurting him. Who knew what vampires were into? Whatever Joe did, it worked, because Tristan opened his mouth to explain. Unfortunately, it was at that same moment that loud footsteps flowed down the hallway and five uniformed men stepped into the apartment. They looked around the room and their shocked faces froze in place as they took in the scene. The killer was on the floor with a broken hand with a random bookstore owner towering over him, and me with my arms crossed next to both of them.

A throat cleared from behind the cops, and they parted, letting Romero walk through. He took one look in the apartment and motioned for two men to approach. As they did, Joe released his boot and Tristan pulled his hand into his chest, whining like a complete baby. I tried not to laugh when one cop twisted his injured arm behind his back aggressively to get the cuffs on. When they walked Tristan out, he watched the floor the entire way, not once looking at me. There was no sweet talking his way out of this one. I doubted Romero would fall for his nonsense like all those poor women did.

The apartment cleared out, the cops leaving dirty boot prints on the floor as they marched. Before walking out, Romero looked at me and tipped his hat, which I assumed was his way of apologizing. I doubted I would ever get an actual apology out of the man, so that was as good as anything. More than likely, I'd be getting a phone call sometime soon to let me know that despite having helped their incompetent police force catch a two-time murderer, I should have minded my own business.

Typical.

"Want to get out of here?" Joe asked.

Elated over the arrest, I almost forgot he was in the room. Arms still crossed, I turned to him, my face made of rigid stone. "I'm not ready to talk about this whole thing yet," I said and waved a hand between us. "And I wouldn't mind a minute alone. To process everything."

"Of course." Joe nodded. "When you are ready, please call me. Day or night. I want to explain."

Somehow, I believed him. While it was true and I wasn't quite at the place where I was eager to sit down with a vampire and hear what he had to say; I couldn't, with all my heart, say I would never get there. If tonight taught me anything, it's that people usually had a reason for the things they did, even if those reasons were often selfish and terrible. None of us were perfect. I looked down at my fingers and tried to make the sparks return, but my magic was as dead as the two people whose justice I helped deliver tonight. I was as far from perfect as a witch could get, so who was I to judge Joe?

Waiting until Joe's footsteps disappeared, I walked over to Tristan's dining table, pulled a chair out, and sat down. My hands shook as the events of the evening washed over me and I placed Rosemary's pendant on the metal table, staring at the purple stone. My fingers grazed the sides of the chair I sat in, running a nail over the inlaid florals carved into the wood. *Such an ugly dining set.*

My jaw locked.

I looked down at the chair, then the one next to it and the one across. Three chairs in a setting for four were odd enough. What was even odder was that these weren't any chairs. I had seen these before, laid out in front of an antique store.

These were Patty's chairs.

The room spun and my breath quivered. Wobbling, I reached for my busted phone, praying it still worked. When it miraculously turned on, I dialed Joe's number, waiting for him to answer. The line rang several times and went to voicemail. *Crap!* "Joe, it's me," I said. "We got it wrong. Tristan didn't do it alone. It was—"

A sharp whack sounded and my headache careened from temple to temple. Pain spotted my vision, the light in the room flickering as my eyelids fluttered open and closed. I tried to hold on to the phone, but it slipped out of my grip and fell to the floor. I turned, a fuzzy shape in the distance coming towards me as my vision flooded with black. "What..."

The world around me fell into darkness.

CHAPTER 29

Everything hurt. My head throbbed, and I pressed a palm to the back of it, pulling away wet fingers. I brought them to my face and winced. Blood. Stomach churning, I peeled my eyelids wide apart. They were so heavy; I couldn't bear to keep them open. I fought against the urge to go back to sleep. Confusion laced through me. Where was I? What happened?

The last thing I remembered was calling Joe, then nothing.

I took a deep breath in and tried to sit up, realizing I was no longer sitting at Tristan's table. Somehow, I had ended up on the floor. Falling when I lost consciousness, no doubt. Beside me, gran's brooch lay under the dining table. Shattered. My stomach pitched violently, and I held a hand to my mouth, preventing myself from getting sick. Tears welled behind my lids, and I choked back gasping sobs, averting my gaze from what was left of the brooch. All our family magic—gone. I was useless as a witch before. And now, well, I wasn't sure what I was. Another human.

My breath tasted of iron, and I licked my lip, which had split open. Fighting the uprising of nausea, I pushed myself up and stopped. I was still in Tristan's apartment, but I wasn't alone.

"Patty," I said, zeroing in on the woman in front of me.

The antique shop owner crossed her arms and watched me struggle to rise. When I stood, she tsked, her left arm rising. There was an object in her hand, silver and clunky, and I forced a swallow, my vision returning. A gun.

Pointing the barrel to the floor, she motioned for me to sit back down and narrowed her eyes. "Don't make me use this."

"I'm not making you do anything," I said. I had some serious bravado for someone who was minutes away from getting her face blown off. But if this was how it ended for me, I wasn't going down without a fight. I looked around the apartment. The front door was closed, and there was no other escape. If I was going to get out of this, I had to keep Patty talking. I prayed Joe listened to his voicemail and caught on. Or maybe Romero would send someone back to the apartment. There had to be an investigation now that they had Tristan in custody. Knowing Romero, it would be ages until things moved along. I only had myself to depend on.

Following Patty's instructions, I slid down. "Why? I thought Rosemary was your friend."

"Oh, you must be kidding. Who are you anyway? You're no friend of Rosey's."

That makes both of us. "I'm someone who figured it out."

She straightened the gun, pulling it higher, so I was staring straight into the barrel. It didn't look new, and I wondered if she pulled it off her store's shelves. Could antique shops carry weapons? I wasn't sure. I hated that this was what I thought of now. Something was seriously wrong with me. When Patty stayed quiet, I said, "You sounded like you missed her. Like you were sorry."

"The only thing I was sorry about was not cutting that snake out of my life sooner," Patty snapped. "Rosey was no friend of mine. The only person she cared about was herself. She had to be on top. Could never let me have anything. She was the queen bee, and we all danced around her like mindless clowns. I was sick of it."

"So, you killed her for it?"

Patty smirked. "I took away what she wanted. I needed her to know she wasn't the most important person in the world."

"You took her life away because she ruined a business deal for you?"

"What? No. I took Tristan."

It was all beginning to make sense now. Tristan and Rosemary didn't break things off. The cheater met another woman, a new shiny trophy to add to his collection. Patty. I swallowed bile. "You mean Rosemary actually liked Tristan?"

"Liked him?" Patty exclaimed. "She was in love with him! Thought he was going to leave his wife for her. When I told her no way that man would do any such thing, she treated me like dirt. Made me out to be a jealous, petty woman and made sure the hotel deal fell through. All to prove that she was better than me."

Acid coated my tongue, and I shimmied my hips, my eyes darting around the room to find anything I could use. This woman was not in her right mind and considering what she'd already done, I knew she wouldn't blink an eye before she shot me. I was trapped. Suddenly, I realized how Harry must have felt every time I chased him around the cafe with a broom. *I promise to treat the petty thief like a prince if I get out of here.* I frowned. Before I made any wild promises, I had to escape. With gran's brooch gone, I had no magic to rely on, so I had to use my wits if I wanted to survive the night. Mind reeling, I checked Patty again. The gun was still in her hand, but it started to sag. She was relaxing, giving me a perfect in. If I could distract her long enough to think of a plan, I might have a shot. "You have it all wrong," I said. "The hotel is going under. Rosemary tried to save you from losing your shirt and you repaid her by killing her. And stealing her boyfriend."

Patty blinked once. Twice. "You're lying."

"I'm not, I swear. One of the hotel staff told me everything. The reason Isabella Beaumont wanted to sell the place to you for cheap was because it was eating money and not turning a profit. She's been trying to get rid of it ever since Rosemary mucked up the deal you two had. You should have been thanking Rosemary."

"No," Patty said, but her speech wavered. "I don't believe you. She was too into herself to do that."

I sighed. "Maybe so, but she was still your friend until the end. Until you killed her."

The gun barrel lifted, and I stared down the hole of doom again. This wasn't working. Patty was all over the place and too irrational to be convinced she was wrong. Maybe if I tried a different approach, pretended to be on her side. "I get it, you know," I said, thinking of Nancy Steeles. "There's someone I know that's like Rosemary. Acting as though she's better than me, flaunting her power all over town. It's frustrating. I understand why you felt you wanted out of the friendship."

"Exactly! All I wanted was to be free of her."

"And you are now," I whispered. "Thanks to Tristan."

Patty scoffed, the gun lowering again. "Turned out the idiot wasn't as useless as I thought. The best part about gold digging fools is how easy they are to manipulate."

"You got Rosemary's lover to kill her for you."

"Poetic justice if you ask me," the gun-wielding psycho said. "All I had to do was convince the cheating moron that Rosemary was in the way of him scoring big with his wife and the pieces fell into place. A few accidental slips of the tongue about how much the antique shop is worth, and he was wrapped around my fingers. He's like a magpie, that one. After the next shiny new thing."

Dimly, I had to admit that Patty had Tristan down to the marrow. All he cared about was getting as much as he could for as little work as possible. If she offered him an easy way to cash out, I could see him turn to putty in her hands. "You promised him money for killing her?"

"Heavens no! The dimwit was supposed to break her heart, not kill her. All Tristan had to do was tell Rosey that what they had was only a fling. I convinced him it was easier this way. That Rosey would have a better time getting over it if she hated him and I would be there to help her through it, talk her out of running her mouth to his wife." She rolled her eyes. "Obviously, I was never planning to help her through anything. I was hoping to rub it in her face how the man she loved used her like a cheap rag and threw her out."

"Was Rosemary planning to talk to Tristan's wife?"

Patty shook her head. "Not at all. One thing I'll give her is she was good with a secret."

So good it got her killed. I wondered if things would have turned out differently if Rosemary told Patty the truth about why she sabotaged the hotel deal. Its possible Patty would never have forgiven her friend, but at least she would have known there was no maliciousness behind Rosemary's actions. Could that have saved her life? My eyes locked on the gun. Probably not.

I wiggled my fingertips, willing my magic to come alive, but all I got were a few loose sparks and a whole lot of nothing else. Defeated, I slumped against the chair leg behind me. My butt wedged on something sharp, and I dragged my palm behind me, keeping my gaze on Patty to make sure she wasn't looking. The tips of my fingers touched cool metal. I paused. Rosemary's pendant. It must have fallen out of my grasp when Patty knocked me out. I wrapped my fingers over the stone and a surge of energy rushed up my arm. Whatever power the necklace held; I could feel the remnants of it around the edges. But how? How could I feel anything magical at all without my family's brooch?

Keep it in the family. Daniel's obscure message for me flashed in my mind, and my grip on the pendant deepened. Could it be the warlock sent the necklace for a different reason than I thought? Maybe it wasn't a clue. Maybe it was a solution. Warlocks had a twisted relationship with time; maybe Daniel foresaw this night and sent the pendant as a precaution? It was a long shot. As long as shots could get.

Memories of gran's famous vampire vanquishing story came flooding back, and I slunk down. If gran transferred the vampire's magic into an object, was there a chance I could transfer Rosemary's family magic into myself? I'd never heard of someone doing that, especially not someone with no magic to do it with. Your family magic was your own, and I wasn't even sure her energy would mingle well with mine. But we were both witches, so it was worth a try. I prayed I had some Addison luck left in me after all.

Light reflected off the barrel of the gun and I huffed out a breath.

I had no other options left.

"So, what went wrong?" I asked, buying myself some time.

"Everything." Patty scratched her curly hair and looked out the window. As she did, I strengthened my grip on the pendant and tried to remember the spell gran used to transfer energy. I had no provisions with me since I was nowhere near my purse and no inner energy to draw from. I'd have to improvise. "Tristan is hot-headed when things didn't go his way and I guess he and Rosey got into it," Patty continued. "He called me in a panic, saying she fell and was really out of it. He kept saying my name, too. I knew if Rosey heard him and word got out that I sent him there, she'd never let me live it down."

My body stayed as still as possible and I tried to summon the energy in the amethyst, but nothing happened. A few stray sparks ignited on my fingers and died away in seconds. "Is that when you told him to kill her?" I asked.

"Uh-huh. My father was a doctor, so I knew my way around a medicine cabinet. I told him what to pick up from the pharmacy and since he already had the keys, it was easy enough. All he had to do was give Rosey enough of the drugs to put her to sleep. I figured since I wasn't in town, I could talk her into thinking she imagined hearing my name later. She'd be pretty knocked out from the drugs, so it was an easy sell."

I tried the pendant once more, with the same disappointing result. "Except it didn't go down like you planned."

"Not even close," she admitted. "The moron gave her too high a dose."

"What about Daniel?"

Patty scratched her head again, confused. "Who? Oh, the hotel manager. That was all Tristan. I told him to leave it alone, but he kept insisting that this guy had a way to prove to the cops what happened to Rosey. Finally, I gave up talking him out of it." She leveled off the gun, checking the safety. "And it all would have been fine if you didn't get involved. How did you know where to look, anyway?"

"Daniel told me," I said, keeping it at that. Staying as indifferent as possible, I continued to try every trick I could to manifest an energy transfer. I scratched the amethyst with my nails, heated it up in my palm hoping to get it started. I even begged the stupid thing to obey. Nothing worked.

Not only was my magic, or lack thereof, garbage, but now it would get me killed.

"Hmm," Patty said. I was glad she didn't ask me to explain further because I was pretty sure there were parts of my story no one would believe. Not even a murderer. She looked at the gun, then at me. "I truly am sorry about all this, but I can't let you leave. I'm sure you understand."

I didn't understand at all. What was increasingly clear, though, was that I only had a few seconds before Patty stopped talking and started firing. Panic penetrated my body and sweat beaded in the curve of my back. My pulse quickened and I could feel its thumping under my sweater. The flash of the gun drew me to Patty, whose head tilted as she tensed her trigger finger. My body convulsed and electricity coursed through my every bone. In my hand, the amethyst warmed and burnt my skin. My eyes shot wide open as a surge of magic blasted through my palm and into the rest of my body.

Before me, Patty released her finger, watching me writhe in pain. I closed my eyes and pictured a wave of electricity flying toward her. When I opened them again, I threw my arms out, acting on instinct. Lightning burst from my fingers and into Patty's shoulder. It knocked her around, making her teeter backward, and she toppled over the side of the couch and to the floor.

Her head smacked against a clunky wooden coffee table, and she went down. Hard.

Trembling, I crawled to where she lay, horrified. For a second, Patty didn't move. Then her chest rose and I slouched beside her, continuing to check for breaths. Patty was out cold, but she was alive.

I surveyed the scene. Tristan was in jail. Patty laid on the floor, passed out from a head injury much like Rosemary was the night she died. My crappy magic miraculously working in time to stop her from getting away with murder.

"Now, this is poetic justice," I said and called the sheriff for what I was hoping was the last time.

CHAPTER 30

Steam hissed out of the metal handle, and I listened to the sound of foaming milk as I made yet another caramel mochaccino. Ever since I put them on the menu—abstaining from naming the drink Mocha à la Joe —they've become the most popular order at the cafe. I added whipped cream, sprinkled some sea salt, and fished out a space-ship shaped cookie to toss on the saucer. The cookies were a recent addition, and I loved how they looked when I delivered drinks to people. A few customers, tourists staying at the Rose Hollow Hotel, even took pictures with them and tagged the cafe on their social media accounts.

That alone got Bean Me Up some serious traction

online, and I spent the last few nights sitting in front of the fire, catching up to messages and comments.

The door opened and a high-pitched bark caught my attention. I looked up from behind the espresso machine to see Sebastian walk in. When my eyes traveled down to Margaret the Third creeping into the cafe, I laughed. Opening a fresh bottle of spring water, I poured some into a bowl and carried it over to Sebastian while he attempted to get the dog to sit down. I slid the bowl across the floor toward Margaret and she immediately stopped barking to drink.

Sebastian rubbed the back of his neck and tied the dog's bedazzled leash to the chair. "Thanks," he said.

"Any time. She knows what she likes," I said, still smiling. "What can I get you?"

"I think I'll try one of the caramel mochas."

Chuckling, I left the water bottle on the table. "Of course."

The day continued at a steady speed. People came in, ordered drinks and baked goods; some stayed, and some left with trays in their hands and smiles on their faces. Shortly after Sebastian came, Cilia and Nancy arrived, and I creeped the three from behind the counter the entire time. Every time Nancy wasn't paying attention, because she was busy casting shade my way, Cilia would look at Sebastian and smile. He'd smile back, glancing away as though he might burst into flames from her attention. It was sweet to see them together. Despite being two of my least favorite people, not counting the two I landed in jail, they were a fitting couple. I hoped one day they'd get over their insecurities and finally come out.

"Why is there salt on my drink?" Nancy complained.

"It's on the menu," Cilia said, coming to my defense. "Drink it and let's go."

Grouchily, Nancy snatched her drink from the counter and sauntered to the table furthest from me, a gesture I was very grateful for. When she left, I handed Cilia her drink, and she thanked me, whispering, "Don't worry about her. I'm working on it."

There was hope for Cilia Craven after all.

By the time the day finished, I made so many drinks and bussed so many tables, my hands got calluses. When the pace of people coming in and out slowed, I took the chance to tape up the *Help Wanted* sign I printed off earlier that morning. Whether or not I wanted to, it was time to admit that I needed help. There was simply too much to do. And with the way business was going, I could afford to hire a part-time employee.

Nerves creeped in as I thought about interviewing people for the job.

I had never been the one on the other side of the

interview table. Sure, I'd sat in plenty of interviews, most of which ended with me not getting the job, but this was different. It was personal. No matter how I attempted to spin it, a lot was riding on me filling this position. For starters, whoever I hired had to keep up with the busy pace of Bean Me Up. Then there was the matter of Harry Houdini, who had become a permanent fixture in the cafe and required a lot of snacks and even more butt-kicking. Lastly, I needed someone supernatural because no way was I going to worry about my new employee finding the stash of magical items I kept in the office.

The pressure was on.

My head spun as I swept up the cafe after the last customer left; remnants of the blow Patty dealt and a constant reminder of that night. The sheriff took little convincing that Tristan didn't act alone, and the police hauled her off as soon as she came to. Turned out, Tristan wasn't as loyal as I assumed. Once the sheriff told him how much time he was facing, he sang like a bird. Even laid out the exact steps he took to drag Daniel's body over to the alley and how he broke into my office; not a difficult task since Harry left the door open again after one of his cookie quests. The way the sheriff explained, Tristan overheard the phone call Daniel made to me before he came over and dumping the body behind Bean Me Up was the first thing he thought of after he strangled the warlock. The rest was as disgusting as I imagined. Tristan shot Daniel up with drugs he stole from the pharmacy after he killed him to throw the cops off. The worst part was, Tristan counted on the police department not following up on his dirty plans. I shuddered to think he would have gotten off Scot-Free if I was a little less stubborn. Given time and a more thorough examination, I was certain the police would have figured out the drugs ended up in Daniel's system post-mortem. Unfortunately, Romero was determined to close the case and it made me sick to think he might handle future cases with the same disregard. Not that I suspected Orchard Hollow to have more murders coming. Not with Tristan Mint out of the picture.

What a nasty piece of work. Patty and he truly deserved each other. I could not understand how Rosemary, Ember, and Isabella—three strong, successful women—ended up with such a deadbeat. I knew I wasn't exactly a dating guru, but Tristan was a questionable choice for anyone.

The door opened, and I tried not to whip around since vertigo and I were best friends these days. "Oh," I said. "Hi, Joe."

My own questionable choice. Brilliant.

Leisurely, Joe closed the cafe door and walked toward me. I noticed he did not display his usual confidence. His eyes drifted, catching on everything except my gaze. The smile he often sported twitched, and he raked his fingers through his messy hair so many times I worried he'd go bald on the spot. Joe was a hot mess. What was going on?

I put the broom down and undid my apron, tossing it on the counter. "Everything alright?"

"Of course. All good," Joe said. He did not look all good. He reached into his jacket and produced a small bundle, and I recognized the ghost on the paper bag right away. "I brought you a gift."

Eyes narrowed to slits, I took the bag from him, pulled out a book, and choked. "You got me *Dracula?*"

"I thought it was funny," Joe said, flushing. "Too soon?"

"Way too soon," I admitted, though I put the book on the counter to read later. Not that I would tell Joe, but *Dracula* was one of my favorites.

"I was hoping I might take you out for a drink. If you're all done for the night, that is."

My smile faltered. "Um..."

"You're not ready," Joe whispered. "Got it."

"No, it's not that! I mean, it is that, but it's not that."

The vampire's eyes darkened, and he looked me up and down. "I don't understand."

That makes two of us. The truth was, I really,

really, really wanted to go out for a drink with him. In fact, I wanted it so badly I was almost willing to forget his blood-drinking ways and coffin sleeping. And yes, I knew vampires didn't actually sleep in coffins; and from what Joe explained in the few minutes I allowed him to speak on the subject, he did not drink human blood. Still gross, but slightly less so I supposed. The problem was that I couldn't get gran's warnings out of my head. I wondered if perhaps her opinions on vampires were tainted because of her own experience, but she wasn't the only one who held such low regard for Joe's kind. And I wasn't ready to jump on the vampire loving wagon yet. I needed time. A lot of it.

I also had other plans for the evening and had no intention of missing them.

Patting the book, I smiled warmly and said, "Some other time, I promise."

We exchanged a few more words and Joe left, leaving me alone in the cafe. I inhaled the lovely smell of coffee and warm milk, made my seventh latte of the day, and headed into the office. "Stella!" I yelled out. "Get a move on! We're starting in five!"

Sparks flew off my fingers and my concentration faltered. I shifted my gaze to the shelf on the wall. Mistake number one. When I tried to recover, my arm wobbled and thrust outward. Mistake number two. Lightning shot from my fingers and blasted the shelf, zapping a box of napkins into oblivion. As it exploded, the box knocked over a bag of chocolate chips and it crashed to the floor, scattering bits of chocolate everywhere.

Instantly, Harry Houdini was all over them.

His grubby fingers collected every chip he could find, and he crammed them in his mouth until his jaw hung open. Chocolate chips fell from his lips as he tried to stuff more inside.

I groaned and slapped my forehead. "Harry, put those down." Then turning to Stella watching from the corner of the room. "It's not working."

"Well, it is working. It simply isn't working as you expected."

Since when was Stella supportive? Super weird.

Twisting my singed fingers around the chain holding Rosemary's pendant, I creased my brow, watching it teeter totter in front of me. "I have zero control over whatever this is."

I had no words to describe the lightning I summoned. It started at Tristan's apartment and now I could almost always bring it back. The problem was I couldn't direct it anywhere specific. The lightning, like the rest of my life, had a mind of its own. Back in the apartment, it worked great, but here: nothing. Stella and I had been at it for four nights trying to recreate whatever I did, and we pretty much burned every inch of the office except the parts we aimed for. And that wasn't even the worst of it.

The absolute worst part was that it wasn't witch magic.

Sure, witches could summon lightning, but not like this. Not without a spell or specific ingredients. Whatever it was I was doing, it seemed to come from inside me; which was impossible since without gran's brooch, all the family magic I possessed should have dissipated. At first, I thought it was the ley lines I was pulling from, but that couldn't have been it. I was nowhere near their core when I first tapped into this power, and besides, you needed to perform some serious magic to tap into ley line energy.

Shivers tripped down my spine.

What was I?

At the base of the shelf, Harry carried off the chips he collected to some dark corner of the universe while my phone vibrated on the desk. I got up from the floor I sat on and looked at the cracked screen, amused.

"Who is it?" Stella asked.

I didn't reply and clicked to answer the call. "Hi, sheriff."

At this, Stella fake yawned and turned around, pretending to buff her nails with an invisible nail file. I could see her making faces as she inspected her fingers. I guessed she never got over not getting that last manicure before she died.

"Miss Addison," the sheriff's gruff voice interrupted my wayward thoughts. "How are you?"

"I'm good. Are you calling about Daniel and Rosemary?"

"Not at all. Though you should know Isabella Beaumont admitted to instructing her employee's silence in the Hayes case."

My lips parted. "Oh. Did she say why?"

"To keep the hotel's reputation intact," the sheriff said. "Since she did eventually file the report, we can't charge her. But I thought you might want to know you were right in your suspicions."

"What about Daniel?" I asked. "Cilia was convinced he didn't deserve the promotion he got. Any chance there was something going on with him and Isabella?"

The sheriff huffed out a sigh and said, "Nothing that requires police intervention. It seems Miss Beaumont hired him to help her market the hotel online. I looked into Daniel's finances and the real estate business was eating a hole in his inheritance. The hotel job helped keep him afloat, though according to Beaumont, he wouldn't have it for long."

"Isabella was going to fire him?"

"Seems he didn't keep up his end of the deal."

Undertsanding dawned on me and I glanced at Stella, motioning to the phone. "Daniel started the rumors of the hotel being haunted, didn't he? To drum up more business."

"He did," the sheriff answered. "And unfortunately, his plan backfired."

In her corner of the office, Stella pointed at the clock on the wall and fake yawned. I cleared my throat. "Well, thank you for calling me," I told the sheriff. "I appreciate the update."

Romero stayed quiet for a few seconds too long. Grumbles sounded on the line, and I couldn't quite make out what Romero said. I was about to ask him to repeat it when he said, "I have a proposition for you."

Stella's back straightened, and she whipped around, suddenly having all the time in the world.

"A proposition?"

"It's rather unorthodox," the sheriff said. The tone of his voice made it sound like he was fighting the urge to hang up. I wondered if someone was holding a gun to his head to make the phone call. I cringed, remembering Patty. *Too soon.* "The recent string of events got me thinking. How would you feel about me calling once in a while, if I have a case that might require your"—he coughed—"specialty."

"My specialty?"

"Yes, Miss Addison. Please don't make me say it."

I knew where Romero was going with this and found it extremely amusing that he couldn't utter the words. The man needed someone in the paranormal community. Someone he could trust. Being someone the sheriff trusted made me all sorts of warm and gooey inside. Lips curled, I rubbed my fingers over the amethyst still in my hands. "You want a witch on the force?"

"Oh, sweet mother of! You wouldn't be on any force, Miss Addison," the sheriff griped. "No one in the department knows about your kind, so this will have to stay between us. And if I do come to you for your expert opinion, I expect you to keep whatever you do under the radar."

I thought over the proposal for about a second and said, "Sure. Does this mean you'll listen to my hunches?"

More grumbled cursing blessed my ears. "I'm going to regret this," the sheriff said. "Have a good night, Miss Addison."

Wishing him good night, I hung up and looked at Stella, slack jawed.

"Didn't know you had expertise enough for an expert opinion," my familiar teased.

I stuck my tongue out. "Ooh! Do you think he'll give me a uniform? I really want a uniform."

"Why don't you worry about getting your happy fingers under control first?" She cast a side eye at the door, following Harry as he wobbled back into the office with an empty mouth. "And that thing."

Whatever. I knew Stella had a soft spot for the cafe's resident thief even if she didn't admit it. That was the thing about Stella Rutherford, a very crucial thing I came to realize after my recent adventures; despite all her complaining, she was there for you when you needed her. In her own way, Stella was the best familiar ever.

"Just because I'm dead doesn't mean I have all the time in the world," she sniped.

The best familiar with the most attitude.

I arranged myself on the floor again and placed the pendant in front of me. Before I started, I looked at Stella over my shoulder. "Hey, can I ask you a question?"

"If you must."

"Did it really take you that long to find Margaret the Third? And how did you know to look for her?"

Stella was gone for longer than I was comfortable with, and she was yet to tell me what happened. Not that she owed me an explanation, but we were stuck together so if something happened, I'd want to know. After she disappeared, Stella had been different. Moodier, but also more present. It was weird, and it made me worry. I cared, sue me.

Long legs stepped into my line of sight as Stella hopped onto the desk, crossing them briskly. "I wasn't looking for the mutt," she said.

"What were you looking for?"

"Nothing, truly. I was at the hotel as I told you and then I was simply... gone."

My pulse sped up. "What do you mean, gone? Where did you go?"

"I don't know," she whispered. "But I appeared in the woods days later and your mutt was staring me in the face."

Well, this was interesting. Why would Stella appear in the woods where she died? And Margaret the Third wasn't mine. I didn't know why, but I felt that was important to emphasize. Before I could, Stella said, "There's another thing. When I returned, I had a memory of what happened to me."

"Stella!" I yelled. "You lead with that! Who taught you how to tell a story? What did you remember?"

"Not much. It wasn't a specific detail, more of a feeling," she said. I noticed her straight posture was slightly hunched. "Like whatever happened to me wasn't an accident."

I opened my mouth to speak, but she shushed me. "Please don't ask me to explain because I wouldn't know where to begin. It's likely the aftermath of being a ghost, constantly feeling as though somebody wronged you. Probably why hauntings are a thing."

"Stella, we can—"

"I have no more information, Piper."

And just like that, the gates were up, and I was locked out from the conversation. Considering how little we knew about ghosts, there was a chance we might never find out what happened to Stella the morning she died. She was right, all she had to go by was a feeling. Besides, Stella had specifically asked me to stay out of her death time and time again, and that was before I got myself looped into being the sheriff's pet witch. If I cared at all for my familiar, I had to respect her boundaries.

Near to us, feral chomping noises pierced the office. I peeled my attention from Stella, focusing it on the chubby raccoon with a face full of chocolate chips. As I glanced back at Stella, her gray body shimmered and solidified. She winked. "Get him."

With one hand on the amethyst, I pictured a bolt of lightning. My fingers prickled and sparks collected on my skin. I cast one last glance at the ghost, then pointed an index finger a foot away from Harry. Lightning flew from my hand, zapping the floor close to where he sat. The raccoon hissed, threw the torn bag of chocolate chips on the floor, and shimmied over a few inches where he continued to stuff his face.

"We'll never be free of him," Stella moaned.

I laughed. I didn't want to be free of him, and I didn't want to be free of Stella Rutherford. Inspecting my fingers, I pictured another lightning bolt, directing this one to the desk where Stella perched. She yelped, jumping up and cursing me out in the process. Chuckling, I looked around the office. Scorch marks covered the walls and shelves. A trouble-making raccoon chewed loudly in a corner, and beside me, a ghost was flipping me the bird.

Life truly couldn't get any stranger. It also couldn't get any closer to perfect.

THE END

MOCHA À LA JOE

Ingredients:
1/2 cup cocoa
2 tablespoons caramel sauce
whipped cream
1/2 cup 2% milk
heavy cream
Double long espresso shot
Optional: a dash of sugar and sea salt

Instructions:
1. Combine cocoa and milk and heat in a double broiler slowly until mixture is creamy. If using a microwave to heat, do so in 30 seconds intervals.
2. Add mixture to espresso and stir.

3. Drizzle 1 tablespoon of caramel sauce inside a glass jar or cup.

4. Pour coffee and chocolate mixture into cup.

5. Froth 1/4 cup of heavy cream and add to cup (add as much as preferred to taste, more cream will create a richer consistency).

6. Add whipped cream on top and drizzle remaining 1 tablespoon of caramel atop whipped cream.

7. Sprinkle cocoa powder to top of caramel and whipped cream.

For an added bite, sprinkle a dash of sugar and sea salt mix.

ABOUT THE AUTHOR

A.N. Sage is a bestselling, award-winning author of mystery and fantasy novels. She has spent most of her life waiting to meet a witch, vampire, or at least get haunted by a ghost. In between failed seances and many questionable outfit choices, she has developed a keen eye for the extra-ordinary.

A.N. spends her free time reading and binge-watching television shows in her pajamas. Currently, she resides in Toronto, Canada with her husband who is not a creature of the night and their daughter who just might be.

A.N. Sage is a Scorpio and a massive advocate of leggings for pants.

For more books and updates:
www.ansage.ca

Connect on social media:
Facebook Group:

facebook.com/groups/945090619339423/

Instagram:

instagram.com/a.n.sage/

TikTok:

tiktok.com/@ansagewrites

YouTube:

youtube.com/c/ANSageWrites

Made in the USA
Middletown, DE
31 January 2023

23022457R00227